VOODOO RIDGE

VOODOO RIDGE

DAVID FREED

THE PERMANENT PRESS
Sag Harbor, NY 11963

For information, address:
    The Permanent Press
    4170 Noyac Road
    Sag Harbor, NY 11963
    www.thepermanentpress.com

Library of Congress Cataloging-in-Publication Data

Freed, David—
    Voodoo Ridge / David Freed.
        pages cm
    "A Cordell Logan mystery."
    ISBN 978-1-57962-355-5
        1. Logan, Cordell (Fictitious character) 2. Pilots—Fiction.
    3. Murder—Investigation—Fiction. 4. Tahoe, Lake (Calif. and
    Nev.)—Fiction. I. Title.

PS3606.R4375V66 2014
813'.6—dc23   2014001648

Printed in the United States of America

For Robert and Rachel

He who binds to himself a joy
Does the winged life destroy;
He who kisses the joy as it flies
Lives in eternity's sunrise.

—WILLIAM BLAKE

VOODOO RIDGE

1956, sixty miles north of Los Angeles . . .

It rained that night as if Noah and his ark were making a comeback. The first real blast of winter. Sleet whipped in cold and hard off the Pacific, pelting the runway at Santa Paula and raking the corrugated metal roof of watchman Herm Hoversten's security shack like machine-gun fire. Not that Hoversten noticed, slumped at his desk, porcine nose bent sideways, drool pooling around his splayed marshmallow lips, fast asleep.

He was a doughy man who'd served briefly in the army, long enough for physicians to diagnose that his snoring through reveille each morning had less to do with draftee malingering than some severe, narcoleptic affliction rarely seen before. Granted a medical discharge and excused from combat duty in Korea, Hoversten soon landed the perfect job for the perfectly lethargic, surrounded by citrus groves, guarding a civilian airfield nearly as comatose as he was.

Not even when the door to the shack cracked open and the wind came howling in loud as a jet engine did he awaken. Only after the stranger booted him off his rickety swivel chair and onto the plywood floor did Hoversten come to. *Don't Be Cruel,* the new tune from that boy from Mississippi with the lips and the hips, the one all the girls were so nutty about, was playing on the radio. The stranger turned it off. He was wearing a dark woolen watch cap. The left sleeve of his navy peacoat dripped blood. In his right hand was a gun.

"You are armed, yes?"

"Mister, I make thirty-nine bucks a week," Hoversten said, rubbing the sleep from his eyes. "I couldn't afford the bullets."

The stranger smiled and nodded toward his bloody sleeve.

"I am in need for you to move a rather cumbersome object that I myself am incapable of lifting under present circumstances. You will please to get your jacket. We will be taking a short, wet stroll."

Hoversten couldn't place the accent. Russian? French, maybe? Hell, it was hard to know. All those foreigners sounded the same anyway. He strained to one knee, then gained his feet unsteadily, eyeing the handgun leveled at his gut.

"I don't want no trouble."

"Do what I tell you. You will be OK."

"Yes, sir."

Hoversten pulled on a greasy yellow slicker.

"I have nothing to lose," the stranger said. "If you run, I will shoot you."

"Don't worry, mister. I ain't run nowhere in years."

The stranger gestured with the gun—let's go—and followed him out the door.

They leaned into the rain, shielding their eyes. Parked on the tarmac ahead of them was a twin-engine airplane made of polished aluminum. It was a Model 18 Beechcraft, with two big radial engines and an amply proportioned fork tail that reminded Hoversten of Marilyn Monroe. He hadn't noticed the plane when he'd come to work that evening, nor the stake-bed pickup truck parked close by it. In the back of the truck sat a wooden crate about the size of one of those ornate "Italian inspired" nightstands that his wife had put on layaway at Montgomery Ward, the ones she said she simply *had* to have because they were pure class.

"You will move that box into that airplane," the stranger shouted over the wind. "If you drop it, it will be the last thing you do."

Hoversten reached into the truck's cargo bed. He undid the ropes holding the box in place and slid it to the edge of the open tailgate, struggling to balance it on his thigh while trying to secure a solid grip with both rain-slicked hands.

"Carefully."

"What d'you got in this thing anyway," Hoversten said, "rocks?"

The crate felt to him as if it weighed a ton. His arms turned quickly to jelly. His legs burned. He took baby steps toward the airplane. Somehow, he held on. With one final, straining push, he hefted the load up and through the fuselage door.

"Your help is greatly appreciated."

"Don't mention it," Hoversten said, bending from the waist, breathing hard.

The stranger holstered his gun and turned to climb into the plane. In that instant, a lifetime of memories welled up inside Herm Hoversten's head, all the taunts and slights he'd ever endured. He was too fat, everyone said, too slow-witted. Even his parents told him he'd amount to nothing. Here was the chance to prove them all wrong. Here was his opportunity to be a hero.

He swept the stranger into a bear hug from behind and squeezed for all he was worth, but the man was strong. Even with his wounded arm, he broke free.

"You're under arrest," Hoversten said, reaching into the front pocket of his baggy trousers.

That's when the stranger fired.

Even over the storm's fury, Hoversten would remember how loud the gunshot was. He felt no pain, only surprise at suddenly finding himself on the tarmac, unable to move his limbs, the rain stinging his face.

The stranger knelt beside him, extracted handcuffs from Hoversten's pants pocket, and flung them angrily away.

"Where is the gun?" he asked.

"I told you. I got no gun."

"I was not going to harm you. I was going to let you go. You are a stupid, stupid man." The stranger shook his head sadly and stepped into the plane.

Hoversten listened as the engines came to life. Propellers whirled, first one, then the other. He saw the Twin Beech taxi to the east end of the field and turn, then come roaring back down the runway and lift off, vanishing in seconds into the low, scudding clouds.

Come daybreak, after the storm had passed and the skies had cleared, a private pilot hoping to practice his landings before work would find Hoversten where he'd fallen. The guard could offer little information that might lead authorities to his assailant. He couldn't remember the airplane's tail number. He couldn't recall what the stranger looked like beyond his cap, coat, and the blood on his sleeve. The stranger's accent was a mystery. The gun, whether a revolver or semiautomatic, its caliber or finish, was a blur.

All Herm Hoversten wanted to do, he whispered moments before gulping his final breath, was sleep.

ONE

2014, West Los Angeles . . .

My ex-wife and I were on our way to see the lady doctor.

"I'm so excited," Savannah said.

"Makes two of us."

The stoplight at South Bundy and Santa Monica Boulevard was red. She glanced over at me from behind the leather-wrapped steering wheel of her platinum Jaguar.

"You don't seem very excited, Logan."

"Are you kidding? My very first visit to a gynecologist? Who wouldn't be excited?"

Savannah pursed her lips, disappointed by what she perceived was the usual acerbic me, which I swear I wasn't trying to be. "He happens to be an *obstetrician*-gynecologist, as well as a fertility specialist," she said. "We're having a baby, Logan. It's supposed to be a joyous occasion. For both parents."

"I'm filled with joy, Savannah. Bursting at the seams with it. I just have a few things on my mind, that's all."

It wasn't a lie. I *was* joyful. Truly, I was. But I was also plenty distracted. I was fast approaching the second half century of my time on this planet, a pathetically underemployed flight instructor with a work history that the United States government prohibited me from divulging to anyone in any detail under threat of a one-way ticket to Leavenworth. Home was a converted garage in Rancho Bonita, California, where I eked out a pauper's existence in one of America's wealthiest communities while rooming with America's dumbest cat who, even in his most sociable moments, pretended like we didn't really know each other. And, at an age in their lives when other guys were pondering whether to buy sports cars and/ or have affairs with their personal assistants, I was approximately seven months shy of becoming a first-time father—with my former wife, no less.

All of which, however, was not what was troubling me most at that moment. It was the couple quarreling directly across from me in front of Starbucks.

She was one of those little heartbreakers you see all over Los Angeles, an aspiring MAW, as they're known in the entertainment capital of America—model, actress, whatever. Spike heels, size double-zero skinny jeans, unlawfully tight tank top, knockoff designer sunglasses.

"Leave me alone!"

He towered over her, trying to snag her waif-thin, 500-calories-per-day wrist.

"Don't you walk away from me."

"Let go. You're hurting me!"

He called her a little bitch. She called him an insensitive jerk. I didn't catch what they were arguing about. It didn't matter.

"Hey."

Slowly, menacingly, he turned and wheeled his head in my direction. White madras shirt open to his navel. A thatch of dark chest hair that would've made Austin Powers proud. Black fatigue pants, black Doc Martens boots. A studly dude who spent way too much time in front of the wall-size mirror in the weight room at 24-Hour Fitness, working on his freakishly oversized biceps.

"What's your problem, *brah*?" he said, glowering at me with three days' worth of carefully managed stubble.

"My problem, *brah*, is that your girlfriend doesn't appear to appreciate the way you're treating her. How about the two of you take it inside, talk things out in a civilized manner?"

"I'm not his girlfriend. Not anymore."

"He's not talking to you, Belinda."

The dude pushed past her and strode toward me, a six-foot-two, 210-pound slab of self-absorbed macho.

"Unless you want to get your punk ass tuned up," he said, "I'd suggest you mind your own damn business, old man."

I opened the Jaguar's passenger door and stepped out.

"Logan, please, we have a doctor's appointment," Savannah said.

"This'll only take a minute."

"Oh, for god's sake." She rolled her eyes and pulled to the curb as the light turned green.

The guy's arms were outstretched scarecrow-style, head cocked, his mouth twisted in a crooked, half smile meant to convey a taste for mayhem.

"You want some of this? Is that what you want?" He pulled his shirt over his head and threw it on the sidewalk. "C'mon, man, let's do this."

He had some good pecs and abs. I'll give him that much.

"With all due respect," I said, "I'd rather just talk this out."

"Good call. Cuz you'd definitely get your ass kicked."

I smiled.

"You think this is funny? C'mon, asshole. Take your best shot."

"Look, much as I'd love to, the Buddha teaches that violence only leads to violence. Compassion, on the other hand, leads to enlightenment. And enlightenment is what all of us should be striving toward in life, don't you think?"

He scrunched up his bad boy face.

"What the hell's that supposed to mean?"

"It means do yourself a favor and stop grabbing women like they're meat. They tend not to like that."

"You telling me what to do?"

"Consider it a friendly suggestion."

"Who do you think you are, man? You ain't jack, OK? You ain't *nobody*." Flared nostrils. Fists clenched. Big vein bulging at the center of his forehead. He was ready to go to war.

"Look, friend, all I'm trying to do is stop you from hurting your lady and making a bigger fool of yourself than you already have. You don't want to listen to sense, suit yourself. Peace out."

I was about to turn back toward Savannah's car when the guy said, "You're the fool," and launched a big, off-balance, overhand right in the general vicinity of my face. I pivoted, palmed his balled fist in midflight with my right hand, turned my hips into him, sunk the fingers of my left hand into his left sideburn, and spun him up against the plate-glass window of the coffee shop.

Pecking away intently on their smartphones, heads down, and sipping their soy iced cinnamon dolce lattes, nobody inside noticed or, if they did, pretended not to. We were, after all, in Los Angeles. Nobody pays much attention to anything in the City of Angels beyond televised car chases and whomever the Kardashians are banging this week.

"Oww! Motherfu--!"

"What's your name?"

"What's it to you, asshole?"

I twisted a handful of sideburn. He screamed like a schoolgirl.

"It's Nitro. My name's Nitro. Jesus!"

"Nitro? Who names their kid *Nitro*?"

"I'm a pro wrestler. My real name's Kenneth."

"Apologize to the lady, Kenneth."

"For what? She started it."

I twisted harder.

"OK, OK, OK! I'm sorry, OK?"

"No, Ken. Not OK. And not to me. To Belinda. Nicely. Like you mean it. Tell her you're sorry for being a jerk. Tell her you want to make it up to her, that you'll buy her the coffee beverage of her choice and a nice bran muffin."

"Cranberry orange," Belinda said. "Low fat."

"Actually, the lady said she prefers cranberry orange. Low fat."

"I know what kind of muffins she likes. For Christ's sake, we only live together."

"Then you should know, in theory, what makes her happy." I yanked his head around by his whiskers so he could address her directly. "You're on, Ken. Remember: *nicely.*"

"I'm really, really, really sorry, Belinda. Can I please buy you the coffee beverage of your choice and a *cranberry orange* muffin?"

"Low fat," I reminded him.

"Low fat," Kenneth said.

Belinda feigned indifference, arms folded, staring up at the sky, milking the moment before she let go a pouty sigh, the kind she'd probably learned in acting class and said, "Fine, whatever."

"Excellent," I said. "How hard was that? Everybody happy? We all good now?"

"Yeah," Kenneth said, grimacing in agony because I was still holding him by his whiskers. "All good."

I let him go.

He scuttled away, putting ten feet between us, rubbing the side of his face. "You're nuts, dude, you know that?" He picked his shirt off the sidewalk and pulled it back on over his head. "Totally nuts."

"A man has to be a little nuts to take action. A reasonably sensible man is satisfied with merely *thinking* of taking action."

I wished I could've taken credit for making such a profound statement, but it was the great French statesman, Georges Clemenceau, who'd said it more or less long before I was born. Regardless, whatever I said or didn't say wouldn't have mattered much. Kenneth and Belinda were already in smooch-and-make-up mode. She stroked his face soothingly where I'd yanked on him and asked if he was OK. He kissed her tenderly and assured her that he was, then held the door open for her.

Belinda looked back and rewarded me with an appreciative smile as the happy couple ventured inside the coffee shop.

I was feeling pretty darned special about my Lone Ranger moment. The feeling evaporated the instant I got back in Savannah's car.

She wouldn't even look at me.

"Did we have fun?"

"You have no idea."

"We should've called the police."

"The Los Angeles police have bigger fish to fry, Savannah, as you well know, being a resident of this fine city."

She exhaled and watched other cars pass by.

"You know, Logan, at some point, you're going to have to stop acting like you're still twenty-five. Someday, you're going to have to grow up."

Had I still been twenty-five, I would've likely sent Ken/Nitro to the emergency room on principle alone. I didn't say that, though, as Savannah cranked the ignition and merged into traffic. I didn't say anything. We were late for the lady doctor.

✝

DR. SHARMA squeezed a puddle of clear goop onto Savannah's tummy from a plastic bottle that could've just as easily dispensed catsup. Then he smeared the goop across her skin with a hand-held transducer while watching a computer monitor propped near the examining table on which she lay.

"There it is," he said enthusiastically in an accent that smelled deliciously of Bombay curry.

I peered at the monitor. The grainy, black and white image on-screen looked like something the Apollo astronauts might've captured on film while orbiting the moon—a dark, irregularly shaped crater.

"There *what* is?" I asked.

Dr. Sharma maneuvered the transducer around Savannah's abdomen like he was grinding pesto until the computer's cursor rested on a small, throbbing mass of pixels at the edge of the crater. He looked over his half-glasses and nodded to his ultrasound technician, a Rubenesque Latina garbed in violet-colored scrubs decorated with butterflies who was standing beside a keyboard attached to the ultrasound machine. As she typed, the words, "BABY'S HEART," appeared on the monitor, followed by, "HI MOMMY AND DAD, CAN'T WAIT TO SEE YOU BOTH!!!"

Savannah wept.

"This," she said, "is the happiest day of my life."

The technician clasped her hands to her mouth and cried happy tears. Dr. Sharma wiped his eyes. I may well have choked up, too, but I was still too much in shock at my life having changed so quickly and radically.

You're going to be somebody's father, Logan. What in the world has the world come to?

We'd been divorced for more than six years, Savannah and I. The murder of my former fellow covert operator, Arlo Echevarria, the man she'd dumped me for, had prompted our reconciliation of sorts. She'd approached me several months earlier and I'd grudgingly agreed to her request to help the Los Angeles Police Department hunt down Echevarria's killer. I knew long after our divorce that I could never stop loving her, but there still remained a part of me that loathed her for having left me to begin with. Which was why, when she told me that she was pregnant with my child, I couldn't decide whether to run to her or as far away as I could. Sitting there in that doctor's office, I still wasn't sure. But looking down at Savannah's ravishing, tear-streaked face as she gazed in awe at the monitor and the image of our seven-week-old baby, I knew one thing: she was right; I'd never seen her so happy.

Dr. Sharma printed out a photo of the fetus and handed it to her.

"Congratulations, Mr. and Mrs. Logan," he said.

Savannah Carlisle Echevarria grasped my hand and smiled through her tears. She hadn't been Mrs. Logan for a long time. She didn't try to correct him, though. Neither of us did.

Through the window of the examining room, across the rooftops of West LA, I gazed toward the gleaming bank towers of Century City. It was one of those perfect autumn mornings in Southern California when the smog drifts off toward Riverside, giving way to clean azure skies and a vaguely defined exuberance that no dream is impossible.

I told myself that fatherhood's a good thing. Perhaps the best of things. Whether I'd be good at it, that was another thing.

☦

WE CELEBRATED pending parenthood over coffee and pie at Du-par's diner in Los Angeles's venerable, midcity Farmers Market, a bustling warren of hole-in-the-wall eateries at Third and Fairfax offering everything from Cajun to Korean.

"Have I ever told you my algebraic theory about why pie is really health food?"

"'Pie is made from fruit. Fruit is good for you. Ergo, pie is good for you.' Only about a hundred times, Logan. We used to be married, remember?"

"We were married? That was you? Really?"

My former wife smiled and licked the last of the lemon meringue from her fork. The restaurant was jammed. Every table and booth filled. We sat at the counter on red leather swivel chairs as waitresses in Depression-era uniforms ferried cheeseburgers and patty melts to hungry customers.

"I never asked you," I said.

"Asked me what?"

"How this happened."

Savannah looked over at me. "How what happened?"

"You. Me. The *three* of us."

"How I got pregnant, you mean?"

— 20 —

I shrugged.

"I'm happy to go through the basics, Logan," she said coyly, "though I have to say, you already seem to have the process down pretty good."

"I just didn't think that it was possible, a woman your age—not that you're old or anything."

She hoisted a disapproving eyebrow.

"Thanks for the compliment."

"C'mon, Savannah. You know what I meant."

She smiled.

"Relax, Logan. I'm just yanking your chain." She reached over and speared a forkful of my cherry pie like a trout going after a fly. "To answer your question, I didn't think I could, either. I wasn't using anything, if that's what you're asking."

"I probably should've asked beforehand."

"A little late for that now," Savannah said.

I nodded.

She ate another piece of my pie. "So, tell me: where do you see yourself fitting in with all of this?"

"Fitting in?"

"Being a parent."

It was time for The Talk: what logistical role did I foresee playing in the care and rearing of the new life we would soon be introducing to the world. Savannah was a former fashion model who barely earned enough income in her new occupation as an unlicensed life coach to cover the groceries. We both knew, however, that she possessed more than adequate resources to comfortably support a child on her own, thanks to her father, a ridiculously wealthy West Texas oilman.

On the other hand, I had virtually no assets except for the *Ruptured Duck*, my ratty old Cessna 172 that recently had been rebuilt by my aircraft mechanic friend, Larry Kropf, after I'd run into a little trouble down in San Diego. I operated a flight school headquartered in an oversized storage closet that I sublet from Larry out of his World War II-era hangar at the Rancho Bonita Airport, but my students, unfortunately, were few—as in none. In other words, I was in no financial shape to support a baby, let alone myself.

"We both know you're in no financial shape to support a new baby," Savannah said.

On top of gorgeous, my ex-wife apparently also was clairvoyant.

The waitress refilled my cup. I waited until she moved off.

"There's more to being a father than paying the bills, Savannah," I said.

Not that I had a clue what I was talking about. I never knew my real father or mother. My childhood was spent as a ward of the state of Colorado, shunted from one foster home to the next. Whatever parental role models I had were no role models at all. They were hardscrabble cattle ranchers and dry-wheat farmers, mostly, who'd welcomed me into their modest homes not because of some abiding Christian kindness, but because I represented help for daily chores, and because the county was paying them to board me. None of my foster fathers ever took me to a ball game, helped me with my homework, or counseled me about the birds and the bees. I was extra income and an extra set of hands. Little more. Still, I believed I had the intuitive makings of a passably respectable dad.

"I can teach him how to catch a football," I said. "That's a start."

"What if it's a girl?"

"Are you implying girls can't catch footballs? That's a rather sexist thing to say, Savannah, don't you think?"

She rolled her eyes. "Logan, all I'm saying is, I don't want you to feel obligated in any way, like it's going to be a burden on you. You can be involved however much you want, or not at all. It's your call."

"What if I want to be fully involved?"

"I'd welcome that." She reached over and ate the last of my pie. "But I think I have a right to know how, specifically, you propose to be all in—other than teaching our child how to catch footballs—when you live in Rancho Bonita?"

"I'm not following you."

"Logan, you live 120 miles from Los Angeles. It seems to me that your location alone would preclude day-to-day parental involvement."

"You could always move to Rancho Bonita."

"I like living in LA."

Part of being human is making pronouncements without weighing their full consequence. Words pass through your lips unfiltered and, suddenly, they're out there, irretrievable, like some unguided missile. I don't know whatever possessed me, sitting there in that loud, crowded diner, at a lunch counter that was anything but romantic, to say what I said. Maybe it was the on-screen image I'd seen of that tiny beating heart. My child's heart. All I know is that the words just came.

"What if we got remarried?"

Savannah paused, sipping her coffee, and turned her head, meeting my gaze.

"What did you just say?"

"We could fly to Lake Tahoe tomorrow," I said, "and get a license. No waiting on the Nevada side."

She searched my eyes.

"Please don't say that if you don't mean it, Logan."

"I meant it. Every word."

Her own eyes were the color of some exotic strain of golden-hewed wood. It felt like they could see straight through me.

"You *do* mean it, don't you?"

I nodded solemnly.

Her arms were suddenly around me. Her lips found mine. I could taste the salt of her tears. We held each other, oblivious to the smiles of other diners.

"OK, then," she said.

"OK, then."

She wiped away her tears and said she was going outside to call her father, to tell him the news—but not before kissing me once more.

I felt good inside. As good as I could ever remember. Watching her head for the door, I was reminded of something I was taught at the academy, how the biggest mistake you can make in war is being too afraid to make a mistake. The same, I suppose, can be said for life in general. I didn't think I'd screwed up asking Savannah to remarry me.

Fate would prove me as wrong as I'd ever been.

TWO

You haven't lived until you've walked in on your octogenarian landlady, a retired gym teacher from Brooklyn, as she grunts out squat thrusts while trying to keep up with some hunky Israeli physical fitness guru on her ancient, black and white console TV.

"Working the glutes," Mrs. Schmulowitz panted, up and down, up and down. "Melting chicken fat like it's going out of style."

Her joints sounded like somebody stepping on broken glass.

"Careful you don't hurt yourself, Mrs. Schmulowitz."

"Don't you worry about me, bubby. I taught physical education for sixty-one years. And the first rule of physical education is, if your legs don't feel like they're falling off your body, you're being a lazy schlep."

With her lime green high-tops, raspberry leggings, tangerine leotard, and a blue New York Giants sweatband, she looked like an eighty-eight-pound Jell-O parfait; one topped with a thinning frizz of hair dyed the color of straw. She sprang off the floor like a woman a third her age, toweled the sweat from her brow, and patted my cheek.

"So, how was Los Angeles?" Then she caught sight of Savannah, walking in behind me. "And look who you brought back with you! Only the most beauteous gal in the whole world."

"You're looking as lovely as ever, Mrs. Schmulowitz," Savannah said.

The two embraced before Mrs. Schmulowitz took a step back and gave her the once-over. Savannah was wearing flat-soled Roman sandals, leather straps snaking up her supple calves, and a pleated peasant skirt. Her perfumed, hennaed tresses cascaded over the shoulders of a simple sleeveless white cotton blouse.

"I'm gonna tell ya something," Mrs. Schmulowitz said. "If I looked that crazy sexy when I was your age, I would've blown off the whole teaching gig and gone straight into porno. My only problem was, they hadn't invented movies yet. People back in my day sat around the campfire, telling stories."

"Right," I said. "The campfire. In Brooklyn."

"You're not *that* old, Mrs. Schmulowitz," Savannah smiled.

"Not that old? What, are you kiddin' me? You know that key Ben Franklin stuck on the end of his kite? It was to my apartment on Bay Parkway."

I tried not to laugh. It would've only encouraged her.

"Savannah and I are flying up to Lake Tahoe tomorrow," I said. "We're getting remarried."

She was momentarily speechless and obviously delighted. It was the first time I'd ever seen Mrs. Schmulowitz at a loss for words.

"Mazel tov! May the both of you find as much joy as I did with my third husband. OK, granted, so the man could get a little kinky at times. You take the good with the bad, am I right?" Mrs. Schmulowitz pecked us both on the cheek, then gave me an affectionate, coach-like slap on the butt. "Way to go, bubby. Smart move. She's a keeper."

I politely declined her offer to cook us a celebratory dinner. My plan was to take Savannah out that night, somewhere romantic.

"Then at least let me watch your cat for you while you're away," Mrs. Schmulowitz said, "unless, of course, you want him in the wedding. I can see it now, that *meshuggener* kitty coming down the aisle, the ring tied around his neck. A kitty

— 26 —

ring bearer. You could get on the Internet. You could get on Letterman!"

As if on cue, my cat, Kiddiot—so named because no feline in history was ever more intellectually challenged—came strolling in from Mrs. Schmulowitz's kitchen looking like an orange balloon mounted on short, skinny legs, with a pipe-cleaner tail that stuck straight up. He made little chirping sounds, like he was happy to see us. He even allowed Savannah to scratch his ears for a few seconds before glancing over at me with a look that I interpreted as disgust, flicked his tail, and strolled nonchalantly back into the kitchen.

"He's decided he enjoys chopped liver," Mrs. Schmulowitz said. "The secret Schmulowitz family recipe. He prefers it on rye bread."

"Toasted?"

"Of course, toasted. How else is anyone supposed to eat chopped liver?"

In the next life, I most definitely want to come back as my cat.

✛

A RESORT community as affluent as Rancho Bonita isn't hurting for fine dining. California Street, the main drag, which ambles up from the beach for a tree-canopied mile before doglegging inland, boasts dozens of restaurants where dinner and drinks can run more than a monthly car payment on a new Mercedes. They're not the kind of eateries that locals like me typically frequent: Mexican greasy spoons that serve up six-dollar smothered chile verde burritos fat as bricks, the kind that camp out in your gut like squatters, leaving you convinced you'll never eat again.

Mrs. Schmulowitz suggested that I take Savannah to Bel Cibo, an intimate, white-tablecloth Italian joint overlooking the water. I was certain Bel Cibo translated to, "Big Ambiance, Small Portions," but that was cool. For once, money was no object, even if I didn't have any. It's not every day a man asks the world's most beautiful woman to marry him again and she says yes.

The menu was in Italian. Not that I could've read it anyway, not in the dim candlelight of our corner table. I was getting to that stage in life where I needed reading glasses. I hated it. Our tuxedoed waiter, an anxious little man with a dented nose and dark, slicked back hair, sounded like a guy from New Jersey trying to sound like a guy from Naples.

"For the *belladona?*"

Savannah held a candle close as she perused the menu. She'd put her hair up—glamour incarnate in gold hoops, heels, and a short, off-the-shoulder cocktail dress, black. I'd trimmed my jail break of a beard and changed into my only dress shirt and khakis. I would've ironed both had I owned an iron.

"I'd like to start with the Mozzarella di Bufala con Pomodoro e Basilico, please," she told the waiter, "then the Tagliolini del Campo as an entree."

"*Eccellente.* And for the *signore?*"

"What do you recommend?"

He recommended the Tortino di Granceaola as an appetizer, followed by Rustichella d'Abruzzo all'Amatriciana. Whatever the hell those were. Both, he assured me, were "*molto delizioso.*"

"I'll take your word for it."

The waiter asked if we'd had a chance to look over the wine list.

"We won't be having wine tonight," I said.

"That's right, we won't." Savannah beamed. "I'm pregnant."

"*Congratulazioni.*"

He suggested a bottle of sparkling water. Savannah said that would be fine.

"You have no idea what you just ordered, do you?" she said playfully after the waiter departed.

"Not a clue. Doesn't matter, though. All I want is you."

She tilted her head, stroking the side of her neck, and smiled demurely. The candlelight danced in her eyes.

"The romantic Cordell Logan. It's so unlike you."

I was on a roll. "You're unbelievably beautiful tonight, Savannah. More so than usual. As if that's even possible. I'm so lucky."

"I'm the one who's lucky."

We held hands across the table. I felt warm and good inside, that sensation when you're living in the moment, where you belong.

Across the restaurant, a busboy spilled a tray of water glasses that shattered on the travertine floor, loud as firecrackers. Every other diner flinched, startled, including Savannah. I didn't. She noticed.

"What is it with you?"

I looked over at her.

"Somebody drops a bunch of glasses and everybody jumps out of their skin but you. Arlo was the same way. Why can't you just be honest with me, Logan?"

"About what?"

"You know what. About *you*. What you did for a living when we were married. The *real* story."

She knew only part of the story, the one before we'd met. That I'd graduated a rare liberal arts major from the Air Force Academy, and that I'd flown combat missions over Iraq in A-10 Warthogs before an old football injury disqualified me from flight status. What she didn't know was that I'd spent nearly a decade after that off the books, much of it while we were husband and wife, kicking in doors as part of a tier one, inter-service counterterrorism unit, code-named Alpha. I could've told her that a man doesn't spend as long as I did shooting people and getting shot at without learning to control his acoustic startle reflex. I also could've told her that Arlo Echevarria had been my boss at Alpha, and that my cover story—working with him at a marketing agency in San Francisco where we all lived at the time—was straight-up hokum. But I kept my mouth shut.

Savannah suspected that the marketing job was a cover story, especially after Echevarria, who'd retired by then, was shot to death in Los Angeles. Now here we were, less than a year after his murder, planning a new life together amid her same old demands of candor and transparency, and my same old obfuscation of the truth. The more things change . . .

"You mind me asking you a question?"

"We're getting married again, Logan. You can ask me anything."

"How many men did you sleep with before we met?"

She sat back in her chair. "What I did before we met is none of your concern."

"I rest my case."

She stared at me with her eyebrows raised and mouth open—that same expression every woman wears when she realizes that the man she's dining with possesses all the smarts of a doorknob.

"Logan, what you did before we were married is absolutely none of my business. And what I did is none of yours. What you did for a living *while* we were married, though, was and *is* very much my business."

"I've told you what I did a hundred times. But for clarification, let's go with a hundred and one: I was a marketing sales rep."

She rewarded my lie with a disbelieving smirk. "A sales rep. With a gun."

"Plenty of people own guns, including sales reps. This is America, Savannah. Mom, apple pie, and guns."

Our special evening together teetered on the precipice. Sparkling water could not have arrived at a more opportune moment. The waiter filled our glasses while the restaurant's sommelier delivered a bottle of wine to an older couple at the next table. He opened the bottle with a flourish and presented the cork to the gentleman for his inspection. Then he dribbled some of the wine into a small silver chalice that dangled from a chain around his neck. He sipped, smacked his lips, pronounced the selection, *"Squisito,"* poured the vino into long-stemmed crystal goblets, wrapped the bottle in a linen towel like he was changing a diaper, set the bottle on the table, bowed crisply from the waist, and left.

"The guy gets paid to chug other people's overpriced grape juice?" I said. "I'm definitely in the wrong line of work."

Savannah exhaled through her nose and looked away. Call it a hunch, but I got the impression she was still mad at me.

✝

BUDDHISTS BATHE their statues of the Buddha. The practice is supposed to improve harmony and inner balance. I owned no such statue but, thanks to Mrs. Schmulowitz, I did have a tub in my garage apartment. And if anybody's harmony and inner balance needed improvement, especially after the tenuous way dinner with Savannah had gone that night, it was mine.

"Think I'll go take a bath."

"Whatever you'd like," she said indifferently. She was stretched out on my bed reading *Psychology Today*, still wearing her cocktail dress, heels off. Kiddiot dozed on her toes like a fluffy, purring foot warmer.

The tub was purple. Ditto the sink and toilet. Mrs. Schmulowitz had picked them all up for a song at the garage sale of some aging rock star who'd decided to redo his McMansion after laboring one season on one of those celebrity rehab shows. Rancho Bonita was crawling with folks like that, famous people who had more money than sense. I shut the bathroom door and ran the water as hot as it would go. I also squirted in a liberal dose of Mr. Bubble, because nothing says "relaxation" like foamy suds, and also because Mr. Bubble is odorless. When you've pulled triggers for a living, there's

— 31 —

something antithetical about going around all day smelling like strawberry or golden-toasted coconut.

I stripped naked and eased into the tub, soaking a forest green washcloth, then spreading it flat across my face as I lay back with my eyes closed. It's in the quiet of such moments that memories intrude. The price, I suppose, for having a clandestine past.

The wet heat conjured memories of a mission to Indonesia, where a certain radical Muslim cleric affiliated with the Malay Archipelago chapter of a certain international terrorist network had proudly claimed credit for helping design especially lethal antipersonnel land mines used against US forces in Iraq and Afghanistan. Rat poison sprinkled among the steel ball bearings dispersed when the mine exploded. Acting as an anticoagulant, the poison prevented blood from clotting, thus reducing a wounded warrior's chances of survival.

The cleric needed to be put out of action.

Following a typhoon and posing as relief workers, five Alpha go-to guys, including me, were dispatched to Jakarta by way of Tokyo and Singapore. The cleric wasn't hard to find. He broadcast a jihadist religious radio show from his mosque twice daily, seven days a week because Allah doesn't believe that Muslims need a day of rest. We waited until he was off air, entered the mosque, ventilated his bodyguard, then him. His last words were, "I am going to paradise," to which one of my colleagues responded, "Happy trails," then put a .40-caliber slug in the bastard's forehead.

I must've nodded off because the next thing I knew, Savannah was in the tub with me.

"Mr. Bubble?" she said, nodding toward the bottle. "Really, Logan? You?"

"It leaves my skin feeling silky smooth."

She smiled, soaped up the washcloth and began gently scrubbing my chest.

"You're totally naked," I said.

"Thanks for noticing."

I smiled. All those nights I lay awake after our divorce, wishing I could see her one more time, just this way. And now, here we were.

"I've been thinking," she said.

"Always a dangerous proposition."

"We should just leave past issues in the past. I won't ask you again what you did, your real job."

I watched a bead of water course the length of her throat and down, seductively, between her breasts.

"You mind if I ask you a personal question?"

"That would be two personal questions tonight, Logan." She leaned closer to me, her hands cupped with warm water, and slowly rinsed the lather from my neck. "I'm not sure we really know each other that well."

"Ever gotten busy in a purple tub?"

She pretended to think about it for a while. "Can't say that I have. You?"

"Never."

Her lips curled mischievously. "Well, you know what they say? There's a first time for everything." Then she leaned in closer and softly kissed my closed eyes.

Beneath the suds, something brushed against my leg and glided northward, to more sensitive anatomical turf.

I knew it wasn't the soap.

✝

SLEEP SHOULD'VE come easily that night. Savannah was snuggled close, her back to my chest, dreaming contentedly in my arms. The rest of our lives lay ahead of us like a golden fairy tale. But I was awake, consumed by introspection and a rare dose of pure self-realization. If the two of us were to make marriage stick this time, I needed to change, shed myself, I realized, of those vestiges that defined who I'd been and what I'd done all those years in the service of my country. As slowly and quietly as I could, I got out of bed, reached between the mattress and box spring, and unlimbered my two-inch, .357 Colt Python revolver.

"Where're you going?" Savannah asked groggily.

"Gotta run a quick errand. Go back to sleep."

"Promise you'll come back?"

I bent down and kissed her shoulders. "Promise you'll be here if I do?"

She smiled.

"Promise."

Kiddiot was curled like a ball on the floor near the bed, his face buried in his tail. He didn't stir as I dressed and left. My watch showed 0335 hours.

Save for a street-sweeping truck washing down the vomit and spilled beer outside the bars and dance clubs on lower California Street that had closed more than an hour earlier, downtown Rancho Bonita was quiet. Not another car in sight, all the way to the beach.

I parked my truck along Magellan Boulevard, got out, and walked across the sand. The tide was out. The moon was gone. The gun was tucked in the small of my back. It had been my primary backup weapon when I served with Alpha—the theory being that a revolver is less prone to misfire than a more mechanically complex semiauto and, thus, more reliable in a pinch. More than once, the little snub nose had saved my life. But that life was behind me now.

I threw it as far into the ocean as I could. Then I drove home.

✝

HEAVY AND hirsute, Larry Kropf trudged out of his hangar at the Rancho Bonita Airport and onto the flight line, grimacing on two bad knees and wiping his greasy hands on a greasy rag.

"Where're you headed, Logan?"

"Lake Tahoe," I said, loading the last of the luggage into the back of the *Ruptured Duck*. "We're getting remarried."

Larry peered at Savannah over the bulletproof-thick lenses of his Buddy Holly glasses, then at me, as if I'd just notified him that we were planning a bank robbery. He was wearing a frayed white T-shirt and bib overalls for a change instead of his usual blue work pants. Pulled down low across his brow was a beat-to-hell, red and white baseball cap that read, "You can't scare me. I have a teenage daughter."

"*Remarried?*" Larry asked. "Nobody in their right mind marries the same woman twice, Logan. Why repeat the same mistake?"

"Uh, hello." Savannah folded her arms indignantly. "I'm right here, Larry."

"Savannah, you remember my mechanic, Larry?"

"Not just your mechanic," Larry said. "The guy you rent hangar space from for your *wildly* successful international flight school."

"Larry's being somewhat sarcastic," I said.

"I would've never guessed," Savannah said facetiously.

He might've fancied himself a badass, but Larry was, in truth, a big softie who'd give you the proverbial size XXXL shirt off his furry back if you needed it. He knew that my "wildly successful" flight school was on the brink of insolvency, and that I owed him about $30,000 in repairs to the *Ruptured Duck*, as well as back rent. He also knew that I had no way to repay him in full given my financial straits, which was why he'd stopped hounding me. Every so often, though, he couldn't help but get a dig in. Call it catharsis. I couldn't say I blamed him.

"Well," Larry said, "I hope you at least got enough cash to pay for the marriage license."

I locked the *Duck's* cargo door and resisted the urge to check my wallet.

"How much does he owe you?" Savannah said.

"Twenty-nine large and change." Larry took off his glasses and wiped them on his T-shirt. "But who's counting anymore, right?"

"How 'bout thirty grand and we call it even?" Savannah asked, digging through her Louis Vuitton shoulder bag. "What would you say to that?"

Larry looked at her like he wasn't sure she was serious. "I'd say, 'Thank you, Jesus,'" he said.

My ex-wife got out a pen and her checkbook.

A real man is supposed to make his own way in the world, relying on no one but himself. A real man's code of honor prohibits him from taking anything except that which he deserves. He doesn't stand idly by, watching his wealthy former spouse casually cover his five-figure IOU like she was buying a few boxes of Girl Scout cookies. But all I could muster was a meek, "You really don't have to do that, Savannah."

"You're right. I don't *have* to, Logan. I *want* to. We're a team now. And, besides, Larry needs the money, right?"

"Putting it mildly," Larry said.

Savannah filled out the check, then handed it to him. He stared at it like it was manna from heaven and muttered something about how he'd never say another unkind word about me as long as he lived.

I told Savannah I could never possibly repay her generosity.

"Take me to Tahoe, flyboy," is all she said.

THREE

Pilots joke that a smooth landing is mostly luck, that greasing an airplane onto the runway twice in a row is *all* luck, and that three in a row is prevarication. Many aviators consider their ability to return a flying machine safely to the ground in reusable condition the ultimate measure of skill. Not me. For me, it's all about passenger comfort. Looking over at Savannah napping peacefully in the right seat, snuggled under my leather flight jacket, her head propped against the door, I had every reason at that moment to consider myself among the greatest pilots who ever lived.

For any good airman, regardless of how relaxing he may claim it is, flying is rarely without worry. You worry about the ever unpredictable variability of weather. The fear of midair collision with another airplane ranks right up there. Little, however, contributes more to a pilot's pucker factor than the potential of some catastrophic mechanical failure occurring miles above the earth, especially in an aging, single-engine bird like the *Ruptured Duck*. Ordinarily, I would've been constantly scrutinizing the gauges, fretting about the occasional creak or groan that all airplanes make—"Indian night noises," the leather-helmeted old timers used to call them—all the while scanning the ground for suitable emergency landing sites in the event of "what-if?"

But not on that day. On that day, flying Savannah up to Lake Tahoe and what would be the beginning of Our Life Together, Chapter 2, my aging four-seat Cessna performed flawlessly. Invigorated by the cold at 10,500 feet, the *Duck* carried us through California's Central Valley on air so silken that I flew virtually hands free, needing only to adjust the elevator trim every few minutes to maintain altitude.

Off our right wingtip, the sawtooth mountaintops of the Sierra Nevada beckoned as though dipped in powdered sugar. I was tempted to wake Savannah, to share the postcard view, but she looked so peaceful that I thought the better of it. She was, after all, sleeping for two. There'd be plenty of opportunities for sightseeing when we were a family. From perpetual foster child to the head of my own real clan. It had taken only more than four decades. I smiled inside.

A family. So this is what serenity must feel like.

After more than two hours in the air, I hooked a right northeast of Sacramento, then followed the highway that wended up from the little Gold Rush-era burg of Placerville, to the airport at South Lake Tahoe. That way, even if visibility deteriorated, which it showed no indication of doing, I could reasonably minimize the chances of becoming personally acquainted with any of the area's 10,000-foot peaks. The Sierra was a veritable graveyard of airplanes whose pilots disrespected Mama Nature and paid the price. The *Duck* and I didn't intend to join them.

We were twelve minutes from landing, according to the Garmin GPS mounted on my steering yoke. Oakland Center had just instructed me to squawk VFR and change to the advisory frequency for traffic pattern entry at South Lake Tahoe, when something on the ground a mile or so ahead of us and slightly to the north glinted brightly, almost blindingly. It looked to me like a signaling mirror, like somebody trying to get our attention. Whatever it was seemed to be coming from deep in the pines between two jagged, granite crests.

"Where are we?" Savannah said, stretching her arms and yawning.

"About ten miles out of Tahoe. Nice nap?"

"Wonderful nap. Very restful. What are you looking at?"

"I'm not exactly sure."

I banked left to get a better look, hugging mountainsides as close as prudence would allow.

Had we taken off from Rancho Bonita one minute earlier that morning, or a minute later, the angle of the sun would've been lower or higher, and I might not have seen what I saw. I wouldn't have seen it had there been more clouds, as the weather gurus initially predicted, or had I been focused on my prelanding checklist, as I probably should've been. The Buddha believes that what happens in life happens for a reason. I still don't know the reason I saw what I saw that morning. But looking down through the pines as I flew over them, I glimpsed a large piece of polished aluminum protruding from the snow.

It looked like the twisted, skeletal remains of an airplane wing.

✝

"South Lake Tahoe area traffic, Cessna Four Charlie Lima is five miles southwest of the field, descending through 8,000 feet. Crosswind entry, runway One-Eight, full-stop, South Lake Tahoe."

I radioed our intentions and instinctively leaned forward in my seat, scanning the sky. If there were any other aircraft landing or departing the field, I couldn't see them. The radio was silent. A good sign.

We turned base at pattern altitude. The view of Lake Tahoe off the *Duck's* passenger side was spectacular. White-caps danced on water the color of gunmetal. Savannah gazed serenely out the window, smiling to herself. That was always one thing I loved about her, her willingness to let beautiful moments speak for themselves, rather than diluting them with the obvious, "Isn't that beautiful?"

"South Lake Tahoe area traffic, Cessna Four Charlie Lima is turning final," I radioed, "runway One-Eight, South Lake Tahoe."

The *Duck* sniffed out the runway and settled onto the asphalt as gentle as a sigh. One of our better landings, if I do say so myself.

"You should think about being a pilot," Savannah said, teasing me. "You're not half bad at it."

"Thanks for the suggestion. I'll definitely give it some thought."

I broadcast that we were "down and clear" of the runway, and taxied toward an arrow and a sign that said, "Transient parking." A tall, gangly ramp attendant in his mid-twenties, wearing faded Levis and a florescent green safety vest over a hooded San Francisco 49ers sweatshirt, directed us to a tie-down spot in front of Summit Aviation Services, the local fixed-base operator. After I'd shut down the engine, he set the wheel chocks and began chaining down the *Duck's* wings to the tarmac, then held Savannah's door open for her.

"I'm Chad. Welcome to Tahoe," he said, brushing his long, unkempt dirty blond hair out of his face. He had sallow eyes, ice blue. "Where're you guys in from?"

I wanted to ask him at what point did people begin referring to both men and women synonymously as "guys?" But I didn't.

"Rancho Bonita," I said, "by way of Los Angeles."

"Sweet. My girlfriend lives down in Rancho Bonita—actually, my *former* girlfriend. We still talk pretty much every day, though. One of those deals where we tell each other pretty much everything. No holding back. Maybe that's why we broke up. Who knows, right?"

"Something to strive toward in any relationship, that degree of openness and emotional intimacy," Savannah said, looking directly at me with one eyebrow raised. "Wouldn't you agree, Logan?"

"Oh, absolutely."

"Maybe you know her," Chad said opening the *Duck's* baggage door and taking out our luggage. "Her name's Cherry

Rosales. She works at Nordstrom, the store downtown. Sells jewelry."

"Actually," I said, "I'm more of a Sears kind of guy."

The air was cold enough that we could see our breath. Chad asked how long we planned to stay and whether we needed any recommendations on accommodations in the Tahoe area. Savannah gave him the name of the local bed-and-breakfast where she'd made reservations.

"As for how long we're staying," she said, "that all depends on how well my pilot and I are getting along."

"We're getting married," I said, clarifying matters.

"Seriously?" Chad's expression implied that people our age were as likely to croak from some incurable disease as they were to get hitched.

"Yeah. Seriously."

"Hey, that's totally cool. Congratulations."

Savannah said we'd need a rental car, to which Chad replied, "No problem." I said that the *Duck's* gas tanks would need to be topped off to which he offered the same response.

"Got your complimentary hot coffee inside, sodas, cookies, peanut butter pretzels, what have you. Feel free to help yourself. Marlene'll hook you up with all the paperwork for the car and your fuel order. I'll bring your bags in. Anything else I can do for you folks today?"

"You can call the local search and rescue team for me. I saw something when we were flying in. West, about 10 miles out, up in the hills. It looked like a downed airplane."

"You're shittin' me. A downed airplane? Really?" Chad promptly apologized to Savannah for swearing and said he was trying to break the profanity habit.

No big deal, Savannah said. She'd heard worse.

"I haven't heard of any planes missing for a while," Chad said, "either coming in or going out of here, but, hey, you never know, right?"

"Could be it's been up there for some time and nobody noticed," I said.

— 41 —

The kid nodded, then snapped his fingers like he'd just thought of something.

"Hey, what if it's Amelia Earhart?"

"Hey," I said, tipping him a five-spot, "what if it's not?"

☩

THE AFOREMENTIONED Marlene, Summit Aviation Services' zaftig, forty-something receptionist, made Chad seem downright rude by comparison. She waived the overnight parking fee for the *Duck* because we were buying gas, and upgraded our rental car from a compact to a GMC Yukon at no additional cost. Then she brewed a fresh pot of coffee and insisted on serving us oatmeal cookies more freshly baked than the ones that had been sitting on her desk.

"And did I mention we have complimentary bicycles for your enjoyment?—though it's probably not the best time of the year to go for a bike ride. Been pretty darned nippy around here."

She leaned over the coffeemaker and poured us Styrofoam cups of hot joe.

The steam fogged the lenses of Marlene's red-frame bifocals and made her brunette shag even shaggier. Her face was soft and full. I noticed faint dark rings obscured by makeup under both eyes. Natural shading, or the result of being punched? I couldn't tell.

"So nice of you," Savannah said. "Thank you."

"Just trying to keep the customer satisfied." Marlene smiled. "I believe that was a lyric in an old Simon and Garfunkel song, was it not?"

"I believe it was," Savannah said.

My ex-wife caught my eye and winked subtly. She knew that I keenly distrusted overtly friendly people until such time as they'd shown their true colors—people like genuinely nice Mrs. Schmulowitz. Geniality, I've learned the hard way, often belies the blackest of instincts, hard-wired impulses that

— 42 —

cruise sharklike behind cordial smiles, ready to surface at little provocation. I've known remorseless murderers who would've been perceived as "nice" by any definition when they were not out slaughtering innocents. I've personally removed a few of those "nice" people from the planet. But that was before I was introduced to the Buddha who is all about giving strangers the benefit of the doubt, including seemingly well-meaning receptionists.

"Another cookie?" Marlene said.

"Don't mind if I do."

The door opened and Chad came in off the flight line, holding his iPhone to his right ear.

"No, ma'am, I'm not the pilot. I just work here. The pilot's right here." He handed me the phone. "El Dorado Sheriff's Department. They want to talk to you."

The voice on the other end identified herself as Sergeant Somebody. I didn't catch her name. She said she was the watch commander on duty. I told her what I'd told Chad, about what I'd seen, and approximately where I'd seen it. If I'd had any presence of mind, I told her, I would've noted the exact location on my GPS receiver, the latitude and longitude, and written it down. But I hadn't.

"Nobody's perfect," the sergeant assured me.

What I'd seen was likely nothing, she said, but department policy compelled her to have the tip thoroughly investigated regardless. Was I willing to talk to a deputy in person? She could have one at the airport in about half an hour.

I was in no hurry, I said, and handed Chad back his phone.

"My lord, a plane crashed?" Marlene's hand was over her mouth as she sat down behind her desk. "I hope everyone's OK."

"We don't know if it's a plane crash yet," Chad said, delivering an invoice to her, documenting how many gallons of fuel he'd pumped into the *Duck*. "It *might* be a crash. Or nothing at all."

I noticed a small, round spider web tattooed on the right side of Chad's neck as he leaned across the counter to hand Marlene his paperwork. Web tats of any kind commonly convey that the bearer has done prison time, but Chad didn't seem like the inmate type to me. I kept the observation to myself.

Savannah said she wanted to drive into South Lake Tahoe and check into the $300-a-night bed-and-breakfast that she'd carefully researched online and insisted on paying for because she knew I couldn't. When I was done talking to the deputy, I would call her. She'd then come back to the airport and pick me up. Time permitting, after that, we would drive to Incline Village at the northeast end of the lake, on the Nevada side, and take out a sixty-dollar license at the Washoe County Marriage License Bureau. Then we'd stop in at the Dream-Maker chapel—where Tom Selleck, among many other Hollywood types, got married, according to Savannah—and retie the knot. No muss, no fuss, she said. I wouldn't even have to change my clothes.

"You're getting married? How romantic," Marlene gushed. "You should've said something." She waddled into a back room and returned seconds later with a box about the size of a Twinkie. It was wrapped in plain red paper with a silver ribbon tied around it. "A small token of congratulations from Summit Aviation Services. We get a lot of people coming up here wanting to get married. Tom Selleck got married up here, you know."

"So I've heard," I said.

"You can open it now if you want," Marlene said.

"Sure. Why not?" Savannah slowly unwrapped the box, careful not to tear the paper, as all women inexplicably do.

Inside was a night light. Embossed on the plastic lens was a full-color rendition of Orville and Wilbur Wright.

"Their eyes light up when you plug it in," Marlene said. "We got a whole bunch of 'em on eBay for next to nothing. Isn't it beautiful?"

Savannah wasn't sure how to respond.

I managed a persuasive smile. And then, if only to wow my ex-wife with my civility, I added, "Thanks for such a lovely gift, Marlene."

Savannah seemed duly impressed.

✝

CHAD SPREAD a copy of the San Francisco-area FAA aeronautical chart on a long wooden conference table in the pilots' lounge. I pointed to the location where I'd spotted what I assumed was wreckage.

"And you're sure that that's where it was?" Deputy Kyle Woo said.

"Affirmative."

Woo leaned over the map, studying it and jotting notes in a black leather binder. He was Asian-American, stocky, in his early thirties. The pumped muscles under his tan uniform shirt told me he was a power weight lifter. His insulated nylon sheriff's jacket matched the deep green of his tactical pants. A .40-caliber Glock rode on his right hip.

"I used to go camping up there off of Chalmers Peak all the time," Chad said. "I'm real familiar with that area. Saw a porcupine up near there once. I'm on this game trail and the dude walks right out in front of me, like, no big deal. Didn't even look at me or nothing. I thought at first maybe it was a wolverine or a beaver or some such, but nope, it wasn't. It was a damn porcupine. Can you believe that?"

Woo looked up at the kid from his note-taking and said, "Pretty weird." His dark, narrow eyes betrayed zero emotion and seemed to miss nothing.

"Yup, pretty weird," Chad said. He seemed nervous under the deputy's gaze. "Well, anyway, I'm outta here. Started work at six this morning. So, unless there's anything else I can do for you gentlemen . . ."

"I think we've got it under control," Woo said.

— 45 —

"Cool, cool. Well, enjoy the rest of your day."

Chad turned and nearly collided with a large man with a ragged haircut who reminded me a little of Fred Flintstone. He was carrying an oversized soda cup with a straw in it and a food bag from McDonald's.

"What're you still doing hanging around here, Chad Lovejoy? You were supposed to be off shift an hour ago."

"I was just—"

"You were just stealing my money, is what you were doing," the man said, cutting him off. "I'm not paying you overtime. How many times I gotta tell you that?"

"Fine. I'm leaving."

"You do that. But before you do, there's a couple boxes in the back of my station wagon. I want you to move them into the supply room."

"You're the boss," Chad said as he left, shooting an anxious glance in the direction of Deputy Woo, who was still writing in his notepad. "I'll get right on it."

Chad's boss was decked out in tan Dockers and a white, oxford-cloth dress shirt, over which he wore a blue, Northface ski parka embossed with the Summit Aviation Services corporate logo. His dour sneer suggested he was not happy at the sight of Deputy Woo.

"So, what's going on?" He plopped his burger bag on the table along with a fat key ring. Attached to the ring was a small metal silhouette of a tailless Australian shepherd dog.

Woo barely gave the man a glance.

"This is Gordon Priest," the deputy said. "Mr. Priest is the manager here at Summit Aviation. He's suing me because I cited his sixteen-year-old daughter for minor in possession."

"She has *one* lousy beer and you treat her like it's her third strike."

Woo kept his calm. "Mr. Logan's a transient pilot. He thinks he may have observed a downed airplane while he was flying in this morning."

"Welcome." Priest unwrapped a Big Mac and devoured half of it in one bite. "What kind of plane was it?"

"Couldn't tell. All I saw was what looked like a section of a wing."

"The Civil Air Patrol routinely notifies us of any missing or overdue planes," Priest said, a bit of lettuce clinging to his lower lip. "Same goes for any ELT signals anywhere in northern California and western Nevada, and we haven't gotten any of those in a long time."

Not everybody files a flight plan, which requires a pilot to list, among other information, the estimated time of arrival at his intended destination. If he's late getting there, the FAA will begin looking for him in short order. Without a flight plan on file, nobody will come looking unless someone reports that plane missing, or saw it go down.

Moreover, not all emergency locator transmitters, which are designed to automatically trigger after a plane crashes, will prompt rescue teams to swing into action. The problem is that most older airplanes are equipped with transmitters that broadcast emergency signals on a frequency no longer monitored by orbiting satellites. In other words, if what I'd seen was, in fact, a missing airplane, there was a good possibility that nobody in officialdom even knew about it. If injured souls were on board, it was imperative to reach the crash site as quickly as possible.

"Where'd you see this supposed wreck?" Priest said, polishing off his Big Mac and unwrapping a second.

I showed him on the chart.

He frowned. "I haven't heard of any airplanes going down in that area in all the time I've been working here. You ask me, if it *is* a plane, it's probably been up there for years, and it's already been reported. Happens all the time, old wrecks getting reported as new."

"I hope you're right. You appear to be a man who usually is."

He was too busy stuffing his face to acknowledge the dig.

Woo asked me if I'd be willing to accompany him on a drive up to the mountains, to give him better perspective of where to begin looking. I said yes. Anyone with any sense of responsibility would've done the same.

The nuptials would have to wait.

✝

Savannah said she more than understood, though I'm not sure she did. Our suite at the romantic Victorian B&B that she'd found online, she told me over the phone, didn't disappoint. We had an antique poster bed with a view of the lake and our own private deck. She wanted to know when I'd be back.

I looked across the center console shotgun mount of Deputy Woo's Jeep Wrangler, with the sheriff's star on the doors, and relayed Savannah's query to Woo as he and I rode west out of South Lake Tahoe on US 50, toward Echo Summit.

"Depends on what we see," Woo said. "Probably around five."

"The marriage license office closes at five," Savannah said.

"We'll pick up the license tomorrow. What's one more day? No big deal, right?"

"Right." She was disappointed, but trying not to sound it.

"I'm not changing my mind between now and then, Savannah. I'm not bailing, if that's what you're worried about."

"I know. It's just that . . . I had everything all planned out for tonight. I wanted it to be . . . special."

"It'll still be special tomorrow night."

"Let's hope so." She cleared her throat. "See you tonight."

"You can count on it."

I slid my phone into the front pocket of my jeans and gazed out at the passing landscape: rocky escarpments to the right and a sheer drop-off into steep canyons to our left. Traffic was sparse.

"You getting married?" Woo said.

— 48 —

"Remarried. We split a few years back. Decided to give it another go."

He said nothing, his dark, expressionless eyes fixed on the road ahead.

I asked him if he was married.

"No."

"Girlfriend?"

"No."

"Boyfriend?"

Long silence.

"You always this chatty, Deputy Woo?"

The right side of his mouth turned upward a couple of millimeters into what I gathered was a smile. That was all I got out of him for the next ten miles or so until the cliffs to the north gave way to dense stands of lodge pole pines on either side of the highway. Woo flipped a switch, activating the flashing red and blue police lights atop his Wrangler, as we came up on a break in the trees, then pulled off the road, onto the shoulder. From under his seat he produced a pair of binoculars.

"Where you pointed to on the map," Woo said, "it's up there."

He checked his mirrors for oncoming cars before getting out. I joined him on a low berm just off the road, affording an unobstructed view of the mountainous terrain to the north. The air was crisp, approaching brisk. I wished I'd thought to bring a warmer coat.

"That's Mount San Carlos on the left and Chalmers Peak on the right," the deputy said, pointing, "and that area between is where you said you saw whatever it was you saw."

He handed me the binoculars. It wasn't difficult to orient myself. Through the magnified lenses, I clearly recognized the bow of craggy, barren rocks linking the two mountains, below which I'd first spotted from the air what I was increasingly convinced were the remains of an airplane. Beyond that, I could make out nothing identifiable other than trees; the forest was too thick.

Woo estimated we were about six miles from the site as the crow flies. He knew of an unpaved logging road that wended about halfway there. The remaining miles would have to be negotiated on foot.

"It'll be sunset in a couple of hours," he said. "Search and rescue can head up first thing in the morning. I'm sure they could use your company."

"Why not fly? Doesn't the sheriff's department have a helicopter? There could be injured people up there."

The sheriff did, in fact, have a helicopter, Woo said, but the conditions of its use in tight budgetary times were extremely restrictive. Unconfirmed reports of downed airplanes apparently fell outside those limits.

"That's all I can do, Mr. Logan." He turned and trudged back down the slope toward his Wrangler, his hands stuffed in the pockets of his jacket.

I scanned the mountainsides with the binoculars one last time. There was really nothing to see beyond those towering peaks and a forest so deep and silent as to be almost unreal.

I'm not a big believer in extrasensory perception. People who claim powers of clairvoyance are con artists half the time, by my experience, and the other half, fruitcakes. But I couldn't shake the powerful sense that *something* was up there, beneath those trees, waiting for me, and that whatever it was, it wasn't good.

FOUR

Johnny and Gwen Kavitch operated Tranquility House, the meticulously kept, Victorian-style bed-and-breakfast where Savannah had booked us a bungalow. They were unbelievably nice in a laid-back, Grateful Dead kind of way. I was immediately suspicious of them.

It was late afternoon. The four of us were commiserating in their parlor. A full-sized concert harp was propped in one corner. The Kavitches had laid out a spread of cheeses on an antique sideboard, paired with bottles of what I assumed was good wine. So far as I could tell, we were their only guests. At 300 bucks a night, there was no mystery as to why.

Gwen was a gaunt blonde gone gray with a world-class overbite and a pair of those shaded, prescription glasses that are supposed to lighten indoors but never quite do, leaving the vague impression that the wearer is either high or hung over. She'd spent nearly thirty years as a special education teacher in San Jose, she told Savannah and me, before budget cuts forced her to take early retirement.

"We're just so pleased you chose to share your special occasion with us," she said. "It's just so *awesome.*"

Gwen said "awesome" a lot, a habit that I found less than awesome.

Johnny was even more pallid than his wife. Garbed in Mexican sandals, faded corduroys and a gray "Old Guys Rule" T-shirt, he rocked a wispy goatee and a shaved head that reminded me more than a little of a hardboiled egg.

Savannah complimented them on their selection of paint color for the parlor's nine-foot walls.

"It's called 'fallen oak leaf,'" Johnny Kavitch said. "Isn't it gorgeous?"

"Looks pretty much like tan to me," I said.

Savannah gave me a look. There was a lull in the conversation. Being a whiz at small talk, I took note of the harp leaning in the corner.

"Musical instruments lend ambiance to a room," I said, like I knew anything about home decor.

I should've said nothing.

Johnny dove into a ten-minute monologue on the ethereal qualities of the harp, its long history, and how he'd always wanted to take lessons, but waited until retiring from the IRS field office in San Jose and moving up to Lake Tahoe, for fear that his fellow auditors might tease him.

"I'd love to play you something," he said.

"Johnny's an awesome musician," Gwen said, beaming at him.

My ex-wife embedded her burgundy fingernails in my forearm before I could say not just no, but hell no.

"That would be lovely," Savannah said.

We sat through Johnny Kavitch's rendition of Barbra Streisand's "Evergreen," which was followed by Barry Manilow's "Can't Smile Without You," replete with Gwen singing along. I was ready to start drinking after that. The only problem was, I stopped drinking years ago. I could tell by her thin smile that Savannah was in agony, too, but there'd be no alcoholic respite for her, either. She was pregnant.

Mercifully, the harp concert was cut short when a surly beanpole in his mid-twenties garbed in saggy jeans, black combat boots, and a Def Leppard sweatshirt barged into the room.

"Who ate my pizza?" he demanded. "It was sitting in the refrigerator last night. Now it's fucking gone."

He was around twenty-seven, six foot three, and all of about 155 pounds. Dark, greasy hair fell to his bony shoulders like strands on a wet mop. Gwen ignored the beanpole's outburst and introduced him pleasantly as their son and resident maintenance supervisor, Preston.

"Preston, these are our guests, Mr. Logan and Ms. Echevarria. They've come all the way from Rancho Bonita to get married—remarried, I should say. Mr. Logan's a pilot. He flew them up here in his own airplane. Isn't that awesome?"

Preston gave me a sidelong glance that was anything but friendly.

"Did you eat my pizza?" he demanded.

"Wasn't me, dude."

"Me, either," Savannah said.

"I cannot tell a lie," Johnny said, carefully leaning the harp back against the wall. "I ate your pizza, Preston, and, boy, was it tasty. But fear not. I'll get you another one." He tried to pat him on the back. Preston pulled away.

"That was my pizza—mine, OK? I paid for it with my own money."

"It's no big deal," Johnny said. "I'll get you another one."

Preston fixed his father with a daggers-of-death glare. "Why don't you do the world a favor and just die. I hate you. Both of you." He swept a pair of brass candlesticks off the parlor's ornately carved mantle and onto the oak floor, stomping out of the parlor. I heard the front door open and slam behind him.

Gwen smiled as she picked up the candlesticks. "He's only like this when he forgets to take his meds. We never take it personally."

"He's really a total sweetheart otherwise," Johnny said.

"I'm sure he is," Savannah said sympathetically.

I was hardly sure. You don't openly speak ill of your parents without having given the idea at least a little thought.

✝

DINNER DID little to lighten my mood. The Kavitches recommended a little sushi place about a half mile up the road. "A bit on the pricey side," Gwen said, "but the most awesome sashimi you'll ever eat."

She was right about the prices. She was flat wrong about the rest.

The restaurant was in a strip mall. Six tables. Posters advertising Kirin beer tacked to the walls. A few sorry koi kites hanging from the ceiling.

"Feels like we're in Tokyo," I said as we walked in.

"I'm sure it's perfectly fine," Savannah said.

The two chefs working behind the counter were white. Not that being born in Japan is a prerequisite for working with raw fish. But both of these guys looked like their only prior seafood experience was eating at Long John Silver's. And both looked to be half drunk.

We ordered miso soup, which wasn't terrible, and a few hand rolls, which were.

"I've had better sushi at Costco," I said.

"What is it with you and Costco?"

"Costco's the American way of life, Savannah. Americans will willingly stand in line for an hour if they think they're saving a buck for a lifetime supply of Spanish olives, even if they hate Spanish olives. It's what the founding fathers envisioned when they wrote the constitution: naked consumerism run amok in a giant metal warehouse."

She picked at a piece of soy sauce-soaked ginger with her chopsticks and smiled one of those smiles where you can tell there's not much happiness behind it.

"We'll go get the license tomorrow morning," Savannah said, "and tomorrow night, we'll have a dinner to remember."

I cleared my throat, sucked down the last of my soup and avoided eye contact. I didn't have the heart to tell her that I'd agreed to guide members of the sheriff's search and rescue team into the mountains at dawn. They needed somebody to show them where the crash site was, assuming it was a crash site. Chances were good I wouldn't be back until after the marriage license office had closed for yet another day.

"There's something you're not telling me, Logan."

Her eyes demanded answers. With good reason. Much of our marriage had been tainted by the nature of my work, the deception inherent in how I once earned a paycheck. You can be a trained prevaricator of the highest order, a first-ballot inductee to the Liars Hall of Fame, as I was back then, and the woman you share a bed with will always know the truth on some subliminal level. Savannah had me dialed in. She always did.

I explained to her the obligation that compelled me to put off our exchanging vows for yet another day, the unspoken bond that compels one pilot to help another in crisis.

"Somebody could still be alive up there," I said. "And even if there isn't, there's got to be family somewhere, relatives, wondering what happened to the people on that plane. They have a right to know, Savannah. If I were up there in those mountains, I'd expect the same effort to be made in your behalf."

She nodded and told me I was doing the right thing. She said my conscientious nature was among the qualities she always found most attractive in me. And she apologized for being petulant without me having accused her of it.

"But I'd be lying," Savannah said, "if I said that I wasn't disappointed. I wanted this trip to be the beginning of the rest of our lives together, Logan. I wanted it to be romantic. All it feels like now is the way things always felt: you going off, doing your thing, regardless of me or my wants. Only in this case, I actually *know* where you're going and what you're doing."

I apologized for disappointing her.

"Don't worry about it," Savannah said. "You'll have plenty of time to make it up to me."

She gave me a wink.

I wanted to kiss her. And did.

✝

H<small>AD</small> I been able to see the ceiling that night in our bungalow at the B&B, I would've lain awake, staring at it. As it was, all I could see over my head was the gingham, rose-colored canopy of our poster bed.

Savannah rolled away from me, taking the covers with her. I was too hot anyway and she was always too cold—opening and closing the bedroom window was often a point of friction during our first marriage. That was before I discovered Buddhism and the duality of life. There can be no up without down, no joy without sorrow, no heat without cold. The sooner we embrace uncomfortable opposites, the more content we'll be.

"I can shut the window if you're chilly," I said.

"I'm OK."

"You sure? I don't want the baby catching cold."

"Babies don't catch cold, Logan, not in the womb."

"Good to know."

Savannah rolled over to face me.

"What if it's a girl?" she said.

"Makes no difference to me."

"You wouldn't be disappointed if we had a daughter?"

"I probably would be when she's a teenager. Larry has a daughter in high school. He says it's like trying to defend a box of raw chicken in a swamp filled with gators."

"It's the male who decides the gender, Logan. Your little swimmers. Sixteen years from now, you'll only have yourself to blame. Just so you know."

"We should be so lucky."

She cuddled in closer. "I love you."

"I love you, too."

"Tell me we're gonna be OK, Logan."

"More than OK."

There was no response. A minute or so passed. I could tell by her slow, sonorous breathing that she'd gone to sleep. I always admired that, Savannah's ability to simply turn off the day, its nagging disappointments, and drift off. My mind, meanwhile, raced in the darkness among myriad ruminations. What would it be like being married again, and responsible 24-7 for a life other than my own? How would I earn a viable income to support my child? What was up there, on that mountain? What if what I saw was nothing? Was I leading authorities on a goose chase?

I closed my eyes. Savannah was in my arms, her soft, warm breath on my chest. It's possible I may have slept.

✛

DEPUTY WOO picked me up before dawn. I'd rolled out of bed quietly, careful not to wake Savannah, and dressed in the dark. Through the front window of our getaway bungalow, I watched a jogger slowly plod the Lake Tahoe shoreline in Spandex leggings, stocking cap and a ski parka. The condensation of his breath clouded in his wake like steam from a locomotive. Definitely cold out there. Part of me toyed with the tantalizing prospect of crawling back under warm covers and snuggling with Savannah, but only fleetingly. Except for my spare boxers, I threw on every article of clothing I'd taken with me.

✛

SUNSHINE STREAMED through the pines. The first light of morning.

Woo navigated his four-wheel drive Wrangler along the rain-rutted logging road he'd pointed out to me a day earlier. Other than exchanging a "Good morning," and, a "Thanks, You're welcome" for the cup of McDonald's coffee he'd brought me, we'd said nothing to each other for more than twenty miles. He wasn't unfriendly. He was merely a man of few words. I respected that. Many of the great writers whose works I had devoured at the academy believed that language is a perishable commodity, that we're allotted only so many words in a lifetime. Once we've used them up, that's it. Game over. Could be Woo read the same books I had. Hard to know. It was hard to know anything about the guy. His face gave away nothing.

We passed an old cabin on our left, its two front windows covered over with tinfoil, a rust-bucket Chevy pickup parked out front. The shingles of its steeply pitched roof were dappled at the joints by green moss. White smoke curled languidly from the chimney. Somebody was home and up early.

The higher we climbed up the mountain, the less road-like the road became. The steering wheel twisted and spun in Woo's hands with each jarring furrow and rut. He maneuvered the Jeep expertly, like he'd negotiated many such roads before. A mule deer, a juvenile, given his immature rack, darted out from the trees to our right, no more than ten meters ahead of us, and flitted across the road back into the trees. Woo said nothing.

"Cold this morning," Woo said after awhile.

"Yep."

The "road" came to an abrupt end after another 400 meters or so, widening into a frost-dusted trailhead, about the size of a residential cul-de-sac, and rimmed on three sides by dense, dark forest. A Ford Explorer bearing El Dorado County Sheriff's Department insignia and the words "Search and Rescue" was parked in the small clearing. Two graybeards in their late fifties and a squat, beefy younger woman, all wearing mountain climbing helmets and florescent orange, one-piece ski suits, were busy hauling backpacks and brightly colored coils of nylon rope out of their vehicle.

Woo pulled in beside the Explorer, got out, and exchanged curt greetings with the search team members. I stepped out—and set foot directly in a patch of cold, sticky mud.

"Careful of the goop," the larger of the graybeards said. "It'll get you every time."

"Now you tell me."

He grinned, which made his bulbous nose, scarred white from bouts of skin cancer, seem even larger.

"Tom Wood," he said, extending his hand. "I'm team leader."

Wood was six foot one, my height, but stockier than my 190 pounds. The other male member of the team was five foot eight and 150 pounds at most. He wore a faded Batman sticker on his helmet and wire-frame eyeglasses. Wood introduced him as Richard Wojewodski.

"And this lovely lady," Wood said, "is Bree Kelly. Better mind your manners. Bree teaches tae kwon do."

"'Preciate you helping guide us in," Bree said. She had the grip of a professional wrestler.

I observed how none of them looked like cops. That's because they weren't, Wood said. They were unpaid civilian volunteers, he said, who coupled their love of the outdoors with passion for public service. Wood taught junior high math. Wojewodski designed software. Kelly was an electrician and part-time ski-lift operator at the nearby Heavenly Mountain Resort.

"I understand you're a pilot," she said.

"Flight instructor."

"Where?"

"Rancho Bonita."

If any of them were impressed by my occupation or city of residence, they hid it well.

"Good luck," Woo said, climbing back in his Jeep.

"You're not coming along?" Wood said.

"Too cold."

The search and rescue folks, Woo said, would give me a lift into town after they'd completed their mission. I watched him turn around and head back down the road, brake lights glowing, the SUV bouncing among the furrows and over rocks, before the forest swallowed him from view and he was gone.

Wood spread out a topographical map on the hood of his SUV, along with various satellite photographs. He asked me to confirm the location where I'd observed aircraft debris. After I did, he punched some buttons on a miniaturized GPS strapped to his wrist. We were looking at a two-hour climb at the minimum, he said, excluding rest breaks.

"You didn't bring any climbing gear of your own, obviously," Wood said.

"I hadn't planned on doing much climbing. I prefer flying over mountains."

He looked down at my low-cut, mud-caked Merrell hiking shoes, the kind favored by many covert operators in the field, including those of us who'd served with Alpha.

"You'll probably be OK in those," Wood said of my choice in footwear. "We'll take along an extra pair of crampons just in case. Might wanna lose some of that mud before we shove off. Your legs'll start to get heavy pretty quick otherwise."

He snapped open a folding knife and handed it to me. I walked across the small clearing toward a large rock, where I intended to sit and clean the soles of my boots while Wood and the others squared away first-aid equipment and shrugged on their backpacks. That's when I noticed fresh tire tracks on the frosty ground.

"Somebody's been up here already," I said.

Wood walked over and took a look at the tread marks. "Nobody was here when we showed up. And that was at five."

"Then they were here before then."

"What makes you think that?"

"Frost forms on clear nights, in early morning hours. Soon as the sun tops those trees, it'll melt off, just like it would've yesterday, given the weather. If you got here at five, then that means they were here sometime last night."

"How do you know we didn't leave those tracks, backing in and out?"

I glanced at the tires on Wood's Explorer, then at the marks left on the ground.

"The turning radius and wheelbase dimensions are different. Also, these tracks were left by smaller tires—a van or a small truck, would be my guess. Plus, you can see where the driver pulled in, put it in reverse, and headed back down the mountain."

Wood squatted for a closer look.

"For a flight instructor," he said, "you sure seem to know a lot about tire tracks."

We learned all about tire tracks at Alpha, along with hundreds of other seemingly trivial topics of study. When you stalk terrorists across the globe in the name of national security, any knowledge, our instructors constantly reminded us, can become an all-powerful weapon, however inconsequential that knowledge might seem in the classroom. Tom Wood didn't need to know all that, though.

"Tires are groovy," I said.

He strained to laugh.

✛

WHERE THE pine forest was thick and the sun could not penetrate the tops of the trees, the trail was hard packed and easily negotiated. Where the trees thinned, enough so that light could filter through, the path devolved into mud. You didn't need to be Tonto to spot two distinctly different sets of man-size footprints embedded in the brown muck. One set of prints was left by heavy-soled boots; the other, what looked like basketball or running shoes. And there was something else: to the right of the boot prints, plowed the length of the trail, were two shallow, thin gouges in the mud, spaced about a foot apart, like someone had dragged something down the mountain.

"Hikers," Bree Kelly said as she followed me up the trail. The same two hikers, she speculated, whose tire tracks I'd noted at the trailhead, now more than an hour's climb behind us.

"Can't be the same hikers," I said. "There's only one set of prints coming back down the hill—the guy wearing the boots."

"Could be the other guy found another way back down," Wojewodski said, bringing up the rear. "These mountains have unmarked game trails going off all over the place."

We stopped five minutes later for breakfast. Wojewodski offered me an apple from his pack. Wood gave me water from his CamelBak. Kelly shared a bag of trail mix. I pretended to eat the raisins, chucking them into the trees when nobody was looking. Why anyone eats dried, shriveled grapes unless they're starving is beyond me.

The trail ascended into a narrow canyon where the sun could not go and the temperature dropped at least ten degrees, then curved northeast along a barren moraine. We traversed across talus, avoiding a modest-sized snowfield, before picking up the path on the other side and climbing in elevation. I didn't complain when Wood stopped to check our bearings on a sun-splashed promontory overlooking Chalmers Peak and the barren granite ridge that ran south-to-north, bridging Chalmers to Mount San Marcos. I needed the rest. My legs and lungs were burning.

Wood studied the terrain ahead with a pair of scratched and dented field glasses.

"You say you saw the wreckage inside the tree line?"

I pointed. "Three hundred meters below that saddle, almost square in the center."

We were no more than a mile from the site, Wood said. The least exhausting way to get there, he concluded, was to find a chute leading to the top of the saddle, cross the saddle to its midpoint, then make our way down the rock face and back into the pines.

"Piece of cake," Wojewodski said, tightening the waist belt on his pack.

It was no piece of cake.

That one mile translated to a grueling, sweat-soaking, seventy-minute endurance test which probably would've taken considerably less time had I not lost my footing and slid about thirty feet down a sheer rock slope, twisting my football-damaged right knee and scraping up my left elbow. Wood and his colleagues had to rope me back up.

"Anything damaged?" Bree Kelly asked, checking me over.

"Only my pride."

I stuffed the pain in a compartment deep in my brain and continued on.

"Anybody who thinks global warming is a hoax needs to come up here and have a look," Wood said as we trudged single file behind him. "Fifty years ago, this whole area was covered with glaciers. They're all melting, going away. Could be that's why you saw whatever it was you saw."

"Assuming you didn't imagine it," Bree Walker said.

✝

WOJEWODSKI SPOTTED the debris first. The four of us had spread out line abreast, twenty meters apart, advancing slowly through the trees, when he yelled out, "Hey, I think I got something!"

I could see instantly what he'd found: remnants of a nacelle, the protective, cigar-shaped structure that protects an airplane engine. The shredded, unpainted aluminum, and what was left of the big radial engine it once housed, were wedged against a large pine and partially buried as though driven into the ground by some great force. Gouged in the earth behind the wreckage was a shallow trench twenty meters or so in length and no more than about a foot deep. This was where the nacelle had first struck the ground and been dragged along like the keel board from a sailboat before slamming to a stop against the tree. The thick blanket of pine needles that had fallen onto the trench and the nacelle, all but obscuring both from above, told me that they'd been there a long time, perhaps decades. The depth of the trench told me that the airplane to which the nacelle had once been attached had probably impacted the earth at a relatively shallow angle, as though the pilot had been flying more or less straight and level when he crashed.

Scattered to my left and similarly buried under years of pine needles, I could easily make out twisted pieces of airplane skin and frame: wing spars and ribs and what appeared to have once been an elegantly rounded wingtip.

"Hey, you guys! Hey, over here!"

I turned and saw Wood in a narrow draw, down slope, far to my right. He was waving frantically, motioning for us to come quickly. I ran as fast as my banged-up knee would allow.

There, in the shadow of the ridgeline that towered above us, partially covered over by snow and broken pine branches, was the mostly intact fuselage of a venerable, twin-engine Beechcraft, a Model 18. The empennage, or tail assembly, looked to have been sheared off.

As I approached it from the rear, I could see that the plane had come to rest on its belly, listing slightly to the left, the ground around it strewn with jagged pieces of aluminum and other debris shed upon impact. The fuselage door, aft of where the wings had ripped away when the plane went into the trees, was canted open, dangling by a single hinge. Inside the door was an open wooden crate, approximately three feet by three feet. On the ground directly outside the door was what looked to be one side of the crate. The tail number—NC1569—was evidence that the plane was more than 60 years old. Federal aviation authorities stopped adding the letter "C" to aircraft "N" registrations soon after World War II.

Through the shattered cockpit windows I gazed down at the mummified remains of the pilot, whose body was only partially decomposed thanks to the glacial conditions where his aircraft had come to rest. He was slumped forward, still strapped into the left seat. The right front quadrant of his chalky skull was missing, along with most of his front teeth—injuries that I assumed he had incurred when his face smacked the instrument panel upon impact. He'd been wearing a woolen watch cap and a double-breasted navy peacoat when he died. Both were now moth-chewed and hanging from his body in tatters. He'd also been armed. The butt of what looked like a .45-caliber, semiautomatic Colt Model 1911A protruded from the right pocket of his coat.

None of that, however, gave me as much pause as what I saw next, and left me wondering what the hell I'd gotten myself into.

Lying beside the wreckage, just forward of the airplane's crumpled nose, was the dead body of a young man. His arms and legs were outstretched, like he'd been making a snow angel.

Lifeless green eyes stared up at a cloudless sky. Around the torso was snow dyed black with blood. Goose feathers poked out from three dime-size bullet holes in the front of his down-filled, shiny black parka.

"Anybody recognize him?" Wood asked.

"His name's Chad," I said, staring down at the young man's face. "He worked at the Tahoe airport."

FIVE

The terrain wasn't flat or clear enough for the El Dorado County sheriff's Jetranger to put down, so the helicopter pilots landed in a meadow about a quarter mile to the west. The homicide investigator assigned to the case hiked in the rest of the way.

Wood showed him where he'd found fresh prints of climbing boots that tracked across a crusty patch of snow, away from the crash site, then accompanied him to Chad's body.

The investigator walked slowly around the corpse, pausing periodically and squatting on his haunches to assess it from different angles, like he was lining up a putt. He was in his mid-thirties, on the stocky side, with sandy, close-cropped hair and a requisite cop moustache that hadn't quite grown in yet. He wore jump boots, green uniform pants bloused at the calves, a tan uniform shirt, and a green tactical vest under a green sheriff's parka. A badge was stitched in gold on the chest, just below his name tag: Streeter.

He snapped on a latex glove and tugged gently on the kid's left hand, which was bent awkwardly inward at the wrist, palm up, fingers outstretched. There was little give in the fingers indicating Chad had probably been dead at least twelve hours—the time it takes humans to reach maximum stiffness after death, depending on their individual physiology and ambient air temperatures. Yet one more thing you learn hunting terrorists.

"Anybody touch anything?" the investigator wanted to know. "Move anything? The body? Inside the plane? Anything?"

All three search and rescuers adamantly shook their heads no.

"Good. Let's keep it that way. We've got patrol units scouring the area for suspects. I'll get the forensics team up here A-SAP." Streeter stood, rubbing his chin with the heel of his hand, and peered in through the broken cockpit window at what was left of the pilot. "Whoa. I'd say this dude's definitely been up here awhile."

"Since October, 1956," I said. "I'm guessing the plane was somewhere out of the LA area."

Streeter turned and gave me a "Who the hell are you?" look.

"This is Mr. Logan," Wood said. "He was the pilot who spotted the wreck yesterday."

"Why 1956?" Streeter said.

"There's a bunch of old newspapers wadded up in the rear of the plane—copies of the *Los Angeles Times*. All the ones I saw were from October '56. 'Cincinnati's Birdie Tebbetts Named National League Manager of the Year.' 'Soviet Troops Invade Hungary.'"

Streeter wasn't happy with me. He asked me my name again. I told him.

"You went *inside* the plane? You contaminated the crime scene, Mr. Logan."

"I touched nothing, disturbed nothing. All I did was take a look. I'd suggest you do the same, Deputy. There's something you really need to see."

I pointed out the side of the plywood crate, lying on the ground outside the fuselage door, and the nongalvanized box nails jutting from the wood, their tips bent and shiny.

"The nails aren't rusty," I said.

"Which means what?"

"Which means they haven't been outside long enough to get rusty. And the plywood's not warped. Somebody pried open that crate and tossed out that piece within the last day."

He looked inside the fuselage door at the crash-damaged crate, sitting open and empty, save for hundreds of balled-up pieces of newspaper scattered in and around it.

"They used the wadded-up paper to pad whatever was inside the crate," I said. "Whatever the shooter found inside that crate was so valuable, it apparently was worth pumping three slugs into that kid over there."

Streeter wouldn't admit it, but I could tell by the way he rubbed the side of his face that I was talking sense.

"What kind of plane is this?" he said.

"A twin-engine Beech 18. Also known as a 'Twin Beech' because of the twin tail. Beechcraft started building them before World War II. Cranked 'em out for more than thirty years. Great airplane. They were the Lear jets of their day. The FAA should still have a record of it on file based on the tail number. They'll know who owned it back in the day. They'll also know when it was reported missing."

Streeter exhaled and said he'd check it out. He clearly didn't like anyone telling him how to do his job.

✝

It was past 1630 hours by the time the sheriff's helicopter flew me back to the South Lake Tahoe Airport, then took off again almost immediately, airlifting two crime scene analysts to the crash scene. I watched the chopper lift off, grateful at not having had to hike all the way back out. I checked on the *Ruptured Duck*, making sure he was securely tied down on the flight line, and patted his nose like the trusty mount that he was. Then, feeling tired and hungry, my knee throbbing, I walked into Summit Aviation Services.

Marlene was sitting behind the reception counter, sobbing.

"One of the sheriff's helicopter pilots said it was Chad they found up there. Please tell me that's not true."

"I'm afraid it is, Marlene."

"I'm sorry," she said, drying her eyes with a Kleenex. "I don't mean to get all emotional. You look like a man who could use a hot cup of hot coffee."

She started to get up. I insisted that she stay put and helped myself to both.

"Such a nice young man." Marlene shook her head and took a deep breath. Her chin quivered. "It's just so terrible. Why'd he go up there? For what? Why would anybody want to hurt Chad? I don't understand."

"Nobody does at this point. Except whoever did it."

She said she'd been trying to reach Summit's manager, Gordon Priest, to give him the bad news, but Priest wasn't answering his cell phone.

"I know he'll take it hard," Marlene said, her voice cracking. "They bickered once in a while, but Gordon was Chad's uncle. He really loved Chad. They were like two peas in a pod, those two."

Priest, she volunteered without me asking, had gone to a big operational meeting at the FAA's Flight Standards District Office in Reno. He'd left a message that morning on the answering machine saying he wasn't sure he'd be back in the office that day before close of business.

"I know he'll be devastated," Marlene repeated.

The Buddha advised great caution when prejudging others, "lest you run the risk of being wrong." That kind of blind, benefit-of-the-doubt benevolence doesn't allow much maneuver room for the kind of gut instinct I was trained to follow when I worked for the government. My gut told me in this instance that it was more than coincidence, Gordon Priest being away at some out-of-town "business meeting" the day after the fatal shooting of his nephew. But if you're a Buddhist, you do your best to let the bad stuff go. You embrace the good in everyone, however much in short supply good may be these days.

And so I tried. Who, after all, murders his own nephew?

✝

"You were busy, Logan. I understand that. But it would've been nice if you'd called to let me know you'd be up there all day."

"I would've, Savannah, believe me, but there's no cell service."

She blew air through her lips and made a right turn off Airport Road, onto Emerald Bay, heading north toward our B&B, after picking me up. I turned on the Yukon's radio to break the strained silence in the car. A country tune was playing. Some guy whaling on his guitar with great earnestness, "Get your tongue out of my mouth 'cause I'm kissing you good-bye."

"Are you mad at me?"

Savannah shook her head.

"You seem mad."

"You were doing what you had to do. I'll get over it—but not if you don't turn off that awful song."

I turned off the radio.

"Thanks for picking me up."

"Of course."

More silence.

"We'll get the license tomorrow," I said, "assuming you still want to."

Savannah glanced over and gave me a smirk.

"I'll take that as a yes."

She almost smiled.

I reached across the seats of our rented Yukon and caressed her silken neck.

"So, what did you find up there? Anything?"

"An airplane."

"Really? Just like you said."

I didn't say anything.

"Anybody alive?"

"The plane had been up there a long time."

I debated filling in the blanks for her. About the skeletal dead pilot. About the mysteriously empty crate. About the dead young man we'd met at the airport the day before. But what purpose, I asked myself, would any of that have served, beyond unnerving the woman I wanted to spend the rest of my life with? We'd flown up to Lake Tahoe to get remarried. Tomorrow, we would. Nothing other than that mattered much in my opinion, not even a murder.

"Were there bodies?"

I looked out the window and didn't say anything.

"I'm just curious, Logan. You don't have to say if you don't want to."

"Yeah. There were bodies."

We rounded a curve doing fifty-five in a forty-five mph zone. A highway patrol cruiser was sitting on the shoulder of the road. Savannah braked, glancing down at the speedometer, then up anxiously in her rearview mirror as we passed by the cruiser. The cop didn't stop us, though. Savannah said it was an omen of good things to come. I attributed it to blind luck. But that's just me. I turned the radio back on to the same country-western station. The song that was playing, near as I could discern, was, "I'm Not Married, But the Wife Is."

Savannah, a native Texan who was not keen on the music she was subjected to as a child, groaned. "What in heaven's name are we listening to?" She reached down and changed stations: a smorgasbord of hip-hop, top-forty, Spanish language, then this:

"... said the wreckage was discovered below Voodoo Ridge, in a remote, mountainous area of the El Dorado National Forest, about eight miles west of South Lake Tahoe. There were no survivors. Officials said they believe the plane may have been missing for several years. Sources familiar with the investigation, meanwhile, told KKOH News that sheriff's authorities are treating the crash site as an active crime scene. Meanwhile, in the nation's capital today, congressional Republican leaders accused the White House of—"

I switched stations.

Savannah glanced over at me with a quizzical look on her face. "The plane's been missing for 'several years,' but they're treating it as an 'active crime scene?' That seems rather strange, doesn't it?"

"Somewhat."

She knew I was holding back.

✝

As Savannah slowed and turned into Tranquility House's small guest-parking area, I could see that the door of our bungalow was cracked open.

"That's weird," Savannah said. "I know I locked it before I went to get you."

"You sure?"

"Yes, Logan, I'm sure."

I told her to wait inside the car, got out, and approached the bungalow.

Among operators tasked with breaching a targeted structure, the first man through the door is known by various monikers. The Point Man. The Bullet Catcher. The Meat Shield. The guy voted Most Likely to Succumb. You never know who or what's waiting for you on the other side. A task for the faint of heart it's not. When you're unarmed and there's only one of you, as I was, the task can be especially daunting. I could've waited out whoever was inside, assuming anyone was, but waiting was never my style. That left two tactical options: storm in or sneak in. I opted for the latter, if only because it was the less confrontational way to go and thus, philosophically, more Buddhist-like.

I pressed my back against the wood siding of the adjacent wall. With my right arm extended, I slowly pushed open the door a few inches, careful to keep clear of the gap and the door itself, where a shooter was likely to fire if his intention was to stop me from coming in. The hinges were well-oiled. They didn't squeak. Nobody shot at me.

Had I still been with Alpha, serving as the point man in a standard, five-man entry team stacked up outside the door, I would've waited for the last guy in the stack to squeeze the shoulder of the guy ahead of him, indicating he was ready for action. That "ready" signal would have been passed up the train until the guy behind me squeezed my shoulder, telling me we were all good to go. Then we would've gone. With my submachine gun or short-barrel shotgun raised to my shoulder and ready to fire, I would've moved to my left, sweeping the room and my field of fire from left to right. The man directly behind me would've entered, shifted to my right, and scanned from right to left. We would've stayed a foot away from any walls because bullets tend to ricochet within six to eight inches of walls. And we would've put multiple hollow-point rounds into the vital organs and skulls of anyone remotely threatening. But, like I said, it was just me, and I was without the comforts of a good gun.

I waited a few seconds, exhaled slowly, and walked in.

The bed had been made. Things tidied up. Nothing looked amiss. Nobody was there. That's what I thought initially. Then, from inside the bathroom, I heard a male voice mutter, "Mmmm. Oh, yeah." I moved quietly and peaked around the corner:

Preston Kavitch, the son of our B&B hosts, Johnny and Gwen, was standing at the pedestal sink, in front of the antique, gilt-framed mirror. He was stroking his crotch with his right hand and caressing his left cheek with a pair of Savannah's black lace panties.

"Hey there, sport."

Startled, he stumbled backward and fell into the claw-footed tub.

"I was just—"

"—Just what? Doing your best Pee Wee Herman imitation?"

"Actually, I was . . ." Preston cleared his throat. His eyes darted in every direction but mine. "I was changing the light bulb over the sink. It went out. Your lady told my mother it was out before she left to go wherever. I'm in charge of maintenance. It's what I do. Only I couldn't find a sixty watt, so I had to get a seventy-five watt, which'll be bright, but that's OK. Not that big a difference between sixty and seventy-five. Uses more energy, but whatever."

His nervous eye movement and his manic elaboration of insignificant, irrelevant details, instead of sticking to the topic at hand—namely, him being a pervert—more than confirmed my suspicions that Preston Kavitch was exactly that.

"Please don't tell my parents, OK?"

"Why wouldn't I tell them?"

Preston had to think about that one for a second. "Because I'm really a nice guy?"

"Nice guys don't go round sniffing their guests' underwear, Preston."

"I wasn't sniffing. I was . . . appreciating."

"Hand 'em over, Preston."

He handed me the panties. Then he started crying.

"They'll kick me out of the house if you tell 'em," he said, crocodile tears flowing, still sitting in the tub with his legs hanging awkwardly over the edge. "I got nowhere else to go. Please, it won't happen again. I swear it."

There was a time when I would've ignored his begging and made a point to teach him a proverbial lesson he'd never forget, one that might've involved the spilling of blood and a broken bone or two. Back then, I didn't feel sorry for many people, including those who got down on their knees and begged me for their lives. I steeled myself against their pleas; they got what was coming to them. But then I started getting older, and maybe, more or less, a little wiser.

"Get up, Preston."

He gripped my outstretched hand and I hauled him out of the tub, just as Savannah came walking into the bungalow.

"Logan?"

"In here." I stuffed her panties in the back pocket of my jeans.

"Please," Preston whispered, "you can't tell her."

Savannah entered. "What's going on?"

"Preston had to change a light bulb."

"That's right," Preston said. He fished the old bulb out of the antique wire trash basket and made a point to show it to her. "Burned out. Just like you said."

"Thanks for getting to it so quickly," Savannah said. "It would've been hard to see in here tonight otherwise."

He gave me a furtive glance, lowered his head and walked out of the bathroom. I waited until I heard the door close and latch.

"You told his mother about the light bulb?" I asked Savannah.

"Yeah. Why?"

"Nothing."

I'd been wrong about Preston Kavitch. He hadn't lied to me. He may have been a disgusting pervert, but he was, at least in this instance, an honest one.

"You've got that look on your face," Savannah said.

"What look would that be?"

"The 'weight of the world' look. I've seen it before, Logan. Innumerable times. And I learned a long time ago that it's pointless, me asking you, 'What's wrong?' Because you'll never tell me, anyway. Now, why don't you slowly undress me and take me to bed?"

I was sorely tempted. I was also plain sore, not to mention exhausted. I couldn't decide which hurt more, my scraped elbow or twisted knee. Both of my feet were blistered. My shoulders felt like they'd been stomped on by contestants from "The Biggest Loser."

"Would you be offended," I said, "if I took a hot bath instead, alone?"

— 75 —

"No, I wouldn't be offended." She tilted her head subtly and her eyes smiled. "I just wish I'd had the presence of mind to bring along your Mr. Bubble."

"I'll survive."

She held my face in her hands and kissed me softly, one cheek, then the other.

"Go take a bath, Logan. Let me know if you need anybody to wash your back."

I assured her I would.

SIX

My phone rang at 0512 the next morning. I was dreaming I was in bed with Savannah. She was curled in the crook of my arm. I could smell the sweet, musky fragrance of her perfume. Her breath warmed my neck. Only it wasn't a dream.

"Logan," I said, still groggy enough that it was a challenge merely remembering my name.

"Matt Streeter, El Dorado County Sheriff's Department. Hope I didn't wake you up."

"No, I'm always up this early. The milkman and me."

"Wondered if I could buy you breakfast."

"I'm staying in a B&B, Detective. The second "B" typically implies breakfast is included with the bed."

"OK, coffee, then. It's important, Mr. Logan. I wouldn't have called this early if it wasn't."

Gone was his recalcitrance from the day before. There was something almost needy in his tone. I asked him where he wanted to meet. He gave me the name of a café and the address. He said it was less than five minutes from where I was staying. I said I'd be there.

Savannah cracked an eye. "What time is it?"

"Time for you to go back to sleep."

I kissed her, said I'd be back as soon as I could, and eased out of bed.

✝

STREETER AND I rendezvoused on Emerald Bay Road, south of town, at a log cabin with a big wooden sign out front that said,

"Steve's Coffee Shop." Virtually everything inside—tables, ceiling, walls—was made from, or covered with, tongue-and-groove planks of knotty pine. Yogi Bear would've felt right at home.

The waitress was a grizzled blue hair easily as ancient as my landlady, Mrs. Schmulowitz. She called Streeter, "Matty," in a raspy voice that bespoke a lifetime of inhaling cigarette smoke. He ordered coffee, biscuits and gravy, with bacon on the side, extra crispy. Then she turned to me with pad and pen poised.

"And for you, sweet cheeks?"

"I'm good with coffee, thanks."

"You got it, Pontiac."

Streeter watched her shuffle off toward the kitchen.

"That's Ruby," he said. "She used to own the place. Sold it to her stepson a couple of years back. He can be kind of a jerk sometimes, but he cooks the best flapjacks this side of Reno."

I pressed my fingers to my eyes and rubbed, still trying to wake up.

"Deputy Woo tells me you came up to Tahoe to get married. Congratulations. You must be very excited."

"You didn't roust my butt out of bed at zero dark to congratulate me on getting married, Deputy. So why don't you just spill it."

"You get right to the point, don't you?"

"One of my many character flaws."

Except for two truckers wolfing down sausage and scrambled eggs at the counter, we were the only customers in the place. But that didn't stop Streeter from glancing nervously over my shoulder, then his, then leaning in closer, to make sure nobody could hear him.

"There's something real weird going on with that airplane up there," he said.

"Aside from the mummy in the pilot's seat and the dead kid, you mean?"

Streeter nodded. He started to say something, then hesitated. "I don't know if I should tell you this."

"If you didn't want to tell me whatever it is you 'shouldn't tell me,' Deputy, we wouldn't be sitting here."

He inhaled and let his breath out slowly. The old waitress brought over two coffees in heavy white ceramic mugs.

"Cream's on the table if you need it, honey."

Streeter gave her a small smile and waited for her to move off.

"It's about that airplane," he said. "What kind did you say it was again?"

"A Twin Beech."

"A Twin Beech, right." He ran a palm over his mouth. "I have reason to believe the government's hiding information on it."

"What makes you think that?"

"You know that plywood from the crate, the piece that was outside the plane?"

I nodded.

"After you left, I turned it over." He fished a smartphone out of his jacket pocket, tapped the screen a few times, then handed it to me. "That was on the side that was lying in the snow."

There was a photo on the phone's screen, a close-up showing a stencil that had been burned black into the plywood. It read:

SSFL
Property of US Government
Extreme Caution When Handling

"I did some digging," Streeter said, spooning sugar into his coffee. "SSFL stands for Santa Susana Field Laboratory. It was a federal research facility. They operated in the hills outside Los Angeles, way back in the 1950s. Classified top secret."

"They designed rocket fuel."

He looked at me. "You've heard of it, then?"

I shrugged.

"Figured you might've, considering your background."

"My background?"

Streeter clearly hadn't restricted his digging to the Santa Susana lab.

"You were tied up in a homicide investigation a year or so ago, back in Los Angeles County," he said. "I saw a newspaper story online. It said you and the victim used to work together in the intelligence community. Some big hush-hush assignment. It said you threatened to punch out a reporter who came snooping around, wanting confirmation. That true?"

I sipped my coffee and said nothing.

Streeter half smiled. "That's what I thought."

He told me that his forensic investigators could find no wallet on the pilot who'd died at the controls of the Twin Beech. Without an airman's certificate or driver's license, there was nothing readily available to identify him. Moreover, the serial number on the .45-caliber pistol stashed in the dead man's coat pocket had been filed off, rendering the gun all but untraceable.

"But that's not the weirdest part," Streeter said.

"And that would be . . . ?"

"The Federal Aviation Administration has a web site."

"That is pretty weird, considering how Neanderthal the FAA is."

"That's not what I meant."

I let him finish.

"The FAA maintains a registry of every plane ever built in the United States. I inputted the tail number to see who owned it and find out when it was reported missing. All I got back was, 'File access restricted.'"

Streeter said he promptly called the FAA's twenty-four hour operations center in Washington, identified himself as a sworn member of law enforcement, and explained that he was actively investigating a homicide. Whoever he spoke to, he said, told him he'd have to write a formal letter of request for any information and send it by registered mail. The request would be reviewed by staff counsel. He could expect a response in six to eight weeks.

"I told her that was unacceptable. She couldn't have cared less."

"Consider yourself lucky. For the FAA to respond to anything in six to eight weeks, we're talking world-record pace."

"You're a pilot," Streeter said. "You tell me: why would they restrict any information on a plane that's been missing that long, let alone an entire file? It's like they're hiding something."

I shrugged. "Your guess is as good as mine."

Ruby brought over a white china plate with five thick strips of hickory-cured bacon and set it down in front of Streeter.

"Matty always likes to eat his bacon first, before anything else," she explained to me. "He's an eccentric, this one."

"I just don't like getting maple syrup on my bacon, that's all," Streeter said.

She gave him an affectionate peck on the top of his head and shuffled outside for a quick smoke, lighting up a Virginia Slims before she was even out the door. Cold air rushed in.

"What about Chad?"

Streeter looked at me like he didn't understand.

"Your victim. The dead kid. From the airport."

"What about him?"

"What was he doing up there?"

Streeter chewed a strip of bacon. "Best guess? You landed, told Chad you'd seen a downed airplane. He calls my department. Deputy Woo buys the call. Woo shows up, you tell him what you saw, correct?"

"Affirmative."

"Chad's standing there. He's listening in. He's local, knows the area like the back of his hand. He gets off work, tells a buddy, and they decide, 'Hey, we'll just hike in there and steal whatever we can from the wreckage before search and rescue can get in.' Happens all the time, people looting downed airplanes. So they get up there. They pry open the crate. Something inside that's worth big money. Only Chad's buddy decides he's not interested in profit sharing. So, like you said yesterday, Chad gets capped and his buddy makes off with the merchandise."

"Sounds like you got it dialed in."

"It's a workable premise. Let's put it that way."

"Why did you want to see me this morning?"

Streeter wiped his mouth with his napkin and picked a bacon bit from the gap between his front teeth. "I need to know why the FAA put a clamp on that file."

"I'm not on real intimate terms with the FAA these days, Deputy. Let's just say we've had our differences."

"But you did work in the intelligence community. You have a security clearance, correct?"

"Hypothetically, if I ever *did* hold a clearance, it would've been revoked when I turned in my resignation papers. That's assuming I ever worked for the government, which I'm not saying I did or didn't."

The deputy's biscuits and gravy arrived, smelling like I imagine heaven smells—the yeasty musk finished off with an irresistible hint of lard. I could feel my arteries congealing just inhaling.

"Enjoy," Ruby said, reeking of tobacco.

Again, Streeter waited until she was out of audio range.

"OK, fine, so you don't have an active clearance. But, assuming you *did* work for the government, like the newspaper said, you'd still have contacts, friends who could do you a favor, correct?"

"That's a whole lot of assuming, Deputy."

Two young men with brown skin and stylishly coiffed black hair walked in and hovered near the door, waiting to be seated. Busy chowing down, Streeter didn't notice them. I did. Some may have mistaken the two for Arabs. I knew them to be Iranians who, I observed in my adventures abroad, are inclined to be taller and slightly lighter in complexion than their Middle Eastern neighbors. Iranian men also tend to be more fashionably attired and more attentive to personal grooming. These guys were all that. Pricey jeans and black leather jackets. No shortage of cologne. Not a nose hair in sight.

The taller of the two caught me looking and tried staring me down. I held my gaze. Dominant males, I learned with Alpha, reflexively maintain eye contact when confronted with what they perceive instinctively as other, socially aggressive males. It goes back to the time when we all swung from the trees by our tails: to see its prey, the hunter must always expose its eyes. When the hunted breaks eye contact, it's a sign of submission that signals, in essence, "Do with me what you will; I won't fight back."

After a few seconds, the taller Iranian looked away, leaned closer to his companion and muttered something in his ear. Pretending to peruse the plastic laminated menu, his friend, a powerfully built fireplug, turned and glared at me. I glared back.

Streeter turned and looked over his shoulder, chewing on a strip of bacon, curious to see what I was seeing. The taller Iranian noticed him and nodded in a not friendly way. Streeter nodded in response and turned back toward me.

"The tall guy's name is Reza Jalali," he said. "Owns a couple convenience stores in town. The other guy, I've never seen before."

"Something hinky about that dude," I said.

"Clearly, you don't trust your fellow man, Mr. Logan."

"I used to. Then I read Lawrence Ferlinghetti, who said that if you're too open-minded, your brains fall out."

Streeter smiled. I watched him dip a piece of bacon in the gravy, stuff the bacon in his mouth, and lick grease from his fingers. Back at the Tranquility House Bed-and-Breakfast, the Kavitches, Johnny and Gwen, would probably be serving up organic granola with reduced-fat yogurt and fresh fruit because that's what B&B owners do—try to convince you that there's something inherently healthier staying with them than at the Comfort Inn, where you cook your own waffles with premixed cups of "batter" that looks a lot like baby spit-up.

Streeter salted and peppered his biscuits and gravy. "So, what do you say? You think you could put a call in for me?"

I told him I'd think about it.

"Either way," I said, "it'll cost you a strip of bacon."

"Knock yourself out."

He slid his plate across the table.

Elevated triglycerides never tasted so good.

✠

Snow was coming down as I walked out of the restaurant. Big soft fluffy flakes that fell slowly through the pines, muffling all sound and washing all color from the morning. I used my arm to brush off the driver's door on the Yukon, got in, started the engine and fired up the heater.

I figured there'd be little harm, making a call or two on Deputy Streeter's behalf. I'll admit, part of my motivation in helping him out was ego driven. I'd seen and done a thousand things in defense of my country. I'd been trained to compartmentalize those things, to keep secret from any and all but my fellow go-to guys the tactics, techniques, and procedures we exercised to do those things. But Streeter had been correct: I did know people in government who enjoyed access to restricted information, including Paul Horvath, an investigator with the FAA's Flight Standards District Office in San Diego.

Horvath had been assigned to determine the cause of my near-fatal accident a few months earlier at San Diego's Montgomery Airport. He'd concluded that an intentional act of sabotage had forced me to crash land the *Ruptured Duck*, and that the incident had been in no way my fault. That, however, hadn't stopped the FAA from tormenting me for months afterward, what with the dozens of reports and sworn declarations

I was compelled to submit just to keep my flight school certified and my pilot's certificate intact.

I found Horvath's card in my wallet and called him.

"Who?" Horvath said, yawning, half asleep.

"Cordell Logan."

I'd forgotten it wasn't yet 0700. It took him a few seconds to remember me.

"What time is it?"

I told him. Then I told him why I was calling.

"Let me make sure I have this correctly. You want me to *give* you confidential information from a restricted agency file?"

"Yes."

"Without going through proper channels? Is that what you just asked me?"

"Proper channels could take weeks, Mr. Horvath. The information is needed in an ongoing police investigation, the murder of a young man in the mountains outside Lake Tahoe."

"Mr. Logan, I'm as law and order as they come. I hope they find the killer and put him away. But what you're asking me to do is to commit a crime, a very serious crime, not to mention jeopardize my career. I'm sorry. I can't help you."

I apologized for having called so early and signed off. Not without some reluctance, I then called my buddy, Buzz.

"This is not directory information, Logan," Buzz grumbled over the phone. "Don't you have any other friends who still work for Uncle Sugar? I'm busy. I have things to do, like saving the free world. Why are you always calling *me*?"

"Because we share a history, Buzz. Because I love you like the deranged, antisocial brother I never had."

"Well, when you put it that way . . ."

Buzz (not his real name) was an opera-loving, former Delta operator who'd been among Alpha's initial cadre of go-to guys—a "plank holder," as they were known. He'd lost an eye to RPG shrapnel on one especially gnarly op outside Benghazi. After the White House shut down Alpha as a potential political liability, he'd ended up working at the Defense Intelligence

Agency, riding an analyst's desk that kept him inside most days, an assignment he'd used to good effect. Buzz cultivated more intra-agency connections over the years and possessed more behind-the-scenes insights about the inner workings of the alphabet agencies than probably any member of the intelligence community who ever lived.

I told him how I'd happened to stumble upon the wreckage of the long-missing airplane, about the murdered kid, the crate from the Santa Susana Field Lab, and the FAA's unwillingness to cooperate with a homicide investigation. Buzz asked me for the plane's tail number. I gave it to him. He said he'd ask around and see what he could come up with. I didn't even have to bribe him, which I usually did.

"You seem like you're in an unusually agreeable mood, Buzz."

"Got busy with the wife last night. First time in a month. I put on a little Pavarotti, she squeezed into something skimpy I got her for Valentine's Day five years ago, which was the last time I *remembered* Valentine's Day, and we rocked the house. The kitchen. Our bed. The *dog's* bed. It was something, lemme tell ya."

"I could've definitely gone all day without knowing about the dog's bed, Buzz."

"Hey, you asked."

"So I did. Live and learn."

"What are you doing in Tahoe, Logan? Tahoe's for rich people. The beautiful people. *Beautiful* is not a word that comes readily to mind when I think of your sorry mug."

"Savannah and I are getting remarried."

There was a long silence on the other end.

"Say again?"

"We're getting remarried."

"To Savannah?"

"Affirmative."

"The Savannah who dumped you for Arlo Echevarria?"

"One and the same."

There was a time when Buzz wouldn't have hesitated to tell me that I'd lost my mind, reconciling with a woman who'd left me for a brother warrior. But for once, he held his tongue.

"I just hope you know what you're doing, Logan."

"Makes two of us, buddy."

He said he'd get back to me with whatever relevant insights he could find on the crashed Beechcraft. I told him I'd be waiting.

The snow was coming down heavier, beginning to blanket the cars in the lot. I envisioned a leisurely breakfast back at Tranquility House with Savannah, followed by a romantic interlude in the privacy of our bungalow with a cozy fire in the fireplace. We'd drive into town after that, take out a marriage license, and exchange vows.

I couldn't have known that by the time I got back, she'd have gone without so much as a word of good-bye.

SEVEN

Nothing seemed amiss.

The damp washcloth draped over the faucet and the water beaded on the tiled walls of the shower stall told me that Savannah had showered shortly after I'd left our bungalow to meet with Deputy Streeter.

There were two bras and two pairs of panties in the plastic bag she used for dirty laundry. That told me she'd apparently dressed for the day and left—but without her long down coat, which was still hanging in the closet. I knew she wouldn't have gone for a walk without it, given the weather.

I also knew she hadn't gone for a run. Her Nikes were still packed in her suitcase, and her iPhone in its pink protective case was still on the nightstand, charging. Savannah never went anywhere without her phone.

I ventured back outside, searching for tracks in the freshly fallen snow, but the only ones I could see were mine. That told me she'd gone before the snow started falling.

"Haven't seen her all morning," Johnny Kavitch said when I· went into the main house. "She didn't come in for breakfast. It's still sitting on the table in the dining room, untouched. Yours, too. Gwen, have you seen Savannah this morning?"

Kavitch's wife emerged from the kitchen, wiping her hands on a red and white striped dish towel. "Listening to the TV. I'm sorry, were you calling me?"

"Have you seen Savannah this morning?" I asked before Johnny could.

Gwen frowned and stared at the floor for a second, trying to remember. "Come to think of it," she said, "I can't say that I have. I'm sure she's around here somewhere, though. Unless she took your car and decided to go into town."

"I had the car. What about your son? Where is he?"

"Preston?" Gwen traded a troubling glance with her husband. "Still sleeping. We let him sleep in. His counselor says it's good therapy."

The acrid taste of bile rose up in the back of my throat.

"Where's his bedroom?"

"Upstairs. Why?"

I bounded up the stairs, taking them three at a time.

"That's our private residence," Johnny hollered after me. "You can't go up there! Hey!"

I ignored him.

Preston's bedroom was down a short hallway decorated with framed family photos, the last door on the left. It was the only one that was locked. I booted it open, splintering the jam, and went in. He bolted upright, shirtless, startled awake. The posters covering his walls were a testament to the blood-fest video games he was apparently into—*Resident Evil* and *Mortal Kombat*.

"Get out of my room!"

"Where is she, Preston?"

"Where's who? I don't know what you're talking about!"

I moved toward him.

"Yes, you do."

"I don't know where your wife is, man!" He pulled the covers up around his pale, concentration camp survivor chest and cowered against the headboard, trying to get as far from me as he could. "How would I know where she is? I told you. Get out!"

"I'm gonna ask you one more time, Preston, then I'm gonna take you apart, one piece at a time. Now, where . . . is . . . she?"

"I told you! I don't know where she's at! Dad! DAD!"

"This is definitely not cool!" Johnny said, bounding in with his wife hard on his heels. He was clutching a ski pole like a spear.

"You need to take a deep breath and calm down, Mr. Logan," Gwen said with her palms outstretched, pleading. "Please. Before someone gets hurt."

"My wife is missing and I'm wondering if Cujo here knows something he isn't telling."

"You have no right to call my son names," Gwen said.

"Mom, I told him. I don't know nothing what he's talking about!"

I might've corrected him on his use of double negatives, but intuition told me that was the least of Preston Kavitch's sins.

✛

STREETER ANSWERED his phone on the second ring. I told him that Savannah had disappeared, and that I was worried.

"How long has she been gone?"

"I don't know. I came back from meeting with you, and she wasn't here."

"We don't usually take missing persons reports until the party's been gone at least twenty-four hours," Streeter said.

"Every hour a kidnapping victim remains missing, the chance of recovering that victim alive declines ten percent."

"How do you know that?"

"It doesn't matter how I know. I'm asking you to help find her."

"Does she jog?" Streeter asked.

"Occasionally."

"OK, so it could be she went jogging. Maybe she stopped for coffee somewhere."

I told him how her running shoes were still packed away in her suitcase.

"There's something else you should know," I said. "She's pregnant."

"How far along is she?"

"Couple months."

Streeter speculated that Savannah may have had a complication with her pregnancy. He said he'd put in a call to the local hospital.

"If there was a medical problem," I said, "she wouldn't have just started walking, and definitely not without her coat. She would've asked the people we're staying with for a ride to the hospital. She didn't do that."

"Well, there's probably some logical explanation," Streeter said. "She'll be back. You just need to be patient."

Patience, unfortunately, has never been my strong suit.

"I have a proposition," I said.

"A proposition?"

"You get a fingerprint tech over here in the next hour and I'll get you the information you want from that FAA file."

"If I didn't know better, Mr. Logan, I'd say you're trying to coerce a sworn peace officer."

"I prefer to call it a quid pro quo."

Streeter drew out a long, slow breath over the phone. "I can't promise an hour," he said, "but I'll see what I can do."

I hung up and stood at the window, gazing out at the white-flocked Currier and Ives landscape. Streeter had asked me how I knew about kidnapping survival statistics. I wasn't about to tell him that of the seven authorized rescue missions I'd participated in as a member of Alpha to rescue the victims of kidnappings, only two resulted in those victims returning home alive. The last mission had been the worst: an airborne insertion into eastern Yemen to save two American missionaries taken hostage by extremists. One of the kidnappers detonated a suicide vest at the last minute as we moved in, blowing himself and the two missionaries to pieces.

I blinked the bloody image from my head.

Where are you, Savannah?

The Kavitches insisted I pay for the door jamb that I'd wrecked, and demanded that I check out by noon. Weirdly, they didn't seem the least bit concerned or even interested in Savannah's welfare. I told them I was sorry for damaging their home and for casting aspersions on their son, Preston, even if he was a creepy slacker. Repentance is a demonstration of wisdom as far as Buddhists are concerned. Admitting guilt and accepting responsibility for one's actions are supposed to lessen the effect of negative karma. Selfishly, I hoped that my feigning contrition would bring Savannah back. But I'd racked up more than my share of negative karma over the years. It would take a lot, I knew, to balance the scales.

Are we rewarded, ultimately, for the good we do in life? What about when we do bad things for ostensibly good reasons? If you pump two rounds into the head of a sociopathic jihadist at point-blank range as he enjoys oysters on the half shell at an upscale French restaurant in Cairo, and one of those rounds exits his skull, killing his otherwise innocent, twenty-two-year-old mistress, does bad erase good? I didn't know. I still don't.

The sheriff's print technician arrived at 0925, crunching into the snowy parking lot of the B&B in a silver Toyota Camry. The car had chains on the front tires. The technician wore UGG boots, gray leggings, and a military-style parka, the hood trimmed in fake wolf fur. With her briefcase kit in hand, she flipped open her ID with a flourish and showed it to me as I opened the door. Brown unkempt hair. Small brown eyes. She was petite and looked about twenty-five. I didn't catch her name.

"I don't know what was so important that I had to drop everything on my day off and race over here," she said, striding past me, inside. "I'm missing my Pilates class."

I shut the door behind her. "I'm missing more than that."

She asked me if I'd touched anything. Door knobs? Plumbing fixtures? Wood surfaces?

"All of the above."

"What about this?" She stooped at the waist and peered closely without handling an empty drinking glass sitting on a nightstand, the side of the bed Savannah slept on.

"Not that I recall," I said.

She opened her kit, got out a small brush, a cold-cream-size jar of finely ground carbon powder, and went to work while I threw on my leather pilot's jacket and went for a walk.

The thermometer had dipped into the high teens. I was sweating. Savannah was in trouble. I could *feel* it. The urge to take control of the situation, to do *something*, was overpowering. In my wallet was a dog-eared picture of her, wearing long gold earrings and a strapless, sparkly purple gown, taken on the day we first met, at the wedding reception for my Air Force Academy roommate. She was unquestionably the most exquisite woman I'd ever known. Even after our divorce, I couldn't bring myself to part with her picture. Sometimes at night, when sleep eluded me, I would take it out and gaze for hours at her perfect face to remind myself how much her leaving had wounded me, hoping my bitterness would swell such that I could force her out of my head once and for all, forever. Only the strategy never seemed to work. The pleasure I derived from staring at Savannah's likeness, knowing that she was once mine, outweighed the pain of having lost her. So I kept the photo. And, now, walking residential streets near the Tahoe lakefront, my hair and beard wet with snow, I stopped to show it to anybody who was willing to look at it.

"Have you seen this woman this morning?"

Nobody had, but everyone I approached expressed concern and assured me that they'd all keep a sharp eye out for her.

A wispy Filipino mail carrier in his US Postal Service Jeep spent five minutes telling me in great detail how his own sister had gone to get milk and eggs at a corner market in Fresno one morning and never came home.

A kindly looking grandfather walking his golden retriever remarked how beautiful Savannah looked in the photo, joking that it would be his lucky day to find her before I did.

A big, rangy-looking sewer cleanout technician wearing a beat-up straw cowboy hat felt compelled to give me a lesson on the fundamental differences between men and women. He was stowing his Roto-Rooter machine in his van and quickly closed the back doors as I approached, like he was in a big hurry to get to his next service call—but not too busy to chat after I showed him Savannah's picture. "Dwayne" was stitched above the left pocket of his stained denim work shirt. He looked to be in his mid-forties.

"You know how women can get sometimes," he said. "My wife's no different. Always mad at me for no logical reason, running her mouth, then running off to her mother's. A day later, she's back, all lovey-dovey." Dwayne rested a reassuring hand on my shoulder. "Dime to a dollar yours'll be back soon enough, too. If I happen to see her around town, I'll be sure and tell her you're looking for her."

I thanked him and moved on.

"Is she, like, in trouble or something?" a high school kid on Sacramento Avenue wanted to know, pausing from shoveling out snow from his parents' driveway to look at the picture.

"Very possibly."

"That sucks." He dug a phone out from under his metallic purple snowboarding jacket and asked me for my number. "I'll hit you up if I see her around."

" 'Preciate it."

I kept going, wandering among businesses along Harrison Avenue.

Nobody had seen anything.

Nobody knew anything.

It was approximately 1130 hours when I left the offices of the Tahoe *Daily Tribune*, where a news reporter named Diane Fairbanks who looked like she'd just graduated from journalism school snapped a photo of me holding the photo of Savannah and said she'd try to get something into the newspaper the next day. Diane seemed intimidated by my presence. I couldn't help but wonder if her promises were intended more than anything to get me to leave.

I'd left the paper seconds earlier and was walking down the sidewalk, not at all sure where I was headed next, when I heard tires crunch in the snow behind me and turned to see an El Dorado County sheriff's Wrangler. Streeter rolled down the driver's window and stuck his head out.

"Tried calling you," he said. "You didn't answer."

"Could be because I need to go to grad school to figure out how my phone works. What's up?"

"Just wanted to let you know we've notified every local law enforcement agency to be on the lookout for your lady. The print tech's wrapping things up back at your room. We'll get results soon as we can."

"OK."

He cocked his head and gave me a hard look. "You didn't have anything to do with any of this, did you?"

"Any of what?"

"Her disappearance."

I swallowed down the urge to do the deputy harm and jammed my hands in the pockets of my jacket.

"You want to polygraph me? Fine, let's go now."

"You might want to talk to an attorney first."

"I don't need an attorney, Streeter. What I need is for you to do your goddamn job. Go find my woman."

Streeter nodded subtly, like I'd just passed some sort of test. "Every suspect, you ask them if they did it, they're always calm. 'No. It wasn't me, officer. I didn't do it.' When you know damn well they did. Nobody ever raises their voice. Nobody looks like they want to punch your lights out—unless they didn't do it. For what it's worth, Mr. Logan, I believe you."

I looked past the Wrangler, hoping I might see Savannah, and said nothing.

"You probably want to change out of those wet clothes," Streeter said.

"Probably."

"I'll give you a lift back to your room."

I climbed in. The heater was on high. It felt good.

Streeter put the Wrangler in gear, checked his mirrors, and headed north toward the lake.

"Could be she got cold feet," he said. "It happens sometimes."

"She walked out when we were married the first time. She wasn't shy about telling me then where she was going, and the reasons why. She wouldn't be shy telling me now, but there was no reason for her to take off. Her leaving wasn't voluntary."

"You think somebody took her. Is that what you're saying?"

I blew on my cupped hands to warm them.

"All I know is she's gone."

A man doesn't do for his government what I did, for as long as I did it, without living in constant fear of retaliation. The fear is with you every day and every night. You constantly scan your surroundings, situational awareness on overdrive, assessing the body language of strangers whose path you cross and whether they pose a threat, until paranoia becomes muscle memory. I didn't rule out the possibility that Savannah's disappearance had something to do with my having once hunted rabid humans across the globe. But that made no sense. If someone had turned the tables, a survivor or disciple of one of my former targets, they would've likely come after me, not Savannah. Regardless, how would anyone have known that we'd be in South Lake Tahoe? The only people I'd told of our travel plans were Mrs. Schmulowitz and Larry, my airplane mechanic. Neither of them would've had any reason to tell anyone else.

"The owners of the bed-and-breakfast where we've been staying have an adult son who lives with them," I said.

"You mean Preston?"

I looked over, surprised Streeter would know him.

"It's a small town. Mr. Logan. Preston Kavitch is well-known among local law enforcement, believe me. Plenty of petty stuff. Drugs, drunk in public. Nothing violent, though, to my knowledge."

I described how I'd caught Preston entertaining himself with Savannah's panties in the bathroom of our bungalow.

"That surprises me," Streeter said. "I didn't think Preston was even aware of women. I don't even remember ever seeing him out with one, tell you the truth. I can take him in for questioning if you think it'll do some good."

"That's your call."

We passed a snow plow rolling in the opposite direction, its amber caution lights flashing, snow arcing gracefully away from its angled blade and splashing onto the roadside like a bow wave from a boat hull.

"Good thing you found that plane yesterday and not today," Streeter said. "Probably wouldn't have been able to get up there in this weather. Wreck's probably been buried over."

Yesterday. It seemed so long ago.

✝

THE PRINT technician was gone by the time Streeter dropped me back at the B&B. She may have been pissed at having missed her Pilates class, but she did her job: there was fingerprint dust virtually everywhere. I stripped, stuffed my wet clothes in Savannah's plastic laundry bag, and took a quick hot shower. After I toweled off, I pulled on dry socks and jeans, a T-shirt, a flannel shirt, and my old Air Force Academy football sweatshirt. My hiking shoes and leather jacket were soaked through, but they were the only ones I'd brought with me. They'd have to do.

I was repacking Savannah's stuff and mine, including her phone and charger, when a key slid in the lock, and the door opened, revealing Johnny Kavitch.

"Just wanted to make sure you'll be out by noon checkout," he said, still clutching the ski pole like a weapon, standing warily in the doorway, keeping his distance.

I checked my watch. "I've still got ten minutes."

"Also, I wanted to let you know that I received an estimate on the door jamb you broke. You're looking at $310 in repair costs."

"A woman, *my* woman, has gone missing. Call me rude, Mr. Kavitch, but I really couldn't give a damn at this particular moment about your door jamb. I told you, I'll pay for the damage."

"I'm sorry she's missing," he said, "but I'm sure she's OK."

"What makes you so sure of that?"

"Because nothing bad ever happens in Lake Tahoe."

No one ever starved underestimating the average human being's capacity to live in denial. I shook my head and continued packing.

"You need to understand something, Mr. Logan. We're running a business here. And we don't appreciate guests coming in and trashing the premises. And I certainly don't need them insulting my son."

I walked toward the door. Kavitch backed up, wearing a fearful expression that suggested I was capable of going berserk at any minute.

"Come back at noon. I'll be gone by then."

I toed the door shut in his face.

My phone rang on the bed as I was zipping up my duffel bag. I nearly sprained a wrist rushing to grab it.

"Savannah?"

"Guess again."

"Hey, Buzz."

The disappointment in my voice apparently was not hard to discern.

"You sound like I usually feel, Logan, which is about two steps removed from a slow, painful death. You doing OK?"

"Yeah. I'm fine."

"You sure? Cuz if this is what 'fine' sounds like, I'd hate to hear 'not fine.'"

"I've got some stuff going on right now I'd rather not talk about." I forced myself to focus. "You make any traction on that matter I asked about earlier?"

"As a matter of fact. Let's just say we never had this conversation, *capisce*?"

"What conversation?"

Buzz sort of snorted. His version of a laugh.

"OK, that tail number you gave me? The plane was reported stolen out of Omaha in October 1956. It belonged to Midwest Mutual. Big insurance company. Pilot went out to the flight line one morning to preflight the bird for a trip to Chicago, schlepping a bunch of corporate bigwigs, and it wasn't there. Gone baby gone."

"Why would the FAA deep six a missing aircraft file for fifty-eight years—unless maybe it was a clerical error?"

"Clerical error my flabby, civil service ass," Buzz said. "There was nothing in error about that file being marked 'eyes only.' That plane was being flown by the Central Intelligence Agency when it disappeared."

EIGHT

Buzz had a friend who had a friend. Buzz always had a "friend" in the know somewhere. In this instance, his contact either was, or worked with, the associate administrator of the FAA's Civil Aviation Security branch in Washington. I didn't get down in the weeds as far as titles or names, and Buzz didn't elaborate. All he said was what his friend had told him: that the file on the stolen Twin Beechcraft that ultimately returned to earth in the mountains outside Lake Tahoe remained under official seal. The file jacket bore a faded, hand-written notation left by an FAA investigator probably long since expired, about something called "Project Short Hair."

"Ever heard of it?" Buzz said.

"No."

"Me, neither. So I called another buddy who, for our purposes, shall remain nameless. He works across the river. I knew it had to have something to do with those dickweeds over there because they always give their ops those goofy, two-name handles—Project Blue Balls, Operation Eat Me. They love all that sexual double entendre crap."

"Across the river" in Buzz's vernacular meant CIA headquarters at Langley. His friend there, he said, had never heard of "Project Short Hair," either.

"So, he tells me he'll have to do some snooping, rummage around the basement where they keep all the dead aliens. He found it, though, the tenacious son of a bitch. I owe him a beer. Which means you owe *me* a beer."

"Put it on my tab."

"Somehow, I could've predicted that would be your response, Logan."

What his friend across the river found, Buzz said, was a briefing paper stamped top secret that CIA officials in 1956 had delivered to then-President Dwight Eisenhower. It outlined the agency's clandestine efforts to arm various nations friendly to American interests in and around South Asia with state-of-the-art weapons that could be used against the old Soviet Union in the event World War III broke out.

"Which countries?"

"We're talking nearly sixty years ago, Logan. Whichever ones they were, I guarantee you the ones that wanted to take warm showers with us then hate our asses now. That's just how the geopolitical worm turns."

"Point taken."

The fact that the Twin Beech had been stolen by the CIA made operational sense. The pilot likely would have been a private contractor who didn't work directly for the agency—a "cutout" in the parlance of covert operations. That way, Langley could deny any direct involvement if the mission went south. Where the plane was coming from or flying to when it crashed, and who shot Chad Lovejoy to death, were the last questions on my mind. I was worried about Savannah. She was really all I could think about.

I felt as helpless as I'd ever been in my life.

"Why don't you just spill it, Logan? You and the little lady are having problems. I can help. I'm a nationally known expert on male-female relations. Me and Dr. Phil."

Buzz was joking around, trying to cheer me up. I knew that. But I was hardly in a cheerful mood.

Somebody just then rapped on the front window of the bungalow. I looked over.

"Twelve o'clock, Mr. Logan," Johnny Kavitch shouted from the other side of the glass, tapping his wristwatch. "Please don't make me call the authorities."

"You've already helped enough," I told Buzz over the phone. "I'll catch you later."

I stacked my duffel on top of Savannah's rolling suitcase and made for the door.

Bundled up against the cold like Mr. and Mrs. Nanook of the North, the Kavitches stood aside as I walked out. Johnny was still holding the ski pole like a weapon.

"I'll be in town as long as it takes to find Savannah," I said. "I'd appreciate you having her call me on my cell, if and when she comes back."

Gwen Kavitch assured me she or her husband would do so, then said she hoped we'd enjoyed our stay.

I said nothing.

I stowed the luggage in the back of the Yukon and started the engine, brushed the snow off as best I could, and scraped the icy windows with my ATM card—a more valid use for the plastic than at any ready-teller, given my paltry account balance. As I got in, my hands freezing, wishing I'd remembered to bring gloves, I caught sight of skinny, bizarre Preston Kavitch, leering at me from the second-floor bedroom window of his parents' Victorian-style inn.

He grinned demonically, raised his right hand, and flipped me off.

✛

WHAT BEGAN as a snowstorm was now a full-blown blizzard. Flakes the size of quarters floated down from a lowering sky, the clouds obscuring the tops of the pines and cutting visibility to a hundred meters at most, draining the day of any color but a flat, opaque white.

For more than an hour I drove around South Lake Tahoe, stopping periodically to ask if anyone had seen Savannah. No one had. Everyone commented on how beautiful she looked in the photo.

The top of my skull throbbed excruciatingly, to the point I could barely focus. In my previous lives as a fighter pilot and covert operator, I would've simply willed the headache away. Maybe it was because I was getting older, or because of the profound anguish I was feeling over Savannah's disappearance, but distancing myself from the pain was no longer a function of mind over matter. I needed to take something before my cranium blew off.

Cruising along Turquoise Bay Drive through a neighborhood of cheap cabins crammed too close together on narrow lots, I happened upon the Dutch Mart Gas and Grub convenience store. If you're American, you know the place—a seedy, shake-shingle storefront with a grandiose gabled roofline meant to convey European refinement. Front windows plastered with posters for Camel cigarettes and twelve-packs of Budweiser. I parked, walked inside, and was immediately engaged visually by whom I assumed to be the store's proprietor—none other than Reza Jalali, one of the two Iranians I'd encountered earlier that morning at the café with Deputy Streeter.

He was standing behind his cash register, ringing up a tin of chewing tobacco and a package of Huggies diapers for an acne-ravaged, dentally challenged meth head who was blathering on about how everything he needed to succeed in life he learned in juvenile detention. A half-opened door behind the counter led to a small office. Inside, I could hear another man laughing. It sounded like he was watching a rerun of *Seinfeld*.

"Aspirin?"

Eyeing me darkly, black hair slicked back, Jalali pointed with his chin toward the back of the store and a pegboard from which haphazardly hung various travel-size toiletries.

I grabbed a packet of two aspirin and, on impulse, a small package of turkey jerky from an adjacent display because it's never smart to take pills on an empty stomach and because nothing says manly like smoked, nitrosamine-laden meat. When I walked back to the register, the meth head was gone and Jalali had been joined by his friend, the fireplug who'd raised my suspicions at the café. I put my purchases on the counter. Jalali rang me up. The fireplug's eyes never left me.

"$8.97," Jalali said.

"Nine bucks for two aspirin and three bites of jerky? That's really promoting customer loyalty."

"You don't want it," Jalali said with an obnoxious, indifferent shrug, "don't buy it."

My head felt like it was splitting apart at the seams. I pulled a ten-spot out of my wallet and slapped it on the counter. Jalali took the bill and made change, his eyes locked on mine.

"You were in the restaurant," he said. "Why did you look at us that way?"

"I'm looking for a woman."

"We are all looking for a woman, my friend," the fireplug said.

I showed him Savannah's picture. "Have you seen her around?"

The fireplug donned designer reading glasses from the pocket of his blue silk dress shirt, took the photo and peered at it intently, then handed it over to Jalali, who studied Savannah's image with similar intensity. For several seconds, they talked back and forth in Urdu, their native language, before Jalali handed the picture back to me.

"No," is all he said.

If I'd understood Urdu I might've been able to assess with greater accuracy whether he was telling the truth. Nothing, though, in his body language or microexpressions suggested he was lying. His friend, the fireplug, was a different story. The small muscles beneath his right eye were in spasm. He couldn't stop glaring at me.

"Who are you?" he said, more of a demand than a question.

"Me? I'm just a guy with a bad headache and a hankering for acid indigestion."

I snatched up the turkey jerky and aspirin and walked out to the car.

To the west, the clouds broke, and for a few fleeting seconds, I could make out mountain peaks—the same mountains where I'd first spotted what remained of a winged phantom lost long ago. The phantom's last flight, according to my spook buddy, Buzz, had been in support of a highly classified mission to arm nations friendly to US interests in and around South Asia—countries that I assumed included Pakistan, India, and, one of America's strongest regional allies back then, Iran. Jalali and his squatty friend, the fireplug, were from Iran. I knew of absolutely nothing to link either man to the murder of Chad Lovejoy, or whatever it was that had been stolen from the wreckage of that airplane. Nor, for that matter, was I aware of one iota of evidence tying them in any fashion to Savannah's disappearance. But when you've spent the majority of your professional life at Defcon 1, suspicious of everyone and their motives, there's no such thing as coincidence.

I drove the neighborhood for a couple of minutes, then circled back to park a block away from the Dutch Mart Gas and Grub where I could establish a relatively unobtrusive surveillance position. With the back of the SUV positioned toward the convenience store, I angled my side and rear mirrors to maintain eyes-on, sat back chewing my overpriced aspirin, and waited to see who came or went. It wasn't much of a plan, but it was better than nothing.

More than anything, I wanted my phone to ring. I wanted Savannah to call. I wanted to hear her voice tell me she was safe. I wanted her to be upset with me for having overreacted at the B&B, booting Preston Kavitch's door the way I had. But the phone remained silent. I checked the call log; there was nothing.

Other men under similar circumstances might've prayed. I'd prayed plenty when I was a kid. I begged God every night to remove me from my latest foster home hellhole, and to find me a family, a *real* family, with people who genuinely cared about me. The Almighty never seemed to hear me, though. Either that or he was always too busy to respond. Soon enough, you stop asking. I knew under present circumstances that the Buddha wouldn't be of much help, either. I realized as I sat there, watching that convenience store, the only power I could rely on was my own.

After nearly an hour observing a procession of ragged but otherwise benign-looking customers pulling in for cigarettes and beer, I turned over the Yukon's ignition and drove on.

Amid the snow, searching for Savannah, traffic on Lake Tahoe Boulevard quickly became slow-and-go—a mile-long backup of four-wheel drive pickup trucks and luxury SUVs mostly, with a few beaters thrown in, many hauling snowboards and skis on their way to the freshly powdered runs at Heavenly Mountain, northeast of town. I rolled down my window, inching along in the right lane, and studied every fogged-up, snow-covered vehicle that rolled past me in the left lane, hoping against hope that I might spot her.

A stocky dude in his early twenties with a sandy crew cut and black ski bibs apparently thought I was checking out his girlfriend and took offense. He rolled down the passenger window on his black Hummer and leaned across her lap, giving me the stink eye.

"What're you staring at, asshole?"

I ignored him.

The inside of my throat was burning. Probably from the aspirin. I needed something to wash it down, and quickly. Up ahead, past a hemp shop where a Jamaican flag hung in the window, was a sign for a bakery. I hooked a right into the snow-covered parking lot.

The bakery was warm and smelled of chocolate. The cherubic girl behind the counter sported a sterling ring in her lower lip and a purple streak in her dark, punk-style hair.

"What can I get you?"

"I'd like some water."

"Bottled or tap?"

"Is bottled faster?"

She didn't understand the question.

"Bottled," I said.

"Bubbles or no bubbles?"

"I have no preference."

"Would you like—?"

"Look, just some water. Please."

She reached into a large cooler behind her and handed me a cold bottle. I chugged it down. My throat felt considerably better.

"Anything else for you today, sir?"

I showed her Savannah's photo.

"Any chance you've seen this woman?"

"Definitely."

My pulse quickened.

"You *have* seen her?"

"Oh, for sure."

"Where?"

"On TV."

"You saw her on TV." I was puzzled. "When was this?"

"Last week." The girl looked at the picture once more. "She's on *Real Housewives*, right?"

I forced a smile. "Not exactly."

"Well, one of those shows, right?"

"She's missing. I'm trying to locate her."

"Oh."

I ordered black coffee along with turkey and Havarti on a baguette. I ate the sandwich quickly. When I was finished, I called Streeter. He didn't answer. I left word on his voice mail that I had some information for him on the downed Beechcraft and asked that he let me know if he'd heard anything from the hospital on Savannah.

"I've checked out of the B&B," I said. "I'm not sure where I'll be staying tonight, but I'll leave my phone on. Call me."

The snow was coming down heavier. I pondered my options and quickly concluded that I had few. Driving around in a blizzard, showing random people Savannah's picture, seemed pointless. The woman at the newspaper said she'd run a notice the next day. That was at least something. I decided to return to Tranquility House, to see if Streeter had gone to question Preston Kavitch, like he said he was going to. As I pulled out of the parking lot onto Lake Tahoe Boulevard, a red-over-silver Subaru Outback drove past from my right to left. The driver, a man of indeterminate age, was wearing a dark-colored baseball cap.

Savannah was sitting in the passenger seat.

I fishtailed out of the lot and across the road, nearly slamming into an eastbound Range Rover and an old Buick heading west. Both drivers hit the brakes, skidding on the snow and laying on their horns as I shot the narrow gap between them.

I couldn't see inside the Subaru—snow obscured the station wagon's back window—but I could tell that whoever was behind the wheel knew how to drive in winter by his lack of sliding. I could also tell that he knew he was being pursued. Repeatedly, I flashed the Yukon's headlights on and off, on and off, pounding on my own horn, trying to get him to pull over, but he did the opposite, ratcheting up his speed to more than forty miles an hour. Half of that would've been too fast given the deteriorating road conditions, but he wasn't about to stop.

We wove crazily through traffic, passing a CVS pharmacy on our right, and blowing through a red light at Fairway Avenue. Fortunately, there were no other cars in the intersection or we would've been creamed.

The Subaru kicked it up close to fifty mph. Snow rooster tails arced from his back wheels, spattering my windshield as I rode his back bumper. Even in four-wheel drive, I could feel the Yukon's front end dancing on the snow. A sane person would've slowed down. He drove faster. So did I.

Up ahead, I could see that the road narrowed to one lane for construction, and that traffic had halted. That didn't stop the Subaru's driver from cutting hard left, into the opposite lanes, with me right behind him. The line of oncoming vehicles parted like the Red Sea, cars and trucks sliding to the side of the road as the Subaru tried to get away.

And then, for once, karma found me.

At Takela Drive, the light turned red and a FedEx truck pulled out moving right to left, directly into our path. The Subaru driver was too quick on the wheel and too heavy on the brakes. He spun—a 360-degree turn, up and over the curb, across the sidewalk and into a stand of juniper bushes, directly in front of the local California Department of Motor Vehicles office.

I slammed my gear shift into "park" at the curb and jumped out as he flung open his door. He was a big dude, around fifty, with a big, lumberjack-like beard in a big, shearling sheepskin coat.

"What in the name of Jesus do you think you're—"

I was on him before he could finish his sentence, grabbing him by his coat, hauling him out, and shoving him face down in the snow in front of the DMV, my forearm around his throat, my knee in the small of his back.

"Move and I'll snap your spine."

I looked over at the woman sitting in the passenger seat. Her hair was dark red and shoulder length, like Savannah's. Only this woman was about twenty years younger, considerably less attractive, with a long, drawn face. She was terrified of me.

"Please, sir, don't hurt my father."

I rolled him over. Under his coat was a cleric's black shirt and white collar. A silver crucifix hung from a leather strand around his neck.

A clergyman.

Way to go, Logan.

"Are you out of your mind?"

"It's been said of me. I'm sorry, sir. I thought you were somebody else."

I helped him to his feet, dusting the snow off of him. For someone who'd just been chased down and assaulted, he seemed surprisingly forgiving.

"We all make mistakes," he said.

"Some of us more than others," I said.

The minister volunteered that his daughter was recently diagnosed with cancer, and more recently divorced from a domestic abuser against whom she'd had to take out a restraining order. They were driving to San Francisco to meet with her oncologist when I showed up in their rearview mirror.

"Her ex-husband has a Yukon just like yours," the minister said. "That's why I didn't pull over."

I showed him Savannah's picture and explained why I'd chased them. The minister commented on how pretty she was. He hadn't seen her around and offered to pray for her safe return. I told him I could use all the help I could get.

The Subaru, from everything I could tell, appeared to have sustained no damage. The minister rocked it out of the snow and I helped push it back across the sidewalk, into the road.

"I'm sorry we had to meet under these circumstances," he said. "You seem like a good man." He handed me his card. "You should think about coming to Sunday services. You'd be amazed, the miracles that can occur when you put your life in the Lord's hands."

"If you say so."

We both knew my going to church would be a miracle in itself.

"I wish you His grace," he said.

"Safe travels. Good luck at the doctor."

The minister's daughter tried to smile.

I watched them drive on, haunted by the expression on her face. I could tell she wasn't long for the world. Call it a gift or a curse. Frequently, I can look at someone and know intuitively they're going to die young. We were studying the Civil War in high school, rotogravure photos of young soldiers, when I first realized I had that skill. Those soldiers who'd been killed in battle all seemed to share the same look as they stared into the camera: a faint, almost imperceptible sadness in their eyes, as if they knew they wouldn't make it to old age. I caught the same look in the eyes of otherwise happy classmates who would die prematurely while driving drunk or by some terrible disease. I saw it in the eyes of fellow pilots, killed in action, and in the eyes of go-to guys who served with me in Alpha, and who never made it home. Sometimes, when I caught my reflection in the mirror, I thought I saw the same look in my own eyes.

A chill came over me and my teeth chattered climbing back into the Yukon. Even with the heat on high, I shook uncontrollably. The weather had nothing to do with it.

Where are you, Savannah? Please be OK.

I studied her photo, her exquisite face. Whatever ominous portend I'd discerned in the eyes of those soldiers and friends whose lives were cut short, I couldn't see in hers. I felt relief, if only for a moment. Then my phone rang. The incoming number registered to "Private Caller."

"Logan."

"I want you to listen very carefully to what I'm about to tell you." The voice on the other end was male, late thirties to early forties. He spoke with a decidedly Australian accent. "We've got your lady. Cooperate with us, mate, you'll get her back. Choose not to, you'll never see her alive again."

NINE

I sucked in as much air as my lungs would accept and let it out slowly, dropping my heart rate, slowing my metabolism, and narrowing my focus, the way I'd been trained to shoot.

"What's your name?" I asked him.

"Right. Like I'm just gonna *give* you my name."

"Doesn't have to be your real name. Give me something. We can at least be civil."

"All right," he said. "You can call me Crocodile Dundee."

"Crocodile Dundee it is. Now, if you would, please do me a favor and put her on the phone."

"You're not dictating terms here, mate. I am."

"Put her on the phone or this conversation's over."

I was bluffing. The last thing I wanted him to do was hang up on him. But if I'd learned anything as an operator, it was that the minute you surrender authority to a killer or kidnapper early on in any negotiation is the minute you'll always wish you could take back.

"Fine," he said, "have it your way."

A jumble of noise filled my ear—scratching sounds and agitated voices, muffled, like Dundee had put his hand over the phone. I heard him say, "Say hello." Then I heard Savannah.

"Hello?" She sounded tentative and afraid, like she'd been crying.

"Don't worry, baby. You're gonna be fine. I promise you'll be home before you can even—"

Dundee was back on the phone.

"Let's get down to business, shall we?"

My whole body shook with rage. I took another breath and let it out slowly.

"You harm so much as one hair on her head, and I swear, after I find you, and I *will* find you, you'll beg for death before we're finished."

He laughed dismissively. "You have no idea who you're dealing with, Mr. Logan. You have no idea what I'm capable of."

I could've told him the same thing, but I didn't.

"What do you want?"

"You'll be delivering a package for me," Crocodile Dundee said. "By air. In your airplane."

"What's in the package?"

"That's none of your concern."

"Deliver it where?"

"We'll get to that, mate. Right now, you only need to know three things: if you talk to the cops, your lady friend dies. If you tell anybody else about our little arrangement before it's concluded, she dies. If you tamper in any way with the package to be delivered, she dies. Do we understand each other?"

I gritted my teeth.

"Affirmative."

"Excellent. Now, here's how it'll go down: the package'll be waiting for pickup at a predetermined location in the Lake Tahoe area. I will send you a text message with the location. Your phone can receive text messages, yes?"

"I assume so. I've never tried texting."

"Then I'd suggest you practice beforehand. If you do not pick up the package within ten minutes of my text, or I smell a hint of bacon in the area, your lady friend dies. We clear?"

"Yes."

"After you've picked up the package, you'll receive another text. It'll instruct you where to fly, the drop-off point. If the package doesn't arrive within half an hour of the specified time of delivery—"

"—My lady dies. Yeah, I get it. When, exactly, are you hoping to pull off this operation? Because nobody's flying in this weather."

"The snow's forecast to let up tonight. Clearing skies the rest of the week. You should be airborne by tomorrow afternoon at the latest, no worries."

"You mind my asking a question?"

"You don't get to ask questions, Mr. Logan."

"What did it feel like to murder that kid from the airport? Was it worth it?"

"I have no idea what you're talking about, mate," Crocodile Dundee said with a nervous little chuckle.

Then he hung up.

He knew exactly what I was talking about. He also knew exactly what he was doing. Whatever it was he'd removed from that airplane and committed murder over, was evidently so precious, or dangerous, that he wanted to minimize his risks at getting caught with it by having someone else transport it for him. With law enforcement officers watching the roads, what better way to get away with the goods than by air?

I closed my eyes and tried to calm myself meditatively, but it did no good. I wanted to kill Crocodile Dundee more than I ever wanted to kill anybody. I wanted to rip out his throat the way I'd been trained, to jam my thumbs into his eyes and implode them like hardboiled eggs. True Buddhists, even in their darkest moments, harbor no such fantasies. I didn't care. He'd kidnapped my woman, terrorized her gentle soul.

He would pay for that with his life.

✛

I DROVE through the cold and snow, back to the bed-and-breakfast, hoping to find Deputy Streeter to see if he'd gone to question Preston Kavitch, but his Jeep wasn't there. With nothing better to do than foment vengeful thoughts, I parked on the street with the engine running, my phone in hand, and attempted to send Streeter my first-ever text message.

My fingertips were too big for the tiny keypad. I kept misspelling words—when the phone's infuriating autocorrect function wasn't misinterpreting them for me. "At Tranquility B&B, need to speak with you ASAP" became "At tranquility choice Neemm too spew Witt you'll," followed by, "Bees to speak with youth," followed by, "Am tranquilizer B&F I homered to spa why you!" Whoever dubbed them "smart" phones must've been pretty stupid. It took me five attempts before I finally was able to hit "send." Streeter responded almost immediately.

"En route your loc 7 min ETA."

Welcome to the Technology Age, Logan, where the telegraph has become the preferred method of human communications.

Streeter arrived exactly seven minutes later, pulling in behind me. I turned off the engine, stepped out of the Yukon, and got into his Wrangler.

"Got your voice mail," he said. "Sorry I didn't get back to you sooner. Crazy day. We got the preliminary autopsy results back this morning on Chad Lovejoy. Looks like Mr. Lovejoy got tapped with a .40-cal, three rounds. We got some good plaster casts, shoeprints leading away from the plane, before the snow covered them up. Fairly unusual tread design."

According to Streeter, law enforcement records showed that Chad Lovejoy had done two tours in the less-than-loving embrace of California's Department of Corrections and Rehabilitation. He'd logged sixteen months at Chino on an intent-to-distribute cocaine beef, and another year at Chuckawalla Valley State Prison for residential burglary. He was on parole at the time of his murder.

"How does a two-time loser land work at a high-end airport like Tahoe?"

"His uncle's Gordon Priest," Streeter said. "Priest is the manager at Summit Aviation Services."

"I already know that. Did you talk to him yet?"

Streeter shook his head. "We're still putting a list together. Lovejoy ran with a pretty sketchy crowd, given his arrest record. He had no shortage of 'friends' who would've slit his throat for a nickel. We're talking to them first."

"What about Preston Kavitch. You talk to him yet?"

"Soon as you and I are done here." The deputy wiped his nose on the back of his hand. "What was so important, you had to talk to me A-SAP?"

Part of me, a big part, wanted to fill him in on the call I'd received from the man calling himself Crocodile Dundee, but I knew doing that would likely doom Savannah. Well-intentioned though they may be, few rural law enforcement agencies have the expertise to bloodlessly resolve real kidnappings. The track record of federal law enforcement isn't much better, which was why I wasn't about to fill in the FBI, either, not with the prospect of special agents flooding Lake Tahoe in their raid jackets and black Chevy Suburbans. The German army marching into Paris was only slightly more conspicuous.

"You wanted information on the locked-down FAA file," I said.

"You got something?"

I filled him in on the downed airplane's apparent ties to the CIA.

Streeter's eyes lit up. "The CIA? In El Dorado County? Oh, man, that's *awesome*."

"If it were my investigation," I said, "the first thing I'd do is try and establish whatever it was that was in that crate. You nail that down, you find out where a thief might fence it. You establish the market, you establish the market's primary players. Then you start squeezing. Hopefully, they lead you to your killer."

"Not to pry or anything," Streeter said, "but you seem pretty familiar with the process."

I opened the passenger door and got out.

"If I hear anything else, I'll let you know. Lemme know if Preston says anything worthwhile."

"I'll tell you what I can," Streeter said.

I started back for the Yukon.

"Mr. Logan?"

I turned.

"We're gonna do our best to find her and bring her back to you safe."

I tried to thank him or at least smile. It would've been the civil thing to do, but I wasn't feeling all that civil.

✝

A MOTEL room is a motel room. All I really cared about was whether the shower produced hot water and the bed was reasonably free of parasites. The thirty-six dollar a night Econo Lodge on Lake Tahoe Boulevard would more than do until I heard back from Crocodile Dundee.

Savannah would've rolled her eyes at the prospect of spending five minutes in such a room, let alone all night. The art that decorated the room—reproductions of badly composed landscapes—would've commanded her attention. The paintings were bolted to the walls. Why, she would have wondered aloud, would anyone in their right mind even *think* about stealing such tacky art? She might've made some snide remark about the floral print bedspread, and how humans occasionally have been known to spontaneously combust rubbing up against that much polyester. She would've accused me of being tight with a buck for having booked us into such a room, while I, in turn, would've accused her of being spoiled by her daddy's oil money. Then we would've thrown the bedspread on the floor and made intense love. Entwined and wholly spent after that, we would've pondered our future together and that of our child. All would've been perfect in our world. For a while, anyway.

A burning, acidic pain traveled up the back of my throat from somewhere deep beneath my sternum. Standing in the

— 117 —

hallway, card key in hand, surveying my new temporary digs, I felt something wet on my cheeks and reached up to wipe it away, surprised by my own tears. The last time I'd cried about anything was, well, I couldn't remember the last I cried.

I took a shower, toweled off, trimmed my beard, put on clean clothes, rearranged the hangers in the closet, lay down to nap and couldn't, paced, did push-ups, gazed out at the snow, forced myself to watch television. Anything to stop staring mindlessly at my phone on the bathroom counter where I'd plugged it in to recharge, waiting for it to ring.

A little dog with a high-pitched yap was barking and whining in the room above mine. I turned up the TV. Five minutes of channel surfing produced nothing that held my interest beyond a few seconds of the Ellen DeGeneres Show—and only because it occurred to me how much Ellen resembled Green Bay Packers' quarterback Aaron Rodgers.

The barking upstairs grew louder, more incessant. I cranked up the volume. Then somebody next door started pounding in protest on the wall. I fantasized about putting my fist through the Sheetrock and teaching whoever was on the other side a lesson in potential life-saving etiquette: never pound on the wall of any motel to complain about the noise because you never know whether it's harmless, hard-of-hearing gramps on the other side of that wall with *Wheel of Fortune* turned up too loud, or members of the Manson family. I turned off the TV, grabbed my phone, threw on my jacket, and left.

Walking through the motel's parking lot toward my car, I looked up and saw the faintest hint of blue sky before the windblown clouds reclaimed their domain. Crocodile Dundee had been right about the forecast; the snow seemed to be letting up somewhat. If all went according to his plan, I'd be airborne in the morning. One step closer to getting Savannah back.

I needed to know as much about him as I could—his motives, his capabilities, everything and anything that might afford me an advantage if and when we crossed swords. No-where, it dawned on me as I pondered what limited resources were available to me in snowy South Lake Tahoe, offered more knowledge than a public library. There was a small one just off Lake Tahoe Boulevard, about a mile and a half west of the motel. I'd noticed it while searching for Savannah earlier in the day. I fired up the Yukon and drove over.

✝

LIBRARIANS ARE among the smartest and often least sociable individuals on the planet. Books are their friends; it's most people they can do without, especially dumb ones. I'd come to that realization the summer between my third and fourth grades in school when I'd been granted a rare day off from farm chores and walked two miles to the local public library, a two-story, turn-of-the-century, red brick fortress that smelled of damp paper.

The librarian, Miss Vanderford, had a long nose and heavy-lidded eyes bunkered behind winged, bejeweled reading glasses. She was ancient. Probably in her forties.

"What're you looking for?" she asked me, from behind the checkout counter.

"A way out."

"A way out, huh? Of what? This? Your life?"

I shrugged and stared at the holes in my canvas basketball shoes.

Miss Vanderford walked over with a cigarette dangling from between her lips, and grabbed a novel off the nearest shelf. "You want excitement? A life of grand adventure? Here. Read this."

She thrust the book in my hand. It was "The Hunters," a fictional account by author James Salter of his experiences flying F-86 Sabre jets during the Korean War. I walked back to the farm, found some shade behind the hay baler, and read

— 119 —

until the sun went down and there was no more light. All I ever wanted to be after that was a fighter pilot.

The South Lake Tahoe Library, a modern, wood-frame structure of spare, architectural utility, offered no inspirations comparable to those of my youth, but the librarian on duty, a willowy blonde about my age with pleasant green eyes, did offer me a cup of coffee and research assistance.

"I'm interested in finding out as much as I can about a plane crash that occurred outside of town, a long time ago."

"The one I heard about on the radio this morning?" she asked me.

I nodded.

"You a reporter?"

"I'm a pilot."

"Just curious about what happened?"

"Something like that," I said.

"Well, you're in luck. We got a call this morning from one of the TV stations in Reno. They're also curious about that airplane. I've already started doing some research for them."

I followed her to the back of the library. She turned toward me as we walked and extended her hand.

"I'm Constance, by the way."

"Cordell Logan."

We shook hands.

"Haven't seen you in here before." She gave me a shy smile. "I think I would've remembered."

"My first visit."

"Really? Well, I hope it won't be your last."

She asked me if I'd come to Lake Tahoe to ski. I told her no. She told me she used to ski, before her divorce, but banged up her knee.

"My kids snowboard," Constance said. "They're always trying to get me to try it. They say it's healthier on the joints."

"Not snowboarding would probably be even healthier."

She smiled, guiding me to a long wooden table with an old, box-shaped microfilm reader resting atop it.

"Well, anyway, I went through every copy of the paper from October 1956. Don't know if it's related to that airplane they found or not, but I found this story very curious."

On the machine's illuminated screen was a front page, photocopied, from the October 25, 1956, edition of the Reno *Gazette-Journal*. At the bottom of the page, below an Associated Press story headlined, "Hungarian Students Rise Up Against Russkies," was another, much shorter wire-service dispatch that ran under the headline:

LOUD BOOM HEARD

Lake Tahoe (AP)—El Dorado County sheriff's officials were investigating reports of a loud explosion heard early Wednesday morning in the remote, mountainous area known as Voodoo Ridge, about 10 miles west of Lake Tahoe's south end.

A handful of area residents reported hearing a thunderous "boom" shortly after midnight. Authorities were exploring the possibility that an airplane may have crashed. However, no missing aircraft were reported. A sheriff's official said a team would be sent to search the area as soon as weather conditions improve. A storm has blanketed the Sierra this week with nearly two feet of snow.

"I went through every copy of the newspaper for a month after that," Constance the librarian said, "but I couldn't find anything more about it. I will say, though, the area described in this article is the same area where they supposedly found that airplane yesterday."

Waiting at the checkout counter with a stack of books, a stooped old man with a cane and a black beret coughed to get her attention.

"Duty calls," Constance said apologetically. "Excuse me."

I sat down at the table and reread the story on the microfilm machine. It offered nothing by way of actionable intelligence:

residents had heard what may or may not have been a plane crash; there was no apparent attempt on the newspaper's part to follow up.

So much for that.

Frankly speaking, the story about the Hungarian uprising that appeared on the same page made for far better reading. We studied the revolt in great detail at the academy, how even though the revolt failed, it came to play a major role decades later in the eventual downfall of the Soviet Union.

The article continued inside the newspaper. I hand-cranked the microfilm, advancing the pages, intending to finish the article. I never got that far.

On the jump page was a list of five, one-paragraph news briefs, each with its own headline, all under a larger headline, "News of the West." The first brief described the winning entry in an Idaho potato-growing contest, the second detailed how officials were assessing small cracks in the Hoover Dam. It was the third story that caused me to sit up straighter in my chair:

AIRPORT GUARD KILLED

Santa Paula, Calif. (AP)—Police are seeking the public's help in identifying the killer of an airport watchman shot to death Tuesday night in this small citrus farming community, about 60 miles northwest of Los Angeles. The suspect is believed to have escaped in a two-engine Beechcraft, Model 18 airplane.

TEN

A security guard is shot to death in Southern California. The suspect flies off in a Twin Beech. Hours later, residents in a remote and mountainous area of California hear an explosion amid a raging snowstorm that they speculate might've been an airplane crashing. More than a half century later, a Twin Beech is found in the same area with a long-dead pilot behind the controls, and with its mysterious cargo recently gone missing. I was no bookie, but the odds told me that it had to be the same airplane.

"Leaving so soon?" Constance said from behind the check-out counter as I headed for the library's front door.

"Got what I needed. Thanks for the help."

"My pleasure." Her smile was one part professional and about three parts lonely.

The storm had let up. Wisps of low-lying stratus clouds retreated to the east, revealing a sunlit, cerulean blue sky so bright it hurt to look at it. The air was cold and felt good down deep in my chest. For an instant, my mind was transported to the frigid Koh-e Baba mountains of the Hindu Kush, where years before the cold had helped wipe from my brain the nauseating bouquet of blood, gastric acid, and partially digested sheep mutton, spilled by the terrorist whose intestines I'd just splattered all over the snow.

I dialed Streeter outside the library and told him what I'd learned about the airplane I'd found, how it may have been involved in a murder in Santa Paula back in 1956. He was stoked.

"If the homicide was never solved, they'll still have a case file down there."

"No statute of limitations on homicide," I said.

"Did the article say whether they ever made any arrests?"

"All I know is what I just told you."

"I'll check it out. Thanks for the tip."

"You talk to Preston Kavitch yet?"

"Finished up with him about ten minutes ago," Streeter said. "He's clean."

"You're sure of that?"

"He's on probation. Wears an ankle monitor. The GPS shows he hasn't left the house all day."

Was Preston Kavitch Crocodile Dundee? I doubted it. Their voices were substantially different. Plus, Preston appeared incapable of tying his own shoelaces, let alone concocting a credible foreign accent and pulling off a major crime like kidnapping. But who's to say he wasn't working with somebody? I ran the theory past Streeter that Savannah could've entered the house, perhaps to grab a cup of coffee while awaiting my return, and run into Preston, who'd then restrained her until his coconspirator arrived.

"I searched the house top to bottom, the surrounding bungalows, and the grounds, and I didn't see anything that jumped out at me," Streeter said. "But I'll go back and do it again, if it'll make you happy."

"Do that. Do *something*."

"I understand you're anxious, Mr. Logan. I'd be, too. We're doing the best we can."

I asked him if he knew whether Preston Kavitch had any ties to Australia.

"Australia?"

"Has he ever been there? Does he hang out with anybody from Australia? Do you know anybody locally who's from there?"

There was a pause over the phone. "Why would you want to know that?"

I knew I was taking a risk. If Dundee found out that I was asking law enforcement such questions, he might well respond violently against Savannah, as he'd threatened to do. On the other hand, I wasn't about to sit idly by and simply hope the sheriff's department did its job.

"I'll explain later," I said.

"If you have information relevant to this investigation, Mr. Logan, I'd strongly urge you to share it. Withholding evidence in a homicide is against the law."

"Duly noted. Are you going to answer my question or not?"

He didn't answer right away, mulling his response. Then he said, "Because you helped us locate a missing airplane, and because you've been of more than a little assistance in this investigation, I feel obliged to reciprocate—to the extent department policy allows me."

I waited.

"I don't know anybody personally from Australia who lives in El Dorado County," Streeter said. "That's not to say they don't exist. I just don't know them."

The only local Australian connection the deputy could think of—and it was a stretch to even call it a connection—was a local kennel club that raised and showed Australian shepherds.

"Great dogs, but they're not even from Australia," Streeter said. "I grew up with one. They're from the Basque region of Spain originally. But, whatever. If you want to know if Preston has any connections to Australia, I'll ask him."

"I'd appreciate you holding off on that for the time being."

"But I thought you just said—"

"I know what I said, Deputy. I have my reasons. I'll explain them when the time's right."

Streeter to his credit didn't push it. We hung up on amicable terms, each promising to keep in touch. I unlocked the Yukon and got in. I was sliding the key into the ignition when I remembered:

Out at the airport, Lovejoy's uncle, Gordon Priest, the manager of Summit Aviation Services, had walked in while I was first pointing out on the map to Deputy Woo where I'd spotted the wrecked Twin Beech. Priest had tossed a bag from McDonald's on the table, along with a keychain. There was a little metal dog attached to the chain. It was an Australian shepherd.

The digital clock on the Yukon's dash read 3:20 P.M. More than nine hours had elapsed since I'd last seen Savannah.

I decided it was time to pay Gordon Priest a visit.

✈

WALKING INTO Summit Aviation Services, I could hear him berating his receptionist, Marlene, over some filing error she'd committed. She stood in his office doorway, taking the pounding without pounding back while trying bravely to smile as Priest ripped into her. She seemed more than relieved to see me.

"Mr. Logan. Come to check on your airplane?"

I lied and said yes.

She looked haggard, her eyes rimmed red from crying.

"I'm having a hard time coming to terms with Chad's death," she said. "I just can't believe he's gone, that he died so violently."

"He had a record, for Chrissake," Priest said, walking out of his office to snatch a cookie off of her desk and ignoring me. "He was a loser."

"My husband has a record, Gordon," Marlene said, clearly miffed at her boss. "He's made a few mistakes in his life, but I would hardly call him a loser."

"A wife beater is more like it," Priest said.

"He's never laid so much as one finger on me. Never."

"When he's sober, you mean."

Marlene sat back in her chair and folded her arms.

"You have no right to talk about him that way."

Priest exhaled. "OK, forget I said anything. I apologize."

She looked away, her arms still crossed, smoldering.

"Look, all I'm saying is, something was bound to happen to Chad sooner or later." Priest took a bite of cookie. "He ran with the wrong crowd. I should've never hired him. I only did it because my sister wanted me to."

"Any idea who might've shot him?" I asked.

Priest glared at me like I was a bill collector.

"Are you the sheriff?"

I said nothing.

"Well, when the sheriff wants my opinion, I'll give it to him. Otherwise I've got nothing to say."

"You seem somewhat hostile, Mr. Priest. I'm going to assume you're just having a bad day, and that you're not always such an insensitive jerk."

My purpose was to antagonize him, to knock him off his game a little. People will often reveal things when they're flustered, little truths that might otherwise remain obscured behind the filters of normal civil discourse.

He strode toward me angrily, half a cookie stuffed in his mouth, his big belly jiggling under his polo shirt.

"That airplane was ancient history. It didn't matter to anybody. If you hadn't spotted it, my nephew would be alive today, and I wouldn't be getting telephone calls from my hysterical sister every twenty minutes. Do you have any idea how much trouble you've caused, how much damage?"

"Actually, I do."

He turned and stormed back to his office, slamming the door behind him.

Whoever it was who'd called me to say he was holding Savannah wasn't Gordon Priest. Crocodile Dundee spoke in a gravelly baritone. Priest spoke in a whiny tenor. You can disguise a voice only so much. Was it still possible that Priest played some role in the murder of his sister's son, and in Savannah's abduction? I wasn't about to rule out anything or anyone. The fact that Priest had left a message the day before on his office's answering machine, informing his receptionist that he'd be away all day at some out-of-town meeting struck me as more than curious. Had he left that message with the intent of establishing a credible alibi, then gone into the mountains to help loot a long-missing airplane, opting ultimately not to share with his nephew the profits to be had in whatever cargo that airplane was carrying? I didn't know, but I definitely intended to find out.

Marlene sat down at her desk and opened the top drawer, revealing an impressive array of candies, cookies, and bags of potato chips. She unwrapped an Almond Joy.

"You mentioned to me yesterday that Chad and Gordon were close," I said, knowing that Priest couldn't hear me with his door closed. "Doesn't seem to me like there was a whole lot of love lost between the two of them."

The receptionist glanced nervously in the direction of Priest's door and crammed half the candy bar into her mouth. "Gordon puts on a big front," she said.

She offered me the other half of the Almond Joy. I declined.

"I'm sorry," she said, stuffing the half I'd turned down into her mouth. "I get really hungry when I'm sad or nervous."

"You don't owe me any explanations, Marlene."

"Gordon's really a big softy. He knows he loved Chad. He gave him a chance when nobody else would."

"I heard he raises Australian shepherds."

"Not raise. Breeds. For money." Marlene licked some chocolate from her fingers.

I asked her why Priest was interested in that particular breed of dog.

"Why not golden retrievers or labradoodles?"

Marlene cocked her head, thinking. "You know, I've never thought to ask him. Are you interested in getting one?"

"Someday maybe. I don't know."

She brightened. "Speaking of beautiful, where's your beautiful girlfriend?"

I probably should have told her the truth—one more set of eyes looking for Savannah couldn't hurt—but I was tired and not in the mood.

"She's around," I said, "somewhere."

Marlene laughed like I'd just made a joke. "Well, I'm looking forward to seeing her again—only this time, with a big fat wedding ring on her finger."

The ring was to have been a surprise. The day before we flew to Lake Tahoe, while Savannah was napping, I'd taken Mrs. Schmulowitz aside and asked if she wouldn't mind picking me out a wedding band that afternoon from her favorite jewelry store in downtown Rancho Bonita. I knew as much about jewelry as I did ballroom dancing, which is to say, nothing. Mrs. Schmulowitz had survived three bad marriages and outlived a fourth. If anybody was an expert on wedding rings, it was she.

"Do I *mind*?" she whispered to me excitedly, careful to not let Savannah overhear. "Bubbeleh, I mind when the Giants miss the playoffs. I mind not being able to find a decent bagel anywhere on this entire *facacta* coast. But do I mind shopping for rings? What are you, kidding me? Now, how much were you planning to shell out for this lasting symbol of your eternal love?"

"I have no clue. How much do rings go for these days?"

"Considering the price of gold? More than you've probably got. What happened to the ring you bought her the first time, you don't mind me asking?"

"She heaved it off the Golden Gate Bridge in the middle of an argument."

"Making a statement. Nice. I always pawned my bling. Why throw good money after bad, am I right?" She reached up and patted my face. "Don't you worry. I'll pick you out a nice ring, bubby—she can always return it if it doesn't strike her fancy. Pay me back when you can."

The ring was still sitting in my duffel bag, in a purple velvet box. My plan had been to pretend on our drive to the wedding chapel that the idea of a ring had simply slipped my mind—just to get a rise out of Savannah. Then I would've grinned, reached into my pocket, and shown her the ring. She would've laughed, kissed me, and all would have been right. That was the plan, anyway. It was now on indefinite hold.

"Think I'll go out and check on my plane," I told Marlene.

"Certainly."

She buzzed me through a glass security door. I pulled the collar up on my leather jacket and walked out to the flight line. Gordon Priest, I decided, could wait. My grilling him about his possible involvement in his nephew's murder would've only antagonized him and probably gotten me in trouble with the sheriff's department, accused of interfering with Streeter's investigation.

The *Ruptured Duck* was tied down directly in front of Summit Aviation, between a Cessna Cardinal and a notoriously unstable V-tail Bonanza—a "Doctor Killer" as they're commonly known in general aviation because more than a few physicians have been known to buy them and die in them. I grabbed a green, six-foot fiberglass folding ladder leaning near the front door, propped it in front of the *Duck's* right wing, climbed up, and began brushing off eight inches of wet snow with my forearm.

"Thought you might want this," Marlene said, emerging from inside, sans coat, carrying a snowbrush in hand.

"'Preciate it."

"You know," she said, "it occurred to me, if you're interested in an Australian shepherd puppy, you really should talk to my friend, Liam. He and Gordon, they're sort of business partners. Liam knows everything there is to know about Aussie shepherds. He's from there, you know, the land down under."

✝

Liam was Liam McMahon, proprietor of Sundowner Sports, a ski and kayak rental shop situated about a half mile from the gondola station at the base of the Heavenly Mountain Resort. Marlene had described him as a middle-aged charmer, an expert snow and water skier popular with the ladies. Sitting in my Yukon outside his small but bustling shop and observing the activities within, it was easy to comprehend why:

A wiry man with Goldilocks tresses that he wore in a ponytail, craggy, sun-burnished features, and a quick, dazzling smile, McMahon moved easily among his customers, teasing and laughing as he fitted them for boots, skis and snowboards. I waited until the crowd thinned before going in. If I concluded that McMahon was in any way complicit in Savannah's disappearance, things could get ugly in a hurry; I didn't want anyone else but him getting hurt.

What I assumed would be a short wait turned into nearly an hour. A steady procession of customers came and went, most of them young and laughing, eager to hit the slopes the next day. As the sun went down, I found myself growing increasingly antsy, unable to sit still—*shpilkes* in my *toches*, Mrs. Schmulowitz called it—needles in my butt. Customers or not, I'd decided I couldn't wait any longer when my phone rang. Caller ID showed a number in Lake Tahoe's 530 area code.

"This is Logan."

"Yeah, you, like, came by and showed me a picture this morning. Some lady you're looking for?"

The voice was young, male. It took me a second: the high school kid who'd paused from shoveling snow out of his parents' driveway as I approached him.

"I remember. What's up?"

"Yeah, well, like, I can't be a hundred percent sure, OK? But I'm, like, pretty sure I saw her this afternoon."

ELEVEN

The kid said his name was Billy. He told me he hoped to be either a firefighter and help people, or a downhill racer on the Pro Ski Tour and get laid a lot. He said he'd ditched his last period chemistry class when he stopped off for a fish taco and saw Savannah try to get out of a van behind the Los Mexicanos restaurant on Herbert Avenue. A man, he said, forced her back inside the van.

"When was this?"

"I dunno. Three hours ago."

"Why didn't you call me then?"

"Had a trumpet lesson I had to go to. Plus, I didn't even think about it until just a couple of minutes ago."

"Did you get the license plate?"

"Um, no."

"What kind of van was it? The make?"

"I dunno. A van."

"What did it look like? How old? What color?"

"I dunno. Green, sorta, I guess—it didn't have any windows, I remember that. Except for, like, you know, the ones on front. What was the other question?"

"How old was it?"

"I dunno. It didn't look new or anything, but not real old."

"A panel van, though?"

"What's a panel van?"

"They don't have windows except for the ones in front."

"Yeah. I guess. Whatever."

Panel vans are popular among small businesses. I asked him if he'd noticed the name of any company advertised on the side.

"Not really."

"'Not really' meaning you *did* see a name but can't remember, or you didn't see anything?"

"I didn't see anything."

"What about the driver? What did he look like?"

"A guy. I dunno. Regular, kind of."

"A regular guy. Young? Old?"

"In the middle, I'd say. Sort of."

I asked him to call me back if he thought of anything else relevant.

"Is there, like, a reward or something?" he wanted to know.

"The reward is in the doing, Billy. The journey is the reward."

"Oh . . . . Cool."

He was in high school. He had no clue what I was talking about.

A green van that wasn't new and wasn't old. A regular-looking guy who wasn't young and wasn't old. A woman who may or may not have been Savannah. Not much to go on, but still, I decided, worthy enough to let Deputy Streeter know, even at the risk of Crocodile Dundee finding out. Dundee had threatened Savannah's life if I went to the police, but it's been my experience that kidnappers and other miscreants rarely keep their word about anything. I called Streeter and left a detailed message on his voice mail.

I doubted the sheriff's department, based on so thin a tip, would flood the area surrounding Los Mexicanos restaurant, hoping to scare up potential witnesses on the thin hope that somebody might've seen *something*. I knew I'd have to do that myself. For the moment, though, I was focused on Australian import Liam McMahon.

✠

A LITTLE bell over the door tinkled as I entered. McMahon was hunched over a workbench, flirting with a twenty-something snow bunny while fitting her rental boots to her rental skis.

"Be with you in a jiff, mate," he said, adjusting the bindings with a wrench and flat-bladed screwdriver. "Just finishing up with this sweet young thing."

The voice was low, like Crocodile Dundee's, but I hadn't heard enough of it yet to persuade me that Dundee and McMahon were the same man.

"Take your time." I looked around the shop, pretending to be interested in skis.

He chatted up the girl for another few minutes, rang her up at the cash register, and even managed to get her telephone number.

"Dinner tomorrow night, love," he said. "I'll call you, deal?"

"OK."

"Have fun out there. Ski safe now."

She gathered up her gear and smiled at me on the way out. McMahon strode from behind the cash register and watched her go, focused on her butt. A fat shark's tooth hung from a gold chain around his neck.

"God help me, I do love the sheilas," he said. "Now, mate, how can I help you?"

"I'm Cordell Logan."

"Pleasure to meet you, Cordell Logan." He had a firm grip and friendly blue eyes. "Liam McMahon's the name. Don't wear it out."

Had McMahon known my name and been genuinely surprised by my presence, his face would have registered telling involuntary muscle movements that scientists call "micro expressions"—an eyebrow lifted almost imperceptibly, the subtle opening of an eye or parting of lips that can speak the truth far more accurately than words alone. But I perceived nothing in McMahon's facial movements, involuntary or otherwise, to suggest that he regarded me as anything other than a paying customer.

"Australian?"

"Born and bred. Ever been?"

"Several times. Good people. How'd you end up in Tahoe?"

"What else? Chasing a sheila. We fell out of love and I fell in love with where she lived."

"A lot of other Australians around here?"

"None at all, hardly. Ten, twelve, maybe. I probably know 'em all. Half are retired buggers. Lack the strength to even stand up. The other half are too drunk or doped up to get out of bed most days. What about you? You're not from around here."

"Rancho Bonita."

"Well, you couldn't have timed it any better, mate, what with all this fresh powder. I can put you on a set of Rossi parabolics that'll blow your mind."

"I'm not here to ski. I'm trying to locate somebody."

I showed him Savannah's picture and explained the circumstances of her disappearance.

"Gorgeous lady," McMahon said. "I'd be bent out of shape, too, if somebody like that had vanished from my life. Tell you what, let me Xerox a copy of that. I'll put it in my window and ask everybody who comes in if they've seen her around."

"I'd appreciate it."

"You'd do the same for me, mate."

He took the photo into a back office where his copying machine was.

McMahon, I realized, wasn't Crocodile Dundee. If what he said was true, that there were no more than a dozen native Australians residing in the greater Lake Tahoe area, then whoever had taken Savannah had to be among the dumbest Aussies who ever lived to front himself the way he did, and Dundee sounded anything but dumb over the phone. The more I pondered it, the more I became convinced that the accent was fake.

I drove over and cruised the strip mall that was home to Los Mexicanos. The restaurant had mirrored front windows and a pretend brick facade painted bright orange. Every employee I approached leaned away from me when I showed them Savannah's picture, fear in their eyes, like they were about to be deported. Nobody remembered seeing Savannah or a green van parked outside that day. The other mall shops were closed for the evening. There was nobody else to ask questions of. I ordered a chile verde burrito to go and ate it sitting in my car.

A few customers drove in, skiers and snowboarders. It seemed pointless to ask them. Shortly after seven thirty, a black, dinged-up Dodge pickup with tinted glass, chrome mag wheels, and a plow blade pulled in and began scraping snow off the lot, piling it along the edges. I got out and walked over, holding up my hand in the truck's headlights. The driver braked and his window came down, giving way to the pungent odor of marijuana, and a glassy-eyed young man of about twenty-two with an Oakland Raider's baseball cap. His earlobes were stretched out like an African tribesman and there was a hole in each the size of a quarter.

"Hey."

"Hey." He waved away tendrils of pot smoke, snubbing out his blunt on the top of a Budweiser can. "What's up?"

I showed him Savannah's picture, explaining what had purportedly happened in the parking lot earlier in the day. He shook his head apologetically.

"I've been sleeping all day, dude. I was supposed to be over here this afternoon, plowing this shit, but I dunno, man. Fell asleep. Next thing I know, it's like, 'Where am I? What planet is this? What time is it?' You know what I'm saying?"

"We all have our off days."

I asked him if he knew anybody in town who drove a green van.

"A green van . . . a green van . . ." He closed his eyes, trying to focus, working the question like a contestant on final Jeopardy. "No, dude," he said after several seconds, "can't say that I do. My buddy, Twitch, he's got this totally tricked-out blue van with a Porta-Potty in it and everything, but it's, like—"

"Blue."

"Exactly."

"Look, if you do happen to spot any green vans, or the woman from that picture," I said, handing him my card, "I'd appreciate a call."

"No worries." He grabbed his own business card from above the sun visor and handed it to me. "You need any snow plowed, firewood, run some errands, there's my number, right there. Ask anybody, OK? I'm, like, totally reliable."

"I'll, like, keep you in mind."

Back inside the Yukon, I glanced at his card in the glow of the dashboard instruments. His corporate DBA was, "The Plowman Cometh."

Clever. I wondered if I'd ever smile again.

✝

THE RED message light was blinking on my beige-colored room phone when I got back to the Econo Lodge. It was Streeter. He'd called about an hour earlier to apprise me that the fingerprint dusting of the room where Savannah and I stayed had proven inconclusive. The only prints the sheriff's technician had been able to find and identify were left by Johnny and Gwen Kavitch, which didn't set off any bells considering the couple ran the B&B and handled room cleaning themselves. Streeter noted that he'd received my message about the green van and had passed it on to his department's patrol units as well as surrounding law enforcement agencies.

"Don't think we're giving up, we haven't even started," he said on the machine. "I'm still confident we'll find her. I also have an update on the Lovejoy homicide I thought you'd find interesting. Call me when you get a chance."

Streeter had been unable to reach me on my cell phone. The thought occurred to me: what if Crocodile Dundee had the same problem—tried to call me with instructions and couldn't get through because I had yet to figure out all of my phone's mind-numbing, over-engineered features. What if he'd taken his frustration out on Savannah? My face felt flush and my mouth went dry.

Walking quickly into the bathroom, I filled a plastic cup with water and gulped it down, refilled the cup, and drank that, too. Suddenly, I couldn't catch my breath. My heart began pounding crazily, like it was skipping beats, and for a moment, I thought I was dying. Not even in a firefight, or diving in on a heavily defended target, had I ever felt anything remotely close to panic. But that's what it was. A panic attack. Complete, unbridled terror.

I went and sat down on the corner of the bed, closed my eyes, and concentrated, trying to will my heart to normalcy. When that didn't work, I rolled onto the floor and did stomach crunches to the point of exhaustion. That seemed to do the trick; the skipping beats stopped. I lay back on the carpet, my right triceps in spasm, too tired to move.

The Buddha believed that fear is the result of attachment— to ourselves, our possessions, the people we love. Everything in life is transient, including life. Embrace that transience, recognize that all those attachments are fleeting, Buddhists reason, and you'll ultimately shed your fear. Could be all of that is true. I don't really know. But if the Buddha had sat in the same room with Savannah for even five minutes, he might've better understood the erratic beating of my heart and my sense of near-paralytic dread at the prospect of never seeing her again.

My cell phone was on the nightstand above me. I pushed myself off the floor and grabbed it, peering closely at the screen, trying to figure out if I'd missed Dundee's call or text message. Whether he'd tried to reach me or not, I couldn't tell; advancements in digital communications are an anathema to the analog me. I lay down on the bed, not bothering to undress or pull down the bedspread, and closed my eyes. When I opened them again, the sun was coming up and my phone was chiming with an incoming text message:

Behind Applebee's. Suitcase. You got 10 minutes. Will call to confirm you have it. No cops or she dies. You're late, she dies.

The room clock read 7:35 A.M. The text had come in two minutes earlier. I grabbed my duffel bag and bolted, throwing open the motel's office door on my way to my car.

"Where's the Applebee's?"

The college kid manning the front desk pushed her stringy brown hair behind one multipierced ear and looked up at me from a copy of the *Hunger Games*.

"Excuse me?"

"Applebee's. Where is it?"

She pointed. "Take a right on Lake Tahoe Boulevard. It's about three and a half miles. But I'm pretty sure they don't open 'til—"

I reached the Yukon, tossed my duffel into the passenger seat, hopped in, fired up the engine, and roared out, onto the boulevard.

The road was still snow packed and icy in spots, but traffic fortunately was sparse. I fishtailed around a garbage truck and a snail-like Mercedes 450 whose driver, a wizened old man, looked to be steering with one hand and conducting Beethoven's Fifth with the other. As I glanced back to pass him, a deer and her spotted fawn bounded out of nowhere, directly into my path. I cut the wheel hard left and slid along the shoulder, fighting to keep 5,200 pounds of SUV from going off the road. How I avoided hitting Bambi and his mother, I'll never know.

The Yukon's odometer told me I had another two miles to go. That was assuming the desk clerk was correct in her distance estimate. Assuming the clock on the dashboard was set correctly, I had six minutes to get there, find a suitcase, and send a text message acknowledging that whatever was in that suitcase was in my possession, or Savannah would die.

The traffic light ahead was red. Vehicles were beginning to back up in either direction. I cut right, laying on the horn and blew through the T-intersection.

Four minutes.

I gunned the accelerator on the straightaways, the speedometer creeping past eighty, and eased up on the curves. Every fiber in me screamed go faster. I probably could've, too, but not without upping the risk past what Indy race car drivers like to call "being stupid." We'd learned all about high-speed and evasive-driving techniques at Alpha from an instructor who'd spent more than thirty years running guns in Latin America for everyone from the Sandinistas to the Medellin Cartel. Jose Camacho was a slight little man with rotted teeth who'd dropped out of school in third grade, but who fathomed inherently and intimately the physics of wheeled vehicles. He didn't drive them so much as strapped them on. "A car is like a woman," he'd tell us, "each different, yet each the same. Learn to touch her in the way she *desires* to be touched. Never push her beyond what *she* desires, and she will fill your heart forever."

Ever so subtly, I could feel the Yukon swaying left and right as the front tires danced on patches of black ice.

I heeded the words of Jose Camacho and slowed down.

Three minutes.

The landscape passed by as a blur. Towering pine forests and minimalls punctuated by stand-alone ski shops, banks, burger joints, cafés, and budget motels. Ordinarily, I would've mentally catalogued them all, consciously and automatically mapping my exfiltration route—the byproduct of escape and evasion training. But I was so laser-focused on making it to Applebee's in time, I barely noticed any of it.

Two minutes.

The road faded left and suddenly I was tapping like crazy on the brakes, hook-sliding on the ice to a stop. An eighteen-wheeler had jackknifed 200 meters ahead of me. The road in either direction was blocked with traffic.

I pulled out of line, bouncing over the sidewalk in front of the Highland Inn, jumped out of the Yukon, and sprinted.

Where the hell was Applebee's? How much farther up the road? I ran like I did back in the day, with lightning bolts on my football helmet. I was never the fastest receiver, but I had good hands and a nose for the end zone. I used that nose now, racing toward my objective as fast as my calcified knees would carry me.

I'd run about 200 meters when Applebee's came into view on my left with its green shingled roof and stone façade. The expansive, snow-covered parking lot in back was empty save for a weathered, silver Honda Civic with Nevada tags. The car was unoccupied.

I looked around frantically. Not a suitcase in sight.

There was, however, a battered gray Dumpster adjacent to the restaurant's rear door.

One minute.

I threw open the Dumpster's hinged steel top. It crashed against the back with a loud clang. Inside, piled high, were plastic trash bags stuffed with fetid table scraps, used paper napkins and the other disposable detritus of dining out. I began heaving bags onto the snow like a homeless man possessed, one after the other.

And there it was: an old suitcase.

I leaned in, hauled it out with both hands, breathing hard, and set it down. It felt like it weighed about fifty pounds. The sides were fabric, scotch plaid, darkened by stains of who-knows-what. A small padlock secured the suitcase's single zippered opening.

My Casio G-Shock showed 0745. I'd made it just in time. I reached for my cell phone, waiting for it to ring with further instructions from Crocodile Dundee. Then I remembered:

I'd left my phone in the car.

TWELVE

How long it took to haul the suitcase back to the Yukon I couldn't tell you, only that I was thoroughly spent by the time I got there, and that my phone was ringing. The first words out of my mouth when I answered it were, "I'm sorry."

"What the hell, mate?" Crocodile Dundee was seething on the other end. "I told you ten minutes. Do you want your lady to die?"

I closed my eyes and tried to slow my heart rate.

"I had a problem. It's been resolved. I've got the suitcase. What do you want me to do with it?"

"How do I know you've got it? Maybe you don't. You'd say anything to save her."

I described it for him. The pattern of the fabric. The stains.

"Yeah, OK, good, you've got it. Not many suitcases look like that piece of shit anymore, do they?" Dundee laughed. "I mean, when you think about it, how long did it take 'em to figure out you could put wheels on goddamn luggage, right?"

His tone was casual, cordial. I fantasized about putting a bullet behind his ear.

"I'm assuming you're smart enough to know that if you try opening it, or tampering with it in any way, she dies."

"Understood."

"You're going to fly it to Santa Maria," Crocodile Dundee said. "There's a hotel right there on the field, a Radisson. You're going to walk in with the suitcase through the back door, through the lobby and out the front door. There'll be a red, four-door Hyundai parked in the third row, closest to the entrance. You're going to slide the suitcase under that car. Then you're going to walk back into the hotel and you're going to sit in the lobby for an hour. You'll be under observation the entire time, so don't think about trying anything, or—"

"She dies. You've made your point."

"It's now eight fifteen. You'll deliver the suitcase by no later than eleven fifteen. That gives you three hours."

"That's virtually impossible. Santa Maria is more than 250 miles from Tahoe. I'm flying a Cessna 172, not a Learjet."

"Not my problem."

"What if I run into a headwind? Or air traffic control starts vectoring me? I can't do it in three hours."

"It's not subject to negotiation, asshole. Three hours. Not a minute later. Whatever goodwill I was feeling for you was just spent being late for the pickup."

I struggled to maintain control, to not threaten him.

"Let me talk to her. I need to know she's still OK."

"Oh, she's *more* than OK, if you know what I mean."

He laughed, like it was all some big game.

"She's pregnant," I said. "Let me talk to her. Please."

"Hang on a sec," Crocodile Dundee said. "Here's the lovely lady right now."

I could hear Savannah over the phone screaming out in muffled agony, as if her mouth was taped shut, followed by pathetic, heart-wrenching whimpering. Pain seared through the left side of my chest as if I'd been stabbed.

I didn't ask what torture Dundee had inflicted on her. I didn't plead with him to not do it again. I knew that no words I could muster would appeal to such a monster because monsters have no humanity. Some human beings are little more than rabid dogs. They can't be rehabilitated. They need to be put down for the better good. Dundee was one of them.

The palm of my left hand felt wet. I looked down and realized I was bleeding: I'd balled my fist so tightly, my fingernails had broken the skin.

"Three hours, mate," Dundee said. "You best get moving. You're burning daylight."

The line went dead.

I promised myself that Dundee would be dead, too, soon enough.

✝

MARLENE WAS playing solitaire on her computer at Summit Aviation Services when I came rushing in from the parking lot, lugging the suitcase. I tossed the Yukon's keys on the counter, said my duffel and Savannah's luggage were still in the back of the SUV, asked her to store them until I returned, that I wasn't sure when that would be, told her to send me a bill, and raced for the door leading to the flight line.

"Gordon wanted to speak with you before you left," she said, glancing anxiously toward the closed door of Gordon Priest's office. I could see Priest through the glass inside, sitting at his desk, on the phone.

"It'll have to wait."

A pilot is required by regulations to thoroughly inspect his or her aircraft before takeoff. You check to make sure that nothing looks like it's about to fall off the plane, that nothing furry or feathered has taken up residence inside the engine compartment or airframe, that the fuel has no water in it. A pilot also is expected to be fully briefed ahead of time on en route weather conditions, as well as those forecast at his intended destination.

I did none of that before hurriedly unchaining the *Ruptured Duck*, tossing the suitcase into the plane's luggage compartment, and jumping into the left seat.

With precious seconds ticking by, I dug the *Duck's* ignition key out of the front pocket of my jeans, swiftly running my hand over the circuit breakers to ensure they were all in. Mixture control knob full forward. Key in the ignition, four strokes on the primer, primer control set and locked, throttle

— 144 —

open one-eighth inch, master switch on. Feet firmly on the toe brakes. Seat belt tight across my lap.

"Clear!" I shouted with my window open—the same warning every pilot yells before starting any piston-driven engine so that no bystander lurking nearby gets pureed by the propeller.

I cranked the key.

The prop turned listlessly, the engine cold and unwilling, then stopped.

I pumped the throttle control in and out and tried the ignition again. Another half-hearted propeller rotation.

Nothing.

"C'mon, *Duck*, not now."

Then I looked down to my right and realized the fuel tank selector valve was in the "off" position. I normally left it on "both" tanks. I could only assume that the late Chad Lovejoy, who'd met Savannah and me planeside when we first landed, had switched the valve handle for whatever reason while refueling my Cessna. I flipped the indicator to "both" tanks, waited another few seconds for the gas to drain down from the wings, and rotated the ignition key once more.

The engine came alive like it was factory new.

I began taxiing immediately, pulling on my headset and rolling toward the freshly plowed runway, faster than I should've, leaning the fuel-air mixture and setting my altimeter to accommodate the 6,269-foot field elevation, while spinning the elevator trim wheel to a slightly nose-up, takeoff setting. To my right, an orange windsock danced limply on the breeze. The wind was out of the northeast—a good sign. It told me I'd be flying with something of a tailwind, at least after takeoff. A tailwind meant faster groundspeed.

It meant I might make it to Santa Maria on time.

I scanned the sky left and right, forward and back, for any other aircraft coming or going. There were none. The radio was quiet. I should've gone through my pretakeoff checklist the way I always did before each flight, testing the control inputs and engine to make sure everything's working correctly, but I did none of that, either. There was no time. The *Duck* was old, there was no denying that, but he'd never let me down in all the time we'd been flying together. I keyed the mic and hoped his dependability held true.

"South Lake Tahoe traffic, Skyhawk Four Charlie Lima is rolling runway three-six with a right downwind departure, South Lake Tahoe."

I squared the *Duck* to the runway's centerline, twisting the directional guidance compass card to align with the strip's magnetic heading, angled the ailerons into the quartering crosswind, then shoved the throttle full forward.

The *Duck* seemed to sense the urgency of our mission as the airspeed needle came alive. He accelerated quickly, faster than normal, it felt like. I lifted his nose in the cold air and we roared into the sky like an F-16. Well, maybe not like an F-16. Maybe not even close. But definitely not like an aging, four-seat airplane with faded paint and a 160-horsepower engine. We were making nearly 1,700 feet per minute in the climb. In a Cessna 172, that's Guinness World Records material. I turned crosswind, then downwind.

"South Lake Tahoe traffic, Skyhawk Four Charlie Lima is departing the pattern to the south. Final call, South Lake Tahoe."

Prudence dictated that I navigate toward Santa Maria in the same cautious manner by which I'd flown into Lake Tahoe days earlier—mainly following passes while purposefully avoiding overflying the peaks of the Sierra Nevada. Mountain flying is ever-unpredictable, offering pilots smooth, uneventful passage one minute and potentially deadly unseen air currents the next. Powerful downdrafts can suck you into the earth almost at will, while spiraling rotor waves of air that wash unseen over crest lines like giant ocean swells can break apart airplanes like so many toys. But, again, there was no time for such worries. I had to fly directly to Santa Maria, regardless of the risk, if I hoped to beat Dundee's deadline. I spiraled upward, leveled off at 10,500 feet, and flew as the crow flies, skimming the tops of peaks, trusting in the *Duck* and fate.

The sky above me was a patchwork of puffy, cotton ball clouds—altocumulus in the meteorology parlance—positioned with precise equidistance from each other, as though someone had purposely arranged them that way. I could see no *altocumulus lenticularis* ahead—thin, lens-shaped clouds frequently touted by National Enquirer photographers as flying saucers, but better known to pilots as harbingers of severe turbulence, best avoided. The air was smooth. The *Duck* was running fine, all engine instruments were within normal tolerance. The GPS showed 235 miles to Santa Maria, with an ETA of 1107. If my tailwind held, I'd get there with less than ten minutes to spare.

I loosened my seat belt a little. For the first time since receiving Dundee's call that morning, I allowed myself to breathe a little easier and pondered the mysterious cargo in the *Duck's* luggage compartment.

Whatever was secreted inside that suitcase had sat untouched for nearly sixty years inside the hulk of a stolen airplane, the result of an intelligence mission gone wrong. The contents had come by way of the Santa Susana Field Laboratory, a since-closed, top-secret federal research facility tucked into the Simi Valley outside Los Angeles. All I knew of the lab was what I vaguely recalled from the one rocket science class I'd taken while at the Air Force Academy. We'd learned how liquid propellant fuels used on NASA's Apollo spacecraft, the ones sent to the moon during the 1960s, had been formulated at Santa Susana.

But it defied logic, the notion that it was rocket fuel I was hauling.

Whoever had looted that crashed airplane regarded its cargo as so valuable that he'd murdered Chad Lovejoy for it. He'd then kidnapped Savannah to force me to fly it out of Lake Tahoe to lessen his chances of getting caught in a police traffic stop or checkpoint. Was he planning to sell those goods on the black market? That was my guess. But who'd buy a miniscule batch of ancient rocket fuel? Propellants have evolved light years since the 1950s. Nobody who knew anything about missile technology today would pay a dime for anything that old.

Something else was in that suitcase. Had to be.

I was so focused on speculating what that something was, I never saw the other airplane.

A white streak flashed from my left to right, perhaps no more than twenty feet above the *Duck's* nose. I turned my head to look, but it was already gone—a twin-engine King Air, headed west, climbing up through my altitude. A millisecond earlier and we would've collided in midair. My heart felt like it was doing jumping jacks.

Maybe it was karma, the reason why it had taken as long as it had to get the engine started when the *Duck* and I were still on the ground. Or maybe it was sheer, dumb luck. Either way, I didn't much dwell on it. I had a deadline, literally, and a delivery to make.

The airspeed indicator was down to less than 100 knots. The tailwind I'd enjoyed departing Lake Tahoe had turned into a headwind, chopping our speed across the ground by nearly one-third. My GPS now showed a projected estimated time of arrival at 1123.

We weren't going to make it.

I tried not to think of the way Savannah had screamed over the phone. I tried not to think of the welfare of the child, my child, she was carrying. I tried to focus instead on the task at hand: getting to Santa Maria before 1115.

My only alternative was to punish the *Duck* and hope he forgave me.

I shoved the throttle full forward, enriching the fuel-air mixture. The RPM needle on the tachometer crept past the red line.

We began to pick up speed.

Going faster came at a price. The oil temperature climbed steadily. So did the exhaust gas temperature. Both climbed well beyond what I would've ordinarily considered safe. But this was no ordinary flight and there was no other alternative. Either I pushed my plane to the brink, or Savannah and our baby might well die. The *Duck's* engine had been rebuilt, thanks to Larry, after our crash in San Diego. I could only hope it would hold up under the strain.

Just this one time. C'mon, Duck, you can do it. I know you can.

I could feel rising heat on my knees and my feet, radiating through the firewall. The engine, fortunately, sounded otherwise normal. I hoped like hell it stayed that way.

Below, the green forested slopes of the Sierra rose up to meet us like a mirage, deceptively soft and benign. If the *Duck's* power plant were to suddenly seize and we went down, I knew there was a good chance I might end up in some inaccessible draw, hoping for rescue or, like the mummified pilot sitting in that Twin Beech, waiting interminably for rescue. Better, I decided, to let somebody know where I was.

I radioed Oakland Center to request flight following. Air traffic controllers would assign me a transponder code allowing them to more readily follow me on radar. Only I got no response. I was probably too low for them to pick me up on their scopes.

Flying without a net, over potentially hostile terrain, wasn't particularly daunting or new. I'd done it dozens of times hunting Republican Guard armor on low-level sorties into Kuwait and Iraq during Desert Shield and Storm. The realization that nobody in the world has any idea where you are can be unnerving if you let it, or oddly comforting. I opted at the moment for the latter, focusing on Savannah, trying to convince myself that everything would work out.

Approaching Mariposa, the weather gods decided to cut me some slack. The headwind I'd been bucking shifted back to the north. The *Duck* responded as if he'd been gulping vitamins. Our airspeed climbed steadily until the GPS showed we were doing 139 knots across the ground—nearly 160 miles an hour. I eased off the throttle, bringing the RPM's back to 2500, cooling the engine, and cruised at a blazing 135 knots.

With our increased speed, the ETA ticked back down to 1107. I figured to make up even more time as we started downhill on our descent.

Maybe we would make it in time after all. I patted the top of the instrument panel.

Nice job, Duck.

At fifty miles out, I radioed Oakland Center and requested radar advisories for any aircraft in my area. At twenty miles out, Center handed me off to the tower at Santa Maria. The controller there told me to plan on making right traffic for Runway 30. At ten miles out, with no other aircraft in the pattern, he cleared me to land. My approach was uneventful; my landing, not the greatest, but it would do. From the air, I had seen the Radisson hotel on the south end of the field where Crocodile Dundee had instructed me to deliver the suitcase.

"Cessna Four Charlie Lima, say intentions," the controller radioed me as I cleared the runway.

"Charlie Lima's going to the Radisson."

"Right on Taxiway Alpha, left on Alpha three. Monitor ground, point nine. Have a nice day."

I repeated his instructions back to him and continued rolling toward the Radisson at high speed. No one told me to slow down. Santa Maria's airport was a mere shell of what it had been during World War II, when it was used as a military training base, crammed with fork-tailed, P-38 fighters. Its vast flight line now sat largely empty.

Parking was plentiful behind the boxy, four-story Radisson; there were no other airplanes on its ramp. I shut down the *Duck's* engine and hopped out. My watch read 1113. Two minutes to spare.

As I was hauling the suitcase out of the luggage compartment, my phone rang.

"Logan."

"Have you not gotten any of my messages? Where the hell have you been?" The urgency in Matt Streeter's voice was hard to miss.

"Have you found Savannah?"

"We're still looking."

A palpable feeling of lament and relief washed over me—they hadn't found her, but they hadn't found her body, either. I began running toward the hotel with the suitcase.

"There's something you need to know," Streeter said.

"Not now. I'm right in the middle of something."

"I'm afraid it can't wait, Logan. That crate in that airplane you found? It was carrying forty pounds of enriched uranium. The kind they use to make atomic bombs."

My mouth tasted like chalk.

Forty pounds of enriched uranium.

During training at Alpha, we were told that nine pounds was enough to construct a portable nuclear device, a so-called "suitcase nuke." Depending on the type and purity of nuclear material used, such a bomb could create a blast radius wide enough to level downtown Colorado Springs or Buffalo, New York.

I slowed to a stop at the back door of the hotel, my heart suddenly palpitating, my brain swirling, and stared down at the suitcase in my hand, staggered by the horrific choice that confronted me:

I could hope to save the love of my life by cooperating with her kidnapper, or I could potentially save the world.

My watch showed 1115.

Out of time.

One second later, my phone buzzed with an incoming text message.

"We had an arrangement, Logan."

THIRTEEN

"I'll call you back," I told Streeter and hung up.

Did Dundee understand the significance of what was in the suitcase? I had to assume so. What did he intend to do with the uranium? Who was the buyer? What would he do to Savannah if I told him that I was on to him, and that I was done playing his game? Would he listen to reason? Recognize the futility of his plan? Let her go?

We had an arrangement, Logan.

I stared at the screen, more afraid than I'd ever been in my life.

Fear is rooted in what the Buddha deemed "delusions"— the distortions with which we look at ourselves and the world around us. By learning to control our minds, we can eliminate those delusions and, eventually, our fears. The truth, though, was that I couldn't think straight. Savannah was going to live or die. The choice was mine and mine alone.

My phone rang. After several seconds, I pushed "answer," slowly raised the phone to my right ear, and listened without speaking.

"You're being watched," Dundee said. "I know you've landed. Now, either you do what you agreed to do, immediately, or the lady's blood will be on your hands."

I scanned the windows of the hotel for any sign of surveillance, but saw none.

"You've got exactly one more minute, Logan. Take the suitcase into the hotel like you were instructed, walk out the front door, put it under the car, and walk back inside, or I swear, she . . . will . . . die."

"Let her go. She's got nothing to do with this."

"You're wasting time. Get moving."

"You'll kill her anyway."

"Fifty seconds."

I saw Savannah's face in my mind's eye. The way she watched me the first time we made love, her eyes locked on mine. The way her lips drew into a slow, satisfied smile, knowing the effect she was having on me. Every fiber of my being as I stood there on the tarmac compelled me to take that suitcase and do as I'd been instructed.

But I couldn't.

Not without spitting on everything that millions of brave and honorable men and women had fought for. Not without imperiling the lives of untold thousands of innocent people.

I couldn't.

"You still there, Logan?"

"Still here."

"Thirty seconds."

"I know what's in the suitcase."

Dundee was seething, barely able to get the words out. "I told you not to look."

"I didn't have to. You know you'll never get away with it. So, let's just call it a day. You let Savannah go, unharmed, and I give you my word that I won't come looking for you right away. What d'you say?"

"I say shit goes downhill and payday's Friday. Fuck you, mate."

And that was it.

✝

I CALLED 911 in a haze, too numb, really, to accept the likely implications of the decision I'd just made.

After the Radisson and several nearby structures had been evacuated, a member of the Santa Maria Police Department's bomb squad, garbed in his "Lost in Space" protective suit, approached the suitcase where I'd left it at the back door of the hotel and gingerly sliced it open. Inside were a dozen, two-foot-long metal canisters, each containing uranium pellets. The car under which I was to have deposited the suitcase had been reported stolen the night before in San Luis Obispo, a half hour away. It had been wiped clean of prints.

"You should've told me," Streeter said over the phone as I sat in the hotel lobby, my legs still shaking an hour later. "We could've at least tried to help."

"There was nothing you could do, not under the circumstances."

I wanted to know how, at the height of the Cold War, nuclear material could have gone missing from a secure government facility.

Streeter said he'd filed a query online with the National Crime Information Center, requesting any records about thefts that may have occurred at the Santa Susana lab in 1956. The NCIC files showed that there'd been what was described as a burglary in October 1956. It was never solved. His query, he said, triggered a call that morning from a US Department of Energy investigator in Washington, who told him their conversation was strictly off the record.

"The DOE guy told me it wasn't a break-in," Streeter said. "It was a staged robbery."

"Staged?"

"Yeah. By the CIA."

The DOE investigator told Streeter that workers at Santa Susana a year earlier had begun secretly constructing America's first operating nuclear power plant, which they euphemistically referred to as a "sodium reactor" to deflect any attention from the press. Five years later, some kind of catastrophic meltdown occurred, Streeter said, and all of Los Angeles came close to being vaporized. Washington was largely successful in covering it all up, and the lab was eventually shut down.

The year the staged robbery occurred, Streeter said, coincided with Pakistan leasing a base to the United States so that American military forces could keep closer tabs on Soviet ballistic missile testing. What Islamabad wanted in return was a small amount of fissile material to build a working atomic bomb that Pakistan could then wave in the face of India, its sworn enemy, who was building its own nuclear weapons at the time.

"Washington couldn't just hand over the stuff without the Indian government going nuts," Streeter said, "so they got the bright idea of planning a heist and making it look like the Russians were responsible. They found some Russian ex-pat, a former military pilot, to do the job. Everybody at the Santa Susana lab was briefed ahead of time. Then, one of the guards got sick. They brought in a temp, some moron, and nobody bothered to tell him what was up. There was a gunfight. He got shot. They think the guy who was working for the CIA got shot, too. Afterward, everybody at the lab had to sign sworn statements saying they'd go to prison if they ever talked publicly about what happened."

The bloodshed didn't end at the lab, according to the DOE investigator.

"That newspaper story you came across, the one about the security guard getting shot at the airport in Santa Paula? They think the guy drove to the nearest airport to Santa Susana, which was Santa Paula, shot that guard to cover his tracks and protect the agency, then flew the uranium out," Streeter said. "The guard, before he died, said it was a Twin Beech. The DOE confirmed that."

Whoever killed Chad Lovejoy and made off with uranium, Streeter speculated, had probably been exposed to a lethal dose of radioactivity. He was worried I might've suffered a similar fate.

"Uranium isotopes are unstable," I said, "which makes the uranium itself barely radioactive. You don't even really need special packaging to protect yourself."

Streeter didn't ask me how I knew such things, and I didn't elaborate. He said his supervisors had formed a task force, assigning three more detectives to investigate the murder of Chad Lovejoy and Savannah's disappearance, which they now considered linked. He said he wanted to make arrangements to have my phone examined forensically in hopes of backtracking Dundee's calls. I suggested he'd probably be wasting his time. If Savannah's kidnapper had any smarts, he would've paid cash for a disposable cell phone and bought calling minutes from one of hundreds of offshore service providers, rendering his communications with me or anyone all but untraceable.

"Never thought of that," Streeter said.

I asked him if his newly formed task force had developed any viable leads that might, in the near term, lead them to Savannah.

He paused. Then, reluctantly, he said, "Unfortunately, not at this time."

I had to hang up. I had to sit down.

Blue-uniformed Santa Maria police were flitting in and out of the lobby, talking urgently on their hand-held radios, questioning hotel employees and guests who'd been allowed back inside after the suitcase had been driven away for closer inspection and the scene declared safe. I watched them go about their work from the comfort of an armchair, like some bit player in a cop movie. Large scale models of World War II aircraft hung from the ceiling over the dining area adjacent to the lobby. I focused on them and tried hard not to think of the choice I'd made.

I honestly didn't know what else to do, Savannah. Please forgive me.

"Mr. Logan?"

Standing over me was a burly Latino police officer in his fifties. He wore silver captain's bars on his collar and a salt-and-pepper crumb catcher on his upper lip. With him was a compact, clean-shaven man of about thirty-five with dark, movie-star features and perfect hair. But for the pistol bulge under the right armpit of his well-tailored gray business suit, he could've passed for a bank executive.

"This is FBI Special Agent Pellegrini from the Santa Maria field office," the captain said. "We've asked the justice department to come aboard for obvious reasons."

"I'd like to ask you a few questions," Pellegrini said.

"Whatever you need."

"I'll leave you two to it," the captain said, shaking the fed's hand and walking off.

Pellegrini sat down in the chair beside mine, removing a small digital voice recorder from his breast pocket and clicking it on.

"You realize," he said, resting the recorder on the arm of my chair, "that you violated any number of federal statutes, flying the contents of that suitcase in here, without proper notice or authorization."

"So nice to meet you, too, Agent. So glad we could establish a warm and trusting rapport before you tried to bend me over."

"I just want to let you know where I'm coming from, that's all."

I wasn't in the mood to be bullied. Especially for no apparent reason.

"Look," I said, "maybe the news hasn't filtered down to the hinterlands, where Quantico typically parks its underachievers: J. Edgar Hoover's dead. They buried him in a pleated skirt. So why don't you knock off the old school, cooperation-through-intimidation G-man routine. Because right now, truthfully, I could give a rip about your 'proper notice and authorization.'"

"I understand she's your former wife," Pellegrini said, "the party who's missing?"

"We're divorced. We were getting remarried."

"I'm told she comes from money."

"Meaning what? That I had some kind of financial motive to do her harm?"

Pellegrini looked at me evenly and said nothing, a standard interrogation tactic: wait for the interviewee to compulsively fill the silence with some inadvertent revelation.

"If I were going to hurt her," I said, "wouldn't logic dictate that I wait until the ink dried on our marriage certificate? California's a community property state. That way, I could legally claim half her assets, no?"

"I don't know," Pellegrini said, "you tell me."

"I just did."

"How did you come to acquire the uranium, Mr. Logan?"

I'd had enough of the guy and his pointless questions. I stood, 'accidentally' brushing his tape recorder on the floor. The back cover fell off and two batteries flew out like victims ejected from a car crash.

"I'm not the bad guy here, Agent Pellegrini. Either read me my rights and hook me up, or this conversation's over."

He stooped to gather the pieces of his recorder and glared at me.

"I'm just doing my job, Mr. Logan."

"If you were doing your job, Agent Pellegrini, you'd go find her."

✝

I REFUELED and flew back to South Lake Tahoe that afternoon to assist Streeter in the search for Savannah. Gordon Priest, the manager at Summit Aviation Services, was gone for the day. Marlene, Priest's receptionist, welcomed my return with a heartfelt hug and fresh oatmeal cookies. They were all out of four-wheel-drive vehicles, she said, but I probably wouldn't be needing one; there was no snow in the extended forecast. She rented me a white Ford Focus at 60 percent off the normal daily rate because, she said, she felt bad for me. The car had an infant seat in the back. I put it in the trunk.

Savannah's disappearance made the local paper that morning, along with a hangdog photo of me holding up my photo of her. Every network affiliate in nearby Reno picked up the story. No mention was made of the stolen uranium. The FBI decided that the information was a matter of national security and squelched any public disclosure about it. When reporters in Santa Maria asked what the hubbub had been about at the airport, they were told that a multiagency training exercise had taken place there. Hotel employees and other civilian witnesses were made to sign nondisclosure agreements and threatened with arrest if they talked.

"Have You Seen This Woman?" notices and pictures of Savannah went up in store windows and on telephone poles throughout the Lake Tahoe area. Platoons of volunteers scoured the surrounding forests, while I knocked on doors and law enforcement personnel interviewed dozens of prospective witnesses. But after putting in twenty-hour days for more than a week, and sleeping four restless hours a night at the Econo Lodge, I realized that faint progress, if that, had been made. Streeter conceded that he and his fellow detectives could find no trace of Savannah and were no closer to identifying the killer who'd called himself Crocodile Dundee than they'd been at the outset of their investigation.

In the interim, I'd become a celebrity of sorts. Residents recognized me on the street. They weren't shy about approaching, offering me encouragement.

"Keep the faith."

"Don't stop believing."

"We're all praying for you."

I tried to respond appreciatively, but I felt undeserving of their moral support. Savannah had vanished because of me. I was entitled to no one's sympathy.

"You doing OK, doll?"

Reeking of tobacco, Ruby, the ancient waitress at Steve's Coffee Shop, patted my shoulder as she refilled my coffee mug.

"Hanging in there," I said.

"If you need anything else, you lemme know."

"Thanks, Ruby."

I stared down at the half-eaten plate of bacon and eggs sitting on the pine table in front of me. My eyes felt heavy from exhaustion. My shoulders ached down deep. I checked my watch for lack of anything better to do: 0649. Another futile day loomed ahead.

"I know you. You're that guy."

I looked up slowly.

Standing beside my table, headed for the register, was a tall man with his breakfast check and a ten dollar bill in his hand. He was wearing a battered straw cowboy hat.

"You don't remember me, do you?"

"I'm sorry," I said. "I don't."

"You were looking for your lady. I was just finishing up a sewer cleanout over on Skyview. It was snowing to beat the band."

"The Roto-Rooter guy."

He extended his hand and said, "Dwayne."

"Logan."

We shook.

"Tell ya what," he said, "it's just a cryin' shame they haven't found her yet. I know everybody around here is pulling for you, putting out the positive brainwaves. Everybody."

I thanked him for his concern and he stood there awkwardly with his hat in his hands, shifting his weight from one boot to another, the way people do when they feel the urge to say more but aren't sure what to say, or how to say it.

"You mind me sitting down for a second?"

I gestured to the other side of the table. He took off his hat and lowered himself into the chair.

"Listen," he said, leaning forward, closer, "I don't mean to speak bad of nobody or anything, but if I was the cops, I'd be looking at all these registered sex offenders they got living around here. There's hundreds of 'em. They're everywhere. You can get their address on line."

"Good to know."

"It's a real problem, and most people, they don't even know about it. I got me one living two doors down. They let him out last year. Six little girls he molested and he gets what, three years? If it was me, I would've hung his ass."

I nodded, in no mood to talk.

"Well, anyway," Dwayne said, "good luck. I hope they find her and the scumbag who took her gets what's coming to him."

"Thanks."

He walked to the cash register where Ruby was happy to take his money.

When I was in the air force, not long out of the academy, a squadron commander who'd earned a Silver Star flying A-1 Skyraiders in Vietnam told me that he could always find enemy ground forces by listening for them from the air. How, I asked him, can you hear the enemy from a Plexiglass-enclosed cockpit, with a big radial engine roaring in front of you and other pilots or air traffic controllers chattering loudly inside your helmet?

"You open your ears," he said, "close your eyes, and just . . . *listen.*"

Years later, on tank-busting missions over Iraq, I did the same thing. I can't explain why, but the tactic often worked.

Talk to me, Savannah. Where are you? Help me find you.

I closed my eyes and opened my ears, listening for her, hoping to *feel* her, but all I heard was the metallic scraping of forks and knives on breakfast plates, and the low murmur of conversations, punctuated by occasional laughter among my fellow diners.

My appetite was gone. I gulped a last sip of black coffee, deposited enough cash on the table to cover my meal and cigarette money for Ruby, and left.

Inn keepers Johnny and Gwen Kavitch, accompanied by their panty-sniffing son, Preston, were walking into the restaurant as I exited. We crossed paths without exchanging words. The elder Kavitches kept their eyes to the ground, pretending not to recognize me. But as Johnny held the door for his wife, Preston turned toward me and leered.

True Buddhists believe in the cultivation of forgiveness and kindness through love. Cultivate enough goodwill, they assert, and you can insulate yourself from the coldest of insults.

I'd like to believe that someday I'll get there. On that frigid morning, I restrained myself from wiping the grin off Preston Kavitch's face and turning him into a human pretzel. Call it progress.

There was little left for me to do in South Lake Tahoe but drive around, dowsing as if for water, hoping divine intervention might somehow lead me to Savannah. It all felt so futile.

I headed to the airport to retrieve Savannah's luggage and the duffel that I'd left behind with Marlene, and to head home.

"You're not listening to me," she kept saying into the phone, bent forward in her chair, rubbing her forehead. She glanced up as I walked in and raised one finger as if to say she'd only be a minute. "We can sell the house. It's not about the bills, honey, it's about making our marriage work. Look, I've gotta go. I'll call you back."

I waited until she signed off.

"Problems on the home front?"

"Money issues." Marlene forced a smile. "What else is new, right?"

She fetched our bags from a closet and offered me some cookies for my flight back to Rancho Bonita, which I declined. Sweets were the last thing on my mind.

FOURTEEN

Piloting a small airplane is not unlike sex. If done well, both can be ecstatic, mind-blowing experiences. Done poorly, embarrassing disaster bodes. Do either long enough, and you learn to perform without consciously thinking about performing, satisfying the needs of the moment while your mind focuses elsewhere.

As I flew the *Ruptured Duck* home that morning, my thoughts remained focused on the man who'd taken Savannah from me. Who was he? Why did he do what he had?

I knew that he had to have been acquainted with Chad Lovejoy, and that he lived in proximity to Lake Tahoe. After all, the two of them on relatively short notice had hiked up to the crash site together. They'd found uranium, realized its potential value, and Lovejoy had lost his life for it. Streeter surmised that Lovejoy had told Dundee all about me, how I was a pilot, how I'd spotted the downed airplane, and how Savannah and I were staying at a local B&B, where Dundee subsequently abducted her to strong-arm me into airlifting his ill-gained treasure out of Lake Tahoe.

The problem was that Lovejoy had done time in state prison. He'd interacted with innumerable other inmates, many of whom, like him, had since been released from custody. Dozens lived in and around Lake Tahoe. Any one of them, Streeter believed, could have been Dundee.

"It's going to take time," Streeter admitted before I took off for Rancho Bonita. "I'd advise you not to get your hopes up."

"What hopes?"

He didn't have to tell me that the more time passed, the more likely it was that Savannah was dead.

"Cessna Four Charlie Lima, contact Rancho Bonita Tower, one-one nine, point six." The approach controller's voice in my headset jarred me from the depths.

"Point six," I responded. The GPS showed a twelve-minute ETA. I switched frequencies on my number two radio. "Tower, Cessna Four Charlie Lima, VFR descent."

"Cessna Four Charlie Lima, descent, your discretion."

One thought consumed me: that after I landed, I had to find a way to identify Dundee. And kill him.

✛

RARELY DO I sleep more than two or three hours at a stretch without waking up in physical or emotional discomfort—the legacy of having played too many contact sports, and of having killed too many people. Sometimes I can nod off again before dawn, but not always; I'm lucky on some nights if two or three hours is all I get. When I got back from Lake Tahoe that afternoon, perhaps ironically, I slept twelve hours straight. Kiddiot was crouched on my chest when I woke up, purring and licking my chin. That was a first, too.

Scientists say pets have a sixth sense when it comes to human behavior. They can detect nuances in mood that even people closest to us typically can't. I had always assumed that Kiddiot was born without any sense. And so, when he seemed intuitively to fathom my depression and sought to comfort me, if that is in fact what he was doing, I was somewhat stunned.

"I take back every insensitive thing I ever said about you."

When I reached up to stroke his ears, he dug his claws into my ribs and spring-boarded out his rubber cat door like his tail was on fire.

The author Robert Heinlein once said, "How we behave toward cats here below determines our status in heaven." As I watched Kiddiot go, the door flapping in his wake, I allowed myself a small smile, but only for a moment; Savannah, after all, was still gone.

A new prospective student named Stefan Weber had left a message on my answering machine in Larry's hangar while I was up north, saying he was interested in flying lessons. We'd made arrangements to meet at 0930 for his one-hour, fifty-dollar introductory flight. My watch showed 0820.

I yawned and stretched, did a few half-hearted push-ups, climbed into the shower and stood under it for a long time, hoping the hot water would steam away my sense of loss. It didn't. I toweled off, dressed, got in my old Tacoma, and drove to the airport.

It was something. And anything was better than dwelling on what had happened to Savannah.

✝

"SWEET JESUS," Larry said. He was peering at me through his thick lenses with his jaws parted, revealing teeth that had never been to the orthodontist. "She was *kidnapped?*"

I nodded.

"Do they know who did it?"

"No."

We were standing outside his hangar, beside the *Ruptured Duck*, waiting for my new flight student to show up.

"I'm really sorry, Logan. I had no idea. It must be hard. I know if something like that ever happened to my wife, much as we'd both like to hire a hit man sometimes to have each other whacked, I'd feel like crap, too." His voice cracked and he swabbed a sausage finger behind the right lens of his glasses. I'd never seen Larry display emotion of any kind beyond anger.

We were both silent.

"Well, at least you got a student," he said after awhile, "something to keep your mind busy, right? Been awhile since you had one of those."

"True."

He shook his head again and said to himself, "Goddamn," staring at his steel-toed work boots, filthy with oil stains. The front of his gray, grease-streaked T-shirt bore the words, "I hate being bipolar. It's awesome!"

"Don't worry about me, Larry. I'll be all right."

He offered to buy me a beer after work. I reminded him I didn't drink.

"OK, a burrito, then."

"Actually, I'm having dinner tonight with Mrs. Schmulowitz."

"Oh, that's right," Larry said. "You and the old lady watch football Monday nights."

"Take a rain check, though?"

"Fair enough." He paused, struggling to come up with something appropriately profound to say. "Well anyway, the sun also rises, or something like that, right?"

"Let's not make assumptions before all the facts are in."

Larry grunted like he was more or less amused and then, in that awkward, halting manner by which heterosexual men typically express affection for each other for fear that anyone might accuse them of being gay, reached out and gripped my left shoulder as if he were squeezing a cantaloupe at the grocery store.

I realized after he walked away that he'd left a greasy, perfectly defined paw print on my last clean polo shirt.

✈

"I'M PRONE to motion sickness," my would-be student, Stefan Weber, said as we flew lazy eights 2,000 feet above the ocean.

I forced myself to break off thinking obsessively about Savannah and looked over at him sitting in the left seat, eyes wide with fear, clutching the control yoke in a two-handed death grip.

"Say again?" I said.

"I said, I'm prone to motion sickness."

Stefan's pallid face, squished between the earphones of the communications headset he was wearing, resembled a loaf of white bread trapped in a vice. He was twenty-five, a balding CPA who'd admitted within the first five minutes of our meeting that he'd never been on a real date, and that the only reason why he was tentatively considering taking flying lessons was because he'd never done one crazy thing in his life, except for the time he'd spray painted "Accountants do it between the spreadsheets" on the wall of his college dorm.

"I think I'm going to be sick."

"It's OK, Stefan, you're doing fine," I said, taking the controls. "I have the airplane."

I leveled the wings and told him to take nice, deep breaths, keeping his eyes on the horizon.

"There's a vent control right there on your left. Why don't you open it up and get some nice cold air going on your face, OK?"

He opened up the vent.

"A little more air, Stefan. There ya go. Just relax now. See? Nothing to worry about."

I reached into the storage pocket of my seat back and pulled out a paper airsick bag. When I looked over at him again, my student was the color of the Chicago River on St. Patrick's Day.

"Here, buddy, take this."

Stefan reached for the bag—a half second too late. He opened his mouth and yodeled a torrent of half-digested nastiness that somehow missed me while splattering him and much of the instrument panel. For a small man, he hurled a prodigious amount of vomit.

"I'm really sorry," Stefan said, wiping his mouth, embarrassed. "I probably should've said something earlier."

"No worries. Happens to the best of us. We probably should head back."

He nodded glumly.

We were on approach to the airport, on base leg, when the *Duck's* over-voltage red warning light suddenly came on. I knew from prior experience that when the light illuminated, there was a problem with the electrical system—a sensor or maybe the master switch. Larry would have to do some trouble-shooting, and that would take time. It would also take money I didn't have. Fortunately, Stefan didn't notice the light. He didn't seem to notice anything except the noteworthy amount of rejected breakfast in his lap.

After we landed, he offered to help clean up the *Duck*. I told him I appreciated the gesture, but that it really wasn't necessary. He wrote me a fifty dollar check and said he'd give thought to the notion of additional lessons. I knew he wouldn't be back. Nobody in the history of general aviation has ever wolfed their cookies on an introductory flight and come back for more.

The sky was virtually cloudless, the breeze nary a whis-per. Another perfect, room-temperature day in paradise. Larry loaned me a pair of rubber gloves, rags, and a spray bottle of cleaner, and said he'd take a look at the electrical system after I de-vomited the *Duck*. He didn't ask how the lesson had gone. He could see and smell the result.

It took me more than an hour to wipe down the inside of the plane. In a weird way, I didn't mind; it kept my thoughts from Savannah, if only for a while. I was tempted to give Streeter up in Lake Tahoe a call after I finished, but I knew he would've called me if there were any worthwhile develop-ments in his investigation.

I watched a gray Cobra gunship come thundering in to settle gingerly down on the tarmac near the Hippo Grill on the field's east side, followed seconds later by another Cobra. The two attack helicopters were up from the Marine Corps' Camp Pendleton, north of San Diego. They flew into Rancho Bonita frequently, ostensibly on training missions that not coincidentally also afforded ample opportunity to flirt with the Hippo's many comely waitresses.

"Thought you could use a cold drink," Larry said, walking up from behind me with a Coke in his hand.

I thanked him, opened the can, and sipped. We stood and watched the four marine crewmen in their tailored flight suits and cool-guy sunglasses stroll toward the Hippo.

"Those guys get all the chicks," Larry said, stroking his Grizzly Adams beard. "Tell ya what. If I dropped a hundred pounds, got Lasik on my eyes and a full Brazilian, I'd give those leathernecks a run for their money."

"I'm sure you would, Larry."

He looked over at me, his brow furrowed.

"No witty retort, Logan? No, 'The day you get girls is the day congress gets anything done?'"

"Not today, Larry."

He nodded like he understood. "I gotta run out for a while. The wife wants me to go carpet shopping. You lemme know if you need anything else."

"Thanks, buddy."

I lingered for a few minutes, buffing dead bugs off the leading edges of the *Duck's* wings, then gathered up the cleaning supplies, dropped the rags in a covered trash can in Larry's hangar and walked back to my cramped, depressing, windowless office. The pile of paperwork atop my government surplus desk demanded to be culled and filed, but I couldn't muster the energy.

I sat down, put my feet up, and stared into space for the better part of an hour. I guess you could call it meditating, though it was really more like trying to put my brain in neutral and not think about anything. After that, I drove home and told my landlady about what had happened. About the wrecked Twin Beech and the dead pilot at the controls. About the young man lying dead beside the wreckage. But mostly about Savannah.

Mrs. Schmulowitz listened with her right hand clasped over her mouth, and wept.

✝

THE GIANTS were playing the Bears that night. Mrs. Schmulowitz served her usual excellent brisket with green beans in cream sauce, which we ate off metal TV trays, while she offered her usual play-by-play commentary on the game, broadcast on her ancient Magnavox console.

"God forbid this guy should actually hold on to the ball," she complained after the Giant's tight end muffed an easy pass. "That *schmegegge* couldn't catch the common *cold* if his life depended on it."

She was garbed in a blue New York Giants hoodie that was about five sizes too big, an oversized Giants baseball cap, a pair of blue Giants sweatpants, and fuzzy pink bedroom slippers that looked like bunnies.

"It's just a game, Mrs. Schmulowitz."

"A game? A *game*?" Sitting beside her on her blue mohair sofa, she looked over at me like it was the craziest thing she'd ever heard. "Football's not a game, bubby. Football is *life*."

I didn't argue her point. Mrs. Schmulowitz came from gridiron nobility—her late uncle was NFL Hall of Fame quarterback Sid Luckman. She certainly knew more about football than any old lady I ever met.

"More brisket, bubby?"

"I'm good, thanks."

"How 'bout beans? I got plenty."

"Not for me, Mrs. Schmulowitz. I couldn't eat another bite. It was all delicious. Thank you." I stood and headed for the kitchen. "Can I get you anything while I'm up?"

"No, nothing, not a thing. I eat one more bite myself, you'll have to call those cute paramedics to come give me mouth-to-mouth. Come to think of it, maybe I will have more brisket. Then you can give 'em a call for me, OK?"

"Whatever you say, Mrs. Schmulowitz."

I knew she was kidding about more brisket, trying to cheer me up. I deposited my plate and silverware in the sink without offering to help clean up because I knew she'd only take offense, as she had after previous offers. Back in the living room, the Giants running back got stuffed for a two-yard loss.

Mrs. Schmulowitz threw up her hands in exasperation.

"Can you believe this interior line play? *Oy gevalt* It's a horror! Even *I* can trap block better than that."

"Just wanted to say good night, and thanks again for dinner."

She gave me a disconcerted look. "It's not even the fourth quarter yet."

"I'm thinking of turning in a little early, doing some reading."

The old lady's cataract-clouded eyes pooled with tears. She said she knew what I was going through, and that her heart ached for me. She told me how one of her brothers had joined the army, gone off to fight in North Africa, and been declared missing in action. Nearly a year transpired before the family received a letter via the Red Cross saying he'd been captured and was in a German POW camp, homesick but otherwise well.

"In the words of Tom Petty," Mrs. Schmulowitz said, "the waiting is the hardest part."

"How do you know Tom Petty?" I asked her.

"How do I know Tom Petty? I know Tom Petty because he's older than I am." She got up and turned off the TV. "Listen, before you go, there's something I need you to do for me, a big favor."

"Name it."

"I need you to come with me to my watercolor class tomorrow."

"I'm not much of a painter, Mrs. Schmulowitz."

"Like anybody in the class is a painter? They're relics, old as dirt, everybody in there. Half the people, their brains have turned to Cream of Wheat. The point's not to paint, bubby. The point is, I just want you to come with me."

"Why?"

"Why? It's a surprise, that's why."

"I don't like surprises, Mrs. Schmulowitz. And I've had more than my share recently."

She put her arms around my waist. I could feel most of the bones in her body.

"You have an obligation to go on living, Cordell. For her. For you. Regardless of where she is right now. The sooner you start doing that, the better off you'll both be."

She promised the painting class would do me good.

"I'm an old lady, bubeleh. Humor me."

Mrs. Schmulowitz was a force of nature. What choice did I have?

✝

KIDDIOT SLEPT on his back at the foot of my bed that night with all four paws up and his tongue lolling out the side of his mouth, while I stared at the ceiling, anguishing over the choices I'd made, replaying on a continuous loop the hours leading up to Savannah's disappearance and my attempts to find her in the hours afterward. What could I have done, short of never spotting that airplane in the first place, that would have let me roll over and find Savannah sleeping contentedly beside me? What clues had I missed? The guilt, incompetence, and helplessness I felt were palpable, weights that pressed like concrete on my heart. I thought I might vomit, but didn't. I got up, drawing a disapproving sneeze from Kiddiot who didn't appreciate being disturbed, and went outside.

The night was still. No moon. I gazed up at the southern sky, through the dark, outlying branches of Mrs. Schmulowitz's oak tree, to the three stars of Orion's Belt. To their right was a V-shaped pattern of stars—the face of Taurus the Bull—and, slightly beyond the bull's face, the star cluster known as Seven Sisters.

To the average eye, the Sisters look like a small, blurry cloud of light. But if your vision is keen, you can discern all seven stars. For centuries, Native Americans used the star cluster as an eye test of sorts; only those would-be fighting men with the acuity of vision to see all seven stars were allowed to join the most elite warrior sects. Often, when I was at the academy, I would walk onto the parade grounds at night, lie down and gaze up at the Sisters, if only to reassure myself that I had the right stuff to be a pilot. Inspiration often followed my stargazing. But as I stared into the heavens that night from my landlady's tidy, postage-stamp backyard, all I felt was lost, adrift amid the cosmos.

More than anything, I felt alone.

FIFTEEN

$\mathbb{M}$rs. Schmulowitz drove a banana yellow Shelby Mustang with an automatic transmission and a vanity plate that read, "BRISKET." She had to sit on two volumes of the 1966 Encyclopedia Britannica to see over the steering wheel, but that didn't stop her from racing down San Miguel Boulevard like she was trying to outrun the zombie apocalypse, garbed in some sort of weird, Annie Hall-like outfit.

We roared past Rancho Bonita's majestic, Spanish-style county courthouse doing fifteen over the posted speed limit.

"You're gonna really enjoy this painting class, bubby," Mrs. Schmulowitz said.

"Assuming we get there alive," I said, bracing myself against the dashboard.

She whipped a sharp left onto Vespucci Street and through the crosswalk, nearly creaming a pair of portly businessmen who literally had to leap for their lives.

"Will you look at that? A parking space, right in front of the rec center. This must be my lucky day."

"Did you not see those guys, Mrs. Schmulowitz?"

"Did I see them? Of course, I saw them. I also saw they could definitely use some exercise. If public schools still had physical education, we wouldn't have this problem! They can thank me later."

The space was impossibly tight, sandwiched between a white Volvo sedan and a Chrysler PT Cruiser. Mrs. Schmulowitz parallel parked like one would expect a nearly ninety-year-old woman to parallel park. She played bumper cars, pounding her way in.

"Perfect," she announced when we were wedged squarely against the curb. "C'mon, bubeleh let's get you some culture."

The weekly painting class was held on the second floor of the Rancho Bonita Parks and Recreation Department's Vespucci Community Center, a stately, two-story red brick building that had once served as a convalescent hospital for wounded soldiers returning from the Great War. The classroom was filled with mostly elderly women, some tethered to oxygen tanks, others reliant on wheelchairs or walkers, all sitting around long tables, glumly slapping thin, wet paint on pieces of watercolor paper.

"Hello, good people," Mrs. Schmulowitz announced as we walked in. "Welcome to Tuesday."

Nobody bothered to look up.

The class instructor, who Mrs. Schmulowitz introduced me to as Meredith Crisp, touted the fact that he'd studied under the late Thomas Kinkade, America's self-proclaimed "Painter of Light." I didn't know squat about fine art, but what I'd seen of Kinkade's saccharine fairy tale villages convinced me that whatever artistic technique Crisp had to teach, I wasn't interested in learning. Not that I had any illusions of becoming the next da Vinci. Far from it. I was only there to keep my landlady happy.

"I'm sorry, Mrs. Schmulowitz, he's really not allowed in here," Crisp said, taking her aside, glancing at me, and whispering a little too loudly with a catty smile that really wasn't a smile. "This is a seniors-only class."

"Who's to know? The geriatric Gestapo? Lighten up, Meredith."

"I'm sorry, Mrs. Schmulowitz. Those are the rules. I really didn't make them up."

He was well past sixty but trying hard not to look it. Flip-flops, too-tight jeans, a Coldplay T-shirt under a fringed leather vest, leather bracelets, a long, beaded earring dangling from one lobe, and purposefully mussed, Rod Stewart-like head of blond, thinning hair that was among the worst dye jobs I'd ever seen.

"I wouldn't bother anybody," I said.

"I'm not sure you understand." Crisp rubbed a hand over his face in exasperation. "I already have thirty-three students in this class, which is ten more than what I was supposed to have. I simply don't have enough supplies for everyone."

"He can use some of my stuff. What's the big deal?"

"The 'big deal,' Mrs. Schmulowitz, is that I'm afraid your friend will distract those of my students who are actually serious about their painting."

"Serious about their painting? Listen, the only thing these relics are serious about is where they can get a good deal on adult diapers. Don't be such a *nudnik*, Meredith. It'll take years off your life."

Crisp knew there was no use arguing with her. He exhaled melodramatically, said, "Fine," and moved off to supervise his other students.

Mrs. Schmulowitz waited until he was out of earshot, then said, "So, I have a confession to make."

Her confession was she'd wanted me to accompany her to class so that she could introduce me to one of her fellow students, a retired psychologist.

"He's a real *mensch*, this guy. And, between you, me and the wall, about the only person in this class with a brain that still works. I thought he could help you get through what you're dealing with," she said, looking around, "only he isn't here yet."

I told her I appreciated her concern, but that I wasn't inclined to spill my guts to a headshrinker, let alone one I didn't know. She patted my cheek and said she understood.

"Just talk to the guy. Ten minutes. He doesn't help you? Fine. Whatever. I tried."

"OK, Mrs. Schmulowitz. For you? Ten minutes."

The psychologist never showed up. For the next half hour or so, I sat with Mrs. Schmulowitz and tried to paint watercolor trees and mountains per Meredith Crisp's direction while the instructor patrolled us, critiquing our work like he actually knew something about art.

"A rather avant-garde use of pigment," Crisp said, assessing my artistic offering with his arms folded and the tip of one index finger tapping his pursed lips. "But I must say, the placement of your seagulls seems perhaps just a tad random."

"Those aren't seagulls. Those are splatters."

"I see."

I needed a break.

There was a wooden bench outside under a big leafy tree. I sat down, spread my arms across the back of the bench, and watched the world go by. The tree was a jacaranda— "jacks," as the locals called them. They produced profusions of delicate, bell-shaped flowers that, for a few weeks in late spring, bathed Rancho Bonita in a violet-colored haze. Many residents condemned them as "messy." They disliked jacks for their tendency to drop sticky blossoms on the freshly waxed Porsches and Benzes of the town's moneyed minions. If for no other reason, they were among my favorite trees.

People came and went: office workers in business suits; tourists clutching guidebooks, with cameras slung around their necks. A shirtless dude of about twenty in grimy jeans, with tattoos covering his toothpick arms and scrawny chest, rolled up on his skateboard to ask if I had any spare change.

"I was about to ask you for some," I said.

He rolled on without a word.

The sun felt good on my face. A middle-aged redhead strutted past me in stiletto boots, wearing too much makeup and some sort of gauzy, gypsy skirt-blouse combo. She gave me a little smile. I didn't notice her, however, as much as I did what she was toting in her right hand: a big brown shopping bag from the Nordstrom department store over on California Street, in the swanky, open-air, Casa Grande mall.

Nordstrom.

My brain flashed back on Chad Lovejoy and what he'd mentioned after Savannah and I landed at the Tahoe airport. Wasn't Nordstrom where he said his ex-girlfriend sold jewelry, the one he maintained an open dialogue with? *What did he say her name was?* It took me a few seconds to remember: *Cherry.*

The mall was two blocks to the west. I walked it.

✠

I'D NEVER been inside the Nordstrom in downtown Rancho Bonita. Or any Nordstrom, for that matter. When fashion and wardrobe are as personally relevant to you as the weather on Venus or who wins the annual World Adult Kickball Association championship, you tend not to do your clothes shopping at such places. Like I said, Sears is more my speed. Only I wasn't shopping.

If platinum smelled, Nordstrom would be what it smelled like—clean and ridiculously expensive. No less than three fresh-scrubbed young sales clerks wished me good morning and asked pleasantly if there was anything they could help me find as I made my way to the first-floor jewelry department.

"Can I help you find something special?"

Late twenties. Blond. Prematurely balding. Wire-frame glasses. Decked out in slacks, suit vest, white dress shirt, a gold tie. He was standing behind a glass display case filled with glittery baubles that I'd never afford.

"Cherry around?"

"She's on her break."

"Any idea when she's due back?"

The clerk checked his oversized divers' watch.

"Should be back any time. Is there something I can do for you? We have a really nice selection of brooches that just came in I'd be happy to show you."

"That's OK. I'll wait."

The women's shoe department was next door. I sat. Mercifully, nobody asked me if I wanted to try on any pumps or anything. I noted an inordinate number of shoppers who were dressed up. That was the difference between Nordstrom and Sears. That and the power tools.

A couple of minutes passed before a round-faced, dark-complected young woman with streaked auburn tresses walked past me to where the clerk in the suit vest was standing behind the display case. She was wearing a black skirt, black ankle boots, and a blousy, zebra-striped top. She and the clerk conferred quietly. He pointed me out and she came over, smiling.

"Hi. Can I help you?"

"Cherry, right?"

"Right." She pushed her hair behind her ear. I noticed a tattoo on the inside of her right wrist. In stylish, cursive script, it said, "Baby."

"My name's Logan. I wondered if I could ask you a couple of questions about your former boyfriend."

"Which one?"

"Chad."

Her friendly expression disappeared. I could see pain behind her dark eyes.

"I'm assuming you heard what happened to him?"

"I heard. You a cop?"

"No."

"Well, I'm sorry," Cherry said, starting to go around me, "but if you're not the police, I really don't think I should be talking to you."

"I was there when they found him."

She stopped and looked back at me.

"You saw him?"

I nodded.

"Did he look really bad?"

"No."

She seemed relieved.

"Chad told me the two of you used to confide in each other, even after you split."

"He was my soul mate," Cherry said, her chin beginning to quiver. "We just didn't get along sometimes, that's all."

"I'm trying to find who killed him."

"What do you care? You said you're not a cop."

"Whoever shot Chad also may have kidnapped someone very close to me. He may be holding her hostage."

She waited until a couple of tall, slim young women in long, flower-print dresses strolled past, each carrying several shopping bags. They were debating the proper pronunciation of *foie gras*.

"Chad was so great." Cherry's eyes glistened. She looked away, wistfully. "We loved each other so much."

"Who do you think might've wanted him dead, Cherry?"

"I don't know."

"Who do you think does?"

She shrugged. "His mom, I'm pretty sure."

"What makes you think that?"

"When she called to tell me what happened, she said she had her suspicions."

"She tell you what those were?"

"Only thing she said was that she was afraid the guy might come after her if he knew she was pointing fingers."

"Where can I find her?"

"I'm not going to get in trouble, am I?"

"No."

Cherry searched my eyes. "I don't know why," she said, "but for whatever reason, I believe you."

✝

CHAD'S MOTHER, Sissy Barbieri, lived in the bedroom community of Thousand Oaks, north of Los Angeles. Why they call it Thousand Oaks is beyond me, considering that most of those one thousand trees appear to have been cut down long ago.

What isn't in short supply in Thousand Oaks are expensive cars and block after block of perfectly manicured lawns surrounding perfectly immaculate, Spanish-themed minimansions. The Stepford Wives would fit right in.

The closest airport to Thousand Oaks was in Camarillo, about thirteen miles away. Flying the *Duck* wouldn't have worked, especially with the plane's electrical problems that Larry had yet to diagnose. So I drove instead down the 101 freeway in my truck.

The address Cherry had given me was on Silver Oaks Drive, which was clearly among one of Thousand Oak's lesser enclaves—modest, single-story ranch-style homes wedged close beside each other on a stretch of bleak, sun-baked real estate a block off the noisy freeway. Sissy's house was noteworthy only for its especially decrepit appearance. Paint was peeling off the siding. A rain gutter hung from over the porch like a hiker clinging to a cliff. A weight bench and bar bells sat rusting on the scrum of devil grass and other weeds that passed for a front yard.

I parked as a matter of practice three houses down the street—far enough away to maintain the element of surprise, yet close enough to get to my truck if I had to in a hurry—walked in, and pressed the bell.

No answer. No sound of a bell ringing inside. I tried the steel-grated storm door. It was unlocked. I opened it and knocked on the front door. A dog began barking crazily inside the house—a small dog, by the sound of it. A few seconds passed, then the door opened, revealing a woman in a maroon, terrycloth bathrobe clutching the nub of a cigarette in the fingers of her right hand. Mid-forties, five foot five, 160 pounds. Her dirty blonde hair was shoulder-length, uncombed and unwashed. Deep sallow creases rimmed blue eyes. She planted her left hand on her hip and shifted her weight, a purposeful move that parted the top of her robe and allowed me a better peak at her pendulous, untethered breasts. You could tell she'd once been beautiful. All she was now was hard.

"Tofu, no!" She turned to yell at a trembling, goggle-eyed Chihuahua barking and snarling at me. Then she looked back at me. "What happened to the regular guy?"

"Pardon?"

"The regular guy? From the dispensary?"

I looked at her blankly.

"I ordered half an ounce of Super Lemon Haze. It was supposed to be here two hours ago. What is *wrong* with you people? Your ad says same-day delivery. Do you know how long I've been sitting around, waiting for my medicine?"

"I'm not from a medical marijuana dispensary."

"You're not?"

"No."

Her shoulders sagged. "Well, do you have any weed on you?"

"Are you Sissy Barbieri?"

She took a drag on her cigarette, eyeing me with sudden suspicion.

"Who's asking?"

"My name's Logan. I was there when they found your son, Chad."

Her demeanor softened instantly.

"You were there?"

I nodded.

"My baby didn't deserve to die the way he did," Chad's mother said.

"I know this isn't easy, Sissy, but I'd like to come in and ask you a few questions about him."

"What kind of questions?"

"Ones that could help bring whoever killed him to justice."

"You a cop?"

"No."

"Then who are you?"

I told her. She asked to see my driver's license.

"You live in Rancho Bonita?" she said, studying it.

"I do."

"You're not a rapist or anything like that, are you?"

"No."

She eyed me, debating my trustworthiness, then handed me back my license and stepped aside. I thanked her for taking the time and walked in.

Barking and snarling, Tofu the Chihuahua held her ground on beige carpet that could've used a steam cleaning, until I reached down to pet her. She flopped over on her back, trembling, legs in the air, and I scratched her tummy. Suddenly, we were BFFs.

Sissy grabbed a quart bottle of Early Times bourbon off a glass-top coffee table and held it up with her eyebrows raised as if to offer me a hit.

"No, thanks."

"You won't mind if I do?"

"Hey, it's five o'clock somewhere."

She filled an orange plastic cup with whiskey and lowered herself onto a sagging, zebra-print sofa, tucking her bare feet underneath her robe. I sat down opposite her on a love seat that matched the sofa. Hanging on the wall behind her was a large oil painting of Paris flanked on either side by framed black-and-white photographs of wild horses running across the Desert Southwest.

"So," she said, "what was it you wanted to ask me about Chad?"

"I understand you may have some insights into who shot him."

Sissy stubbed out her cigarette in a frog-shaped ashtray overflowing with butts and fired up another one with a red Bic lighter sitting on the coffee table, next to a glass bong. She inhaled deeply, turned her head, expelled the smoke over her left shoulder, and sat back again, massaging her lower face.

"Who told you that?"

"I'd rather not say."

"It was Chad's girlfriend, wasn't it? That little bitch."

I didn't say anything.

"She's making shit up. We never talked about anything like that."

"You're scared, Sissy. I can see it in your face."

"I do not know what you're talking about."

"You're lying, Sissy. You've stopped looking at me. You're covering your mouth, scratching your nose. You just placed that bourbon bottle between you and me like a barrier. All of that tells me that you're being guarded. What are you guarding, Sissy?"

"Who *are* you?"

"That doesn't matter. What matters is that you help me find who killed Chad before he kills somebody else."

Tears began to stream down her cheeks.

"You don't understand," she said.

"What don't I understand?"

She shook her head no and wiped her nose with the back of her right hand.

"I do understand, Sissy. I understand that this is your son we're talking about. I also know you don't want anybody else to die the way Chad did. No mother would want that."

She began to weep, rocking and wailing uncontrollably, covering her eyes.

I got up, gently took the cigarette from her hand, and set it down in the ashtray. I told her I was sorry for having upset her. I was patting her back, trying to console her and get her to talk to me.

That's when the front door flew open and a stout man burst in, armed with a skinning knife.

SIXTEEN

He came at me growling, teeth clenched. Five foot ten, 220 pounds, early forties, grizzled red beard, blue do-rag on his head, jeans, Harley T-shirt, heavily tattooed arms, a biker's keychain, black leather motorcycle boots. Frankly, I was focused more at that moment on his weapon of choice—a ten-inch hunting knife with a curved blade and stag horn handle—than on who he was or why he seemed bent on slicing me like deli ham. What I needed was a weapon of my own, and I had about two seconds to find one.

The first rule of unarmed combat is never be unarmed. Hollywood would have you believe that a body trained in martial arts, ala Bruce Lee, is itself a lethal weapon. Unfortunately, martial arts are rarely, truly effective in stopping an armed assailant beyond the confines of a film studio lot, and only when the cameras are rolling.

Table lamps are a much better bet.

The one on Sissy Barbieri's end table was made of frosted glass and shaped like an electric guitar, the body of which lit up when turned on. I grabbed it by its neck and swung, connecting with my attacker's center mass like a batter chasing a fastball. Pieces of lamp flew, along with the knife, as he flopped head first into the coffee table.

"What are you doing?" Sissy screamed. "He's my boyfriend!"

She pushed past me and knelt beside him, trying frantically to revive him.

"Russell, wake up! Oh, my god, wake up, baby, please!" She looked up at me, seething. "He was only trying to protect me. You didn't have to hurt him!"

I turned him on his back, checking his carotid pulse, which was strong. Aside from a good-sized cut on his right cheekbone where he impacted the coffee table, I could see no other injuries.

"He's not moving."

"Do you have a washcloth?"

"He's dead! Can't you see that?"

"He's not dead, Sissy."

"Russell, wake up!"

"He'll wake up when he's ready. Now, go get a washcloth. Please."

"What for?"

"For his cheek. Unless you want him bleeding all over your carpet."

Reluctant to leave his side, Sissy got off her knees, wiping away tears, and made her way to the bathroom.

Russell groaned and held his head.

"What the hell happened?"

"You got a guitar lesson. Let's get you sitting up. It'll slow that bleeding."

I hoisted him off the floor and over to the couch.

Russell looked over at me woozily, head wobbling. "Who are you?"

"I'm looking for the guy who killed your girlfriend's son. He also kidnapped my girlfriend."

"Cool."

Sissy returned with a damp washcloth and sat down beside him. She asked him if he wanted to go to the hospital. He shook his head no.

"Why'd you try to stab me?"

"I thought you were him," Russell said.

"Who's that?"

"Chad's friend," Sissy said, holding the washcloth to Russell's cheek, "if that's what you want to call him."

As she explained it, Chad's "friend" had called the day after Chad's body was found. He told her that he'd done state time with Chad, and that the two of them, along with unnamed others, had become involved in some sort of impromptu business venture that had gone terribly wrong.

"The guy told me the police would be asking questions—who Chad knew, who he hung out with," Sissy said. "He said the best thing I could do for my own good is to say I didn't know anything. He said he knew where I lived cuz my son told him. He said he'd be checking up on me to make sure I played it smart and kept my mouth shut."

"So you go and let some dude you don't know inside the house?" Russell said to her accusingly, gesturing toward me. "That wasn't playing it smart, Sissy. That was plain stupid."

Put off by his remark, she grabbed his right hand and made him hold the washcloth to his cheek himself. "It wasn't stupid, Russell. I knew it wasn't the guy."

"How'd you know I wasn't the guy?" I said.

Sissy stood and began picking up pieces of the electric guitar lamp, depositing them on the love seat.

"Because you don't sound like him," she said.

"What did he sound like?"

"Like he wasn't from here."

"He had an accent?"

She nodded.

"What kind of accent?"

"I don't know. England or somewhere."

"Could he have been Australian?"

"Maybe. Who knows?"

"Foreigners," Russell said. "They're all assholes."

I asked Sissy if her son had any friends from Australia.

"If he did, he never said nothing to me about it." She reached over, still on her knees, and gulped down some bourbon. "Not that he told me anything after awhile. My mother told him I was a bad mother. She had him convinced I was the reason for every shitty little thing that went wrong in his life. Who knows? Maybe she was right."

"You got skills, baby," Russell said, "but mothering ain't exactly one of 'em."

"You go to hell, Russell."

Sissy got off her knees, stormed down a hallway, and slammed a door behind her.

Russell looked at me like he couldn't understand why she was upset.

"How's your head?" I said.

"I'll live."

I checked his pupils. He seemed OK.

"Sorry about the knife, man. I saw you through the window and I got scared, that's all."

"No worries." I walked over, snatched his knife off of the floor, and handed it to him, hilt first. "Sorry if I scared you."

"Picked this bad boy up at the flea market in Pasadena," Russell said, stashing the blade in his left boot. "I know the guy who sells 'em, if you're interested."

"Thanks. I'll keep it in mind."

As I walked toward the door, he said, "Listen, you didn't get this from me. OK?"

☩

WHAT I "didn't get" from Russell was the name, telephone number and last known address of Jethro Murtha, a convicted armed robber and Chad Lovejoy's cellmate at the California Institution for Men at Chino. To celebrate the two of them both being paroled, Chad invited Murtha home to his mother's house in Thousand Oaks, where he introduced Murtha as his best friend. The two ex-cons sat in the backyard that night working on a case of Budweiser and debating the most efficient ways to knock off banks.

"If anybody on this earth knows anything about what happened to Chad up there," Russell said before I left, "it's Jethro Murtha. Just watch your ass. He struck me as dangerous."

"I'll keep it in mind. Thanks for the help."

The address he gave me correlated to an apartment tucked above the A-1 Super Fine Discount Golf Shop on Olympic Boulevard, in the densely packed, Mid-Wilshire neighborhood of Los Angeles known as Koreatown. Two open-air flights of stairs adjacent to the shop led from the boulevard to the second floor. I parked at a meter on the street, walked up, and knocked on the door. There was no answer. It was 4:10 P.M. Assuming Murtha still lived there and held down a day job, I figured him to be home shortly after five.

I'd wait.

In the golf shop below, a clerk in beige golf shorts with long dark hair, lively eyes and a name tag in Korean pinned to her fuchsia-colored Callaway golf shirt, tried to sell me a $350 titanium putter, the head of which was only slightly smaller than a land-mine detector.

"The stainless steel head has a thicker face and top line," she said in an accent that was more Sherman Oaks than Seoul, "so the feel is a lot more solid when you make contact with the ball. It'll take three strokes off your game, guaranteed."

I took the club if only to humor her and made a few practice putts while keeping an eye on the street.

"Sole weights at the heel and toe," she said, "so you can change the head weight however you like. Sweet, right?"

"Very." I handed her back the putter.

"I'll make you a great deal. Even throw in a free cover, because if you take care of your putter, it'll take care of you." She smiled, her tongue flicking the side of her mouth provocatively.

"I don't play golf."

"Just learning?"

"No. Actually, golf seems like a giant waste of time to me."

She looked at me funny. "But this a golf shop."

"So it would appear."

"Why come in if you don't play golf?"

"I'm waiting for the guy who lives upstairs to come home. His name's Jethro Murtha. You wouldn't happen to know him, would you?"

The clerk thought hard for a second. "Big dude. Kinda angry all the time. Got these little tats . . ." She tapped her left cheekbone.

"Teardrops?"

The clerk nodded.

"You a cop?"

"Do I look like a cop?"

"Pretty much, yeah."

I thanked her for her time and told her I'd definitely be back if I ever got into the game of golf. We both knew that would be never.

There was a donut place two doors to the west, past a dry cleaners and a cash-only dental office. The lady behind the counter was friendly in a minimum-wage kind of way. She wore a hairnet. I ordered a plain cake donut and a small coffee.

When I returned to my truck, there was a parking ticket under the left windshield wiper. Expired meter: sixty-three dollar fine.

"Proud to be an American."

I stuffed the ticket in my jeans, wolfed down my donut, transferred what change I had in my pocket into the meter, and tried hard not to think about Savannah as I sat behind the wheel, watching the approaches to Murtha's apartment. I checked my phone for any calls I might have missed, but there were none.

At 5:20, an orange and silver MTA bus rumbled by and pulled into the stop up the block. Two Asian girls stepped off, giggling teenagers, followed by an older Asian woman, and a hulking construction worker of about thirty-five with a shaved head and a tool belt slung over his shoulder. He walked past my truck with tired, downturned eyes. He was lugging a plastic bag filled with groceries. The teardrops tattooed above both of his cheekbones were easy to spot.

I got out and fell in behind him.

"Jethro, you got a second?"

He glanced over his shoulder at me, dropped his groceries, and bolted.

In my prime, I would've caught him easily. Not even broken a sweat. But the years can rob a man of speed, along with his desire to achieve it. I stopped and watched him grow smaller as he fled down the sidewalk, glancing back at me periodically, his billiard ball head bobbing above a sea of Asian pedestrians along Olympic Boulevard.

I picked up the bag he'd jettisoned and looked inside: a box of Froot Loops, a dozen dinner rolls, two cans of tomato soup, and a plastic jug of cheap, off-brand vodka.

Jethro would be back for the booze. I was pretty sure of that.

✛

I LEFT his groceries, less the vodka, in the bag outside his door above the golf shop, parked my truck in a twelve-dollar-a-day lot two blocks away, and established an observation post inside a KFC almost directly across the boulevard from his apartment. Nobody would question my presence or kick me out as long as I was a paying customer, so I ordered a bucket of original recipe chicken and a soda with free refills. I was gnawing four hours later on a thigh, floating in a somewhat uncomfortable ether of salt, processed sugar, and saturated fat, when the ex-con I was eager to speak with came home.

He approached his apartment with an almost vaudevillian wariness, slowly looking this way and that, like a big cat slinking toward a watering hole, before cautiously ascending the stairs to his apartment. The top of the stairs was obscured from my vantage point at the KFC, but I knew that he'd gone inside because interior lights came on behind the shades in the two small windows over the golf shop.

I waited about fifteen minutes for him to settle in, wiped the grease from my mouth and hands on a half-dozen moist KFC towelettes, fetched Murtha's jug of vodka from my truck, and returned to his apartment.

The grocery bag I'd left on his stoop was gone. Either he'd taken it inside when he'd returned home, or someone had stolen it. I climbed the stairs slowly, quietly, my eyes trained on the door above me, pausing every few seconds to listen. Amid the urban cacophony of cars, jetliners, and the faint, sing-song strains of people conversing in Korean, I could make out twangy country music coming from Murtha's place—Merle Haggard's "Okie From Muskogee."

I rapped my knuckles on the door, careful to stand well to the side, lest I be greeted with a shotgun blast.

The tune inside stopped. The windows went dark.

I waited, then knocked once more.

No answer.

"If I were a cop, Jethro, do you really think I would've picked up your groceries and left them for you?"

Silence.

"I just want to talk," I said.

Five seconds passed.

"About what?" came a voice from the other side of the door.

"Chad Lovejoy."

"I don't know no Chad Lovejoy."

"You know that vodka you bought?"

"Wouldn't know nothing about that, either."

"Good. Then I guess I'll have to drink it myself."

More silence. Then the door opened with the security chain in place. Murtha eyed me up and down through the crack. He spied the jug of vodka in my hand.

"You got any ID on you?"

I slipped him my driver's license and a business card. The door closed.

"A *flight instructor*?" I could hear him slip the chain off. The door opened wide. "You're a flight instructor?"

"I am."

"Hell," he said, standing there in his stocking feet. "I was thinking about taking some flying lessons. Soon as I save me some money."

"Come up to Rancho Bonita. We'll make a pilot out of you."

"What's this about Chad?"

"Can I come in?"

Murtha glanced at the vodka jug in my hand.

I gave it to him.

"Welcome," he said, stepping back with a grand, exaggerated sweep of his hand, "to the Taj-fucking-Mahal."

His apartment was one room. Toilet and shower stall partitioned by a hanging green bed sheet. Soiled clothes strewn about the floor. A brown corduroy foldout couch, a card table and two folding chairs. A red velvet recliner that looked like it had been retrieved from some curbside. A Lynyrd Skynyrd poster. A fifty-inch flat screen TV resting on cinder blocks.

"Nice crib you got here, Jethro."

"Yeah, right. Have a seat."

I parked myself at his card table while he fished a chipped blue ceramic coffee cup out of the sink, rinsed it out, and filled it with vodka.

"You want one?"

"No, thanks. Why'd you run from me?"

"Thought you was parole. Didn't feel like getting piss-tested today." He gulped some vodka. "What's so important, you hanging around here for four hours, wanting to talk to me about Chad?"

"I was hoping you'd tell me."

He wiped his mouth with the back of his left hand. "The little prick didn't tell you I still owed him money, did he?"

I said nothing, studying Murtha's face and body language, looking for signs of obfuscation. I saw none.

"Chad's dead," I said.

He paused in midgulp and chuckled, like he thought I was kidding around.

"Sure he is."

"Outside Lake Tahoe. He was shot. A little more than a week ago."

Murtha studied me.

"Are you bullshitting me? He got *shot*?"

I nodded.

"Shit." Murtha downed the rest of his drink, refilled it, and settled into his red recliner, making a face like his lower back hurt. "I should've seen it coming, man."

I said nothing.

More than a month had gone by since they'd last spoken, Murtha said. Chad had called to tell him that he'd been hired by his uncle Gordon at minimum wage, catering to rich assholes at the Lake Tahoe airport. Chad had said he hated the work.

"I told him, 'Hey, at least you got a job,'" Murtha said. "Steady work for ex-cons, that don't come along every day, you know?"

I nodded.

"Don't get me wrong," Murtha said, "Chad wasn't complaining none. He said his uncle was letting him sleep on a cot where they keep the airplanes or some shit. Wasn't even charging him nothing to stay. Free rent. Beer money. Sounded like a pretty sweet setup to me. But, like I said, I didn't see it coming. Should've said something to him. Only I didn't, goddammit."

"Tell him what, Jethro?"

"To watch his back. His uncle Gordon? The dude's dirty as they come. Up to all kinds of nasty shit."

"How do you know that?"

"Chad told me." Murtha propped his hands behind his head and his feet on the floor in front him, facing me directly—body language that conveyed openness. "I'll tell you something else he told me, too. You know Iran?"

"I've heard of it a time or two."

"Yeah, well, Chad's uncle, he's running some kind of scam with some hardcore Iranian dudes living up there in Tahoe. It had Chad freaked the fuck out."

"What kind of scam?"

"He wouldn't tell me. Too scared." Murtha lit a Camel, exhaled smoke through his nose, and eyed me through blue tobacco haze. "So what *are* you doing here, anyway, Mr. . . . Logan, is it?" he said, glancing at the business card I'd given him. "Chad worked at an airport. You're a flight instructor. That tells me something."

"It tells you nothing." I got up and headed for the door. "Thanks for your time, Jethro."

"I'm definitely interested in taking flying lessons," he said. "Soon as I make some bank."

"Or rob one."

"Exactly."

He grinned as I left.

✛

So Chad Lovejoy's Uncle Gordon was up to no good. I'd wondered about him all along. Murtha's insights gave me new direction, new hope, a viable lead to follow. Walking to my truck, I was feeling reenergized, almost exuberant, when my phone rang.

"Logan."

"It's Matt Streeter."

I could feel my pulse quicken.

"What's up, Deputy?"

He asked me where I was.

"I'm in LA. Why?"

"How soon can you make it up to Lake Tahoe?"

His voice sounded different, an odd flatness to it.

"Why?"

"I'd prefer we talk in person."

"I'd prefer we talk now."

Streeter paused, as if gathering his courage.

"We've located some remains."

SEVENTEEN

With the *Duck* still suffering electrical system issues and out of commission, I drove through the night as fast as my truck would carry me from Los Angeles to South Lake Tahoe. Four hundred and eighty miles. Nearly seven hours, excluding two brief pit stops for octane and caffeine. I focused on the far reaches of my headlights and fought to keep submerged the anguish that threatened to overwhelm me.

The drive was no scenic tour. The Golden State Freeway, which constituted more than three quarters of the route, runs the length of California's semiarid Central Valley like a concrete spine. In daylight, it is a featureless, litter-strewn highway upon which most everyone flagrantly ignores the posted speed limit, anxious to escape as fast as possible the wasteland surrounding them. Driving the route in darkness might seem a blessing—but not when the eyes and brain are denied distraction. A man can keep his thoughts in neutral for only so long before his mind automatically slips back into gear.

Please God, Buddha, Allah. Don't let it be my woman.

I passed a tractor trailer, a Kenworth, hauling a load of lemons. The lemons reminded me of the time a few weeks after we were first married when Savannah decided to bake me a meringue pie and left it in the oven too long. It looked like something left over from Hiroshima. She laughed at my teasing, a good sport, then went into the bathroom, locked the door, and sobbed. It was the last time she ever baked me anything.

I shouldn't have said what I said. You were doing something nice for me and I was a complete jerk. I'm sorry, Savannah. For what I did. For everything I didn't do.

The road ahead seemed to blur. For a second, I thought the windshield had fogged up. Then I realized I was crying. I wiped away the tears angrily and drove on.

A light snow was falling as I turned off the freeway near Elk Grove onto US 50, south of what was once Mather Air Force Base, and began climbing into the rising sun. The highway remained ice-free for the most part, even as the weather turned colder. Air temperature lapses an average three and a half degrees for every thousand feet of altitude gained. I can't say how cold it was on the valley floor a mile below me, but by the time I reached South Lake Tahoe a little before 0700, the digital thermometer outside Alpine Bank and Trust on the town's far western approach showed eighteen degrees.

Streeter wanted me to contact him as soon as I pulled into town. I called from the bank's parking lot. He was there inside of five minutes. He got out of his Jeep and into my truck with a manila file folder under his right arm, his expression grim.

"Thank you for coming up. I know it's a long way on short notice."

I nodded.

His jaw muscles were tight. He wouldn't make eye contact. He no more wanted to do what we were about to do than I did.

"It's all right," I said. "Just tell me."

He nodded, appreciative of my straightforwardness, and gazed down at the file folder now resting on his left thigh.

"Some of these pictures may be very graphic in nature to you. I apologize in advance."

"I've been to a few rodeos," I said as evenly as I could.

He hesitated, then handed me the folder.

I opened it. I had to force myself to breathe.

The first photos were of a woman's sweater, a bra, a pair of panties, and a pair of brown suede boots. They'd all been badly burned.

"Do you recognize any of those garments?" Streeter asked.

"No."

After the pictures of clothing came autopsy photos, more than a dozen in all. They were of a dead woman. Like her clothes, she, too, had been burned. What was left of her hair appeared to be dark red, like Savannah's. Her face was charred, unrecognizable. Her nose was gone. Her eyes were gone. The jaw was parted. The teeth were white and perfect. Like Savannah's.

"Where did you find her?"

"Down a ravine, south of town. A car caught fire. She didn't have any ID on her. We're having some trouble getting good prints, given the extent of injury. I figured you'd want to know."

I flipped slowly through the photos. Burned hands. Long, elegant fingers, like Savannah's. Burgundy fingernails, like hers. Burned legs. Blackened arms. The limbs really didn't look like Savannah's. Or did they? I couldn't be certain. Nausea floated up from my stomach. I let out a breath, struggling to remain focused, trying not to cry.

"Were you able to establish a cause of death?"

"Not yet."

"Was she violated sexually?"

"We won't know that until the coroner comes back with his full results."

A photo of the left leg caught my attention. A patch of skin on the inside of her upper thigh had been spared from the flames that had consumed much of the rest of her. When Savannah was a teenager, long before it had become a social requirement that every young person in America get tattooed, Savannah had gotten inked—a small, delicate red rose that took me by surprise when I first discovered it, kissing my way up her leg.

"You don't strike me as the provocative, renegade type," I told her at the time.

"You want provocative?" she said alluringly, both of us naked. "I'll show you provocative."

And then, to my great pleasure, she did.

I held up the photo of the leg and looked closer:

There was no tattoo. I suddenly felt light-headed.

"This isn't Savannah."

"Are you sure?"

I explained to Streeter why I was.

He sat back and exhaled. He seemed almost more relieved than I was, but I doubted it.

It was possible, he said, that the woman in the photographs hadn't met with foul play, that she'd simply lost control of her car on a patch of ice and rolled into the ditch where her car caught fire. It happens all the time in winter, in the mountains.

"I'm sorry you had to go through this," he said. "It's just, we had to know."

I told him what Jethro Murtha, the ex-con, had passed along to me about Chad Lovejoy's uncle, airport executive Gordon Priest, and Murtha's assertion that Priest was involved in some sort of scam with Iranian immigrants living in the Tahoe area.

"Did he tell you that Priest or these Iranians killed Chad?" Streeter asked.

"All he said was that Chad found out what Priest was up to and that Chad was spooked. I'm pretty certain he didn't know the kid was dead until I told him."

"I do not want you approaching Gordon Priest. Let us do our job. Is that understood?"

I nodded.

The deputy dug a phone out of the pocket of his green sheriff's jacket and asked me for Murtha's telephone number, along with the ex-con's address. He typed them into the phone with his thumbs while telling me about the weapon that had been used to kill Chad Lovejoy.

Forensic examination showed that the bullets had been fired from a .40-caliber Glock, among the more common handguns on the market these days. The rounds, Streeter said, had been checked against ballistic databases in both California and Nevada to determine if the Glock had been used in any other crimes. No matches came up.

"Have you made any progress in finding Savannah? Anything tangible?"

"We still have plenty of people left to talk to," the cop said, "but I think it's safe to say at this point there aren't any arrests imminent."

I was rapidly coming to dislike anything and everyone, including Deputy Streeter. I was exhausted and hungry. My shoulders ached. My knee ached. The pounding pressure inside my skull felt like I was diving on a shipwreck.

"Did you get any sleep last night while you were driving in?" he asked me.

"No."

"You're more than welcome to crash at my place if you want. I've got an extra bedroom."

Considering the depth of my exhaustion and the fact that motels don't usually allow check-in before midafternoon, I thanked him for his hospitality.

"The least I could do," Streeter said, taking a slip of paper out of the file, jotting down his home address, and handing it to me, "making you drive all the way up here for essentially nothing."

Streeter roomed with Deputy Kyle Woo. He said he'd call to see if Woo was home, and to let him know I was coming over.

✝

THE TWO cops lived not far from the airport in a rented, three-bedroom, chalet-style house with a steeply pitched cathedral roof and a floor-to-ceiling moss rock fireplace. Their guest room, cluttered with moving boxes and exercise gear, was on the first floor, off the kitchen. The bed was a futon outfitted with a patchwork quilt that Woo said his grandmother had sewn.

"There's towels on the shelf in the bathroom," he said. "Help yourself to whatever's in the fridge, assuming you can find anything that's not moldy. We don't do much cooking around here."

"Sounds good."

He was getting ready to go to work, strapping on his holstered Glock and sliding a hammerless .38-caliber Smith & Wesson, his backup weapon, into an ankle rig under the right leg of his uniform trousers.

"We've had some burglaries in the neighborhood," Woo said. "Just remember to lock the front door and turn down the heat before you leave."

"Will do. Thanks for letting me stay."

He nodded, his affect flat, and left.

I curled up on the futon without taking my shoes or clothes off, pulled the quilt up around me, and closed my eyes. For the better part of an hour, I lay there, unable to sleep. Too tired. Too tortured, my brain filled with thoughts of Savannah. For lack of anything better to do, I decided to get up and get myself something to eat.

The stove looked like it had never been used. The refrigerator housed a variety of condiment bottles and jars—mustard, catsup, steak sauce—a quart of milk, a six-pack of Miller Lite, various vitamins, a deli package of mold-covered ham, and a Styrofoam takeout container with a leftover enchilada slathered in a congealed goo of green sauce and sour cream. A refrigerator for bachelors. Clearly, no women lived there. I grabbed the milk—miraculously not past its "use by" expiration date—found a box of Shredded Wheat in the cupboard above the dishwasher, a clean bowl and a spoon, and ate standing up over the double stainless steel sink.

I wondered about the emotionless, enigmatic Deputy Kyle Woo.

Chad Lovejoy had been shot with a .40-caliber Glock. Woo packed a .40-caliber Glock. When we'd first met, at the South Lake Tahoe Airport, Woo said he had often gone camping in the mountainous area where I'd spotted the downed Beechcraft, and where Chad's body was found the next day. Woo's sheriff's uniform included military-style tactical boots. Somebody had left tread prints of military-style tactical boots in the snow at the scene.

None of that, of course, would've come close to explaining why Woo would've had any reason to murder Chad Lovejoy. And I knew of nothing even remotely to suggest that he'd disguised his voice, passed himself off as Australian, and that he was the killer who'd dubbed himself Crocodile Dundee. But that didn't stop the cogs in my head from grinding in Woo's direction. When you're a hammer, as they say, all the world's a nail.

I walked upstairs and down the hall, past Streeter's bedroom, to Woo's room.

A neat freak Woo was not. The bed was rumpled and unmade, cluttered with boxes of pistol ammunition, gym clothes, and a pair of thirty-five-pound dumbbells. A wet towel was draped over the brass headboard. The beige carpeted floor presented an obstacle course of running shoes, boots and more free weights. The only other piece of furniture was one of those pressboard, put-it-together-yourself dressers from Ikea that even Einstein would've found all but impossible to assemble without leaving parts out. On the dresser was a Blu-ray disc player. A flat-screen TV rested atop that.

The top drawer was crammed with underwear and socks. The middle drawer held boxes of ammo, a collapsible police baton, handcuffs, two holsters, and four pornographic DVDs, including one entitled, "An Officer and a Genitalman." T-shirts were stuffed haphazardly into the bottom drawer.

Two of the T-shirts bore logos from pubs in Sydney, Australia—Lord Nelson and the Bavarian Bier Café on O'Connell Street.

Somebody probably gave him the T-shirts as gifts. Or maybe he picked them up as souvenirs on vacation. They don't mean anything, Logan. Why can't you ever give people the benefit of the doubt?

I put the T-shirts back, closed the drawer, and moved on to Woo's closet.

Several uniforms hung in dry-cleaning bags that obscured the back of the closet. I pushed them aside to find propped against the wall an M-4 assault carbine with a laser site and collapsible stock. On the shelf above the carbine was a small plastic box with the word, "Glock," stylishly embossed on it. I took the box down, set it on the bed, and opened it. Inside was a .40-caliber, semiautomatic identical to the Model 22 Woo carried on his hip. I grabbed a corner of the top sheet and, careful not to leave any prints, lifted the pistol out of the box, ejected the magazine and pulled the slide back to make sure that the firing chamber was clear. It was. I swabbed the muzzle with my little finger and held the finger to my nose: cordite. The weapon had recently been fired.

The pistol was still in my hand when I heard movement in the hallway and turned toward the doorway.

Woo was standing in a two-handed combat crouch, his semiauto leveled at my chest.

EIGHTEEN

"Drop the weapon."

"It's not loaded."

"Drop it NOW!"

"You got it."

I lowered the gun to the floor.

"What're you doing in here?" Woo demanded.

My impulse was to ask him what he was doing back home. But when you're standing uninvited in a cop's bedroom after perusing his personal possessions, and you're staring down the business end of his service weapon, the only proper response is a contrite one.

"I'm hunting a murderer."

Woo eyed me through his gunsights and asked me what in the hell I was talking about. I laid out all the circumstantial evidence that had left me suspicious of him.

"You think *I* shot Chad Lovejoy?"

"Did you?"

He holstered his pistol, strode past me, and picked up the Glock I'd dropped on the carpet.

"Either you got some balls or you're the dumbest guy on the planet, Logan, tossing my room, then calling bullshit on me without a gun in your hand."

He put the Glock back in the box and returned the box to the shelf in the closet where I'd found it.

"What're you doing back home? Thought you were going to work."

"I came to pick you up. Sheriff wants to see you."

"About what?"

"I'm not at liberty to say."

"Is it about Savannah?"

"I'm not at liberty to say."

"Well, what *are* you at liberty to say, Deputy Woo?"

"That the sheriff's waiting there," he said, his expression giving away nothing.

"'There' meaning where?"

Woo looked at me blankly, his face an emotionless mask.

"Sorry, I forgot. You're not at liberty to say."

The sheriff's waiting there.

Reading tea leaves and Woo's words, I convinced myself that the only possible reason the sheriff wanted to see me was to deliver the good news personally: Savannah had been found. She was alive and unharmed!

Then I remembered how long she'd been missing, and how the chances of surviving a kidnapping begin to plummet the longer the victim's been gone. Whatever optimism I enjoyed vanished instantly—only to rebound just as quickly.

Maybe, I thought, the reason the sheriff wanted to see me in person was because his investigators had identified Crocodile Dundee. They'd taken him into custody, prepping him for my questioning him. Suddenly, I was fired up and depressed at the same time—pumped because they'd caught the monster; depressed because I hadn't caught him myself, before they had.

I envisioned the interminable, dragged-out trial Savannah would have to endure. To what extent would we be expected to testify? Would I be able to contain myself, staring at Dundee from across the courtroom, or would I lunge, bailiffs struggling in vain to restrain me, while I happily ripped out his windpipe with my fingers?

Woo followed me into the hallway and pulled his bedroom door closed behind him. I apologized for having gone through his stuff. He offered no response.

I grabbed my jacket and followed him outside to his Wrangler, parked in the driveway. The snow was coming down again, swirling like white cornflakes borne on a hard wind. The air had a bite to it, and I could feel the skin on my cheeks burning from the cold. I thought I caught the wisp of a sad smile on his poker face as the deputy unlocked the passenger door for me. I took it as anything but a hopeful sign.

In silence we headed south and west out of town on the same two-lane highway Woo had taken that morning more than a week earlier, when we'd driven up to the trailhead to rendezvous with the sheriff's search and rescue team. I didn't ask this time where we were going. Maybe I already knew.

Don't ask how long it took to get there. It may have been fifteen minutes. It might've been twice that long. I was focused on the frost that had collected on the outside of the passenger window, trying to keep my rising fears in check.

We crossed over a cascading stream, its banks dappled with patches of ice—the South Fork of the American River, the sign said. Beyond the river, on our right, was an unmarked dirt road rising north into the snow-covered pines. Woo put his signal on and turned up the road. Another hundred meters or so and our journey came to an end. Assembled in the roadway was a collection of sheriff's vehicles, grim-faced deputies, perhaps a dozen or more, including Matt Streeter, and a coroner's van.

What happened beyond that remains largely obscured in my mind. I remember my heart racing. I remember how time slowed to a crawl.

A tall, older man wearing a green sheriff's parka gripped my shoulder as I stepped out of Woo's Jeep. I recall neither his name nor his title. He said something about how the hardest part of his job was having to convey bad news to family members of crime victims.

I remember Streeter and other deputies watching me with sad eyes as the tall man led me to a shallow ditch running along the east side of the road. I remember the tall man saying something about kids hunting rabbits and finding instead a grave.

I remember looking down, very briefly, and seeing Savannah's nude body. She was curled on her left side, the color drained from her mud-strewn face, her red hair matted with snow and dirt, splayed about her head as though she were underwater, her exquisite mahogany eyes gazing serenely at nothing, the white sclera red with ruptured blood vessels, the dark bruising around her throat, suggesting she'd been strangled.

I remember the gray duct tape binding her wrists behind her back.

"Do you recognize her?" I remember the tall man asking me.

"Savannah Carlisle Logan Echevarria," I whispered, the best I could do. "We used to be married."

I remember him saying something about how very sorry he was for my loss. At least I think that's what he said. I was listening more to several ravens, cawing in the trees above us. I remember thinking, *Those birds are trying to tell me something.*

Tracking terrorists through forests and jungles, it was the birds which always let us know when we were closing in on our targets. The closer the target was to us, the more agitated the birds grew, or the more silent. Whatever those ravens were saying was beyond my ability to comprehend. All I really fathomed amid my shock and grief at that moment was the crushing realization that the only woman I'd ever really cared about was gone forever.

✝

THE BAR on Lake Tahoe Boulevard was named McJ's Irish Pub, but it was apparent that its owner had never set foot on the Emerald Island. McJ's was a straight-up, ski-town beer hall with blaring rock music, antique toboggans on the walls, and two floors of tall stools and sticky tables packed with mostly twenty-somethings, all looking to hook up after a fun-filled day on the slopes. I'd gone there that night for two reasons. One, because it was an easy walk from the Econo Lodge, where I'd checked back in, too devastated to drive back to Rancho Bonita that night. The second reason was that I planned to get good and drunk.

I'd sworn off liquor after Savannah left me for Arlo Echevarria. Not even so much as a beer. That was more than seven years ago. But if ever there were a good time to nose-dive off the wagon, I convinced myself, this was it.

Camped out alone at a corner table, I stared down at the double shot of Cuervo the young waitress with the black lipstick had dropped off. I wanted so badly to feel the tequila burn all the way down my throat and into my stomach, to cloud my mind and help me forget as only tequila can, if only for one night.

I picked up the glass. I held it to my lips. I set it back down.

Over and over, the exercise repeated itself until sobriety ultimately won out. I never took a sip. Not because I feared that after so many years of being clean, I might end up in detox, and not because the Buddha warned that practitioners of his teachings should keep their minds clear and lucid at all times. No, what deterred me from getting smashed that night was unadulterated rage.

I couldn't very well find and kill the man who'd murdered Savannah and Chad Lovejoy if I were inebriated.

"Hi."

I looked up from my drink. Standing across the table, smiling at me, was a buxom, thin-waisted brunette in her mid-twenties. Gray-green eyes. Nice full lips. Black turtleneck. Black ski jacket. Jeans tucked into calfskin knee boots. She was no beauty queen, but nobody, as the old saying goes, would've tossed her out of bed for eating crackers.

"You mind if I sit here?" she said. "This place is crazy crowded."

I gestured: have a seat.

"Great, thanks." She pulled out the stool to my right and offered me her hand. "I'm Jessica, by the way."

"Logan." We shook. "You want some tequila, Jessica?"

"Sure."

I slid my glass over. "Cuervo. Haven't touched it."

Bon Jovi's "Wanted Dead or Alive" was playing on the bar's megaspeakers.

"You don't want it?" Jessica asked over the music.

I shook my head no.

"Can't let premium liquor go to waste," she said.

She slugged it down like a marine.

"Is Logan your first or your last name?"

"Last."

"You come to Tahoe often?"

"Hardly ever."

"You seem sad to me."

"Do I?"

"You do. You have this, like, aura or something. It's pretty creepy, really."

I told her it was a long story, and that she seemed like too nice a young lady to be burdened by it.

"Well, whatever it is," she said, resting a comforting hand on mine, "I'm really, really sorry."

A tall, skinny white guy with dark, greasy hair came barging through the crowd, sloshing a sixteen-ounce glass of beer. Black jeans. Black hoodie. Black Oakland Raiders cap pulled down low over his ears, Compton gangster style.

"What the hell, Jessica," he said accusingly as her hand quickly retreated from mine. "You said you were with me."

"Dude, chill," Jessica said. "I just needed a place to sit down, that's all."

I recognized him before he did me: Preston Kavitch, the panty-sniffing creeper from the Tranquility House Bed-and-Breakfast. Even in the dim light of the bar, I could see the blood drain from his face as he realized who I was.

"What're *you* doing here?"

"I was just leaving."

I stood to go.

"Thanks for the drink," Jessica said.

"This guy trashed my parents' house, and you let him buy you a drink?" Preston was pissed, slurring his words, a little drunk. "He thinks I killed his chick. Can you believe that?"

"He thinks you did *what?*" Jessica stared at him with her mouth open, then at me.

I walked on—or tried to, anyway.

"Hey, where you going, man?" Preston said. "I'm talking to you, asshole."

Blame what happened next on muscle memory. He clamped his hand on my right arm as I walked past him. In one fluid motion, I drove my right elbow into his midsection, shrugging off his grip, turned back, and snagged his wrist, bending it outward. With no option other than following the direction of his wrist or feel it splinter like a turkey bone, Preston crashed to the floor as the après-ski crowd scurried to get out of the way.

"Did you see that?" he screamed to no one in particular, sitting on the floor and holding his wrist, writhing in pain. "He assaulted me!"

"You deserved it," Jessica said as she slid off her stool and made her way toward the ladies' room.

"Call the cops! I'm filing charges!" Preston shouted.

Everyone seemed to ignore him as I headed for the exit. Nobody tried to stop me.

✛

THE RED message light was blinking on the room phone when I got back to the Econo Lodge. Gil Carlisle, Savannah's mega-wealthy oilman father, had called, weeping. At the crime scene that morning, Deputy Streeter had offered to notify Savannah's next of kin so that I wouldn't have to. I'd given him Carlisle's name. Streeter in turn apparently had given Carlisle my number at the motel. Carlisle wanted me to call him back as soon as possible, to fill him in on the details of his daughter's death.

I had a moral obligation to do so. I understood that. I'd been married once to his daughter. I probably should've alerted him when she first went missing. It would've been the decent thing to do, certainly the less cowardly. Yet I hesitated. How do you explain to your former father-in-law, a captain of industry used to having his way in virtually everything, that the death of the child he loved more than anyone on this planet was fundamentally your fault? In what manner do you initiate that dialogue? I was too spent to sleep, too numb to cry. So I simply sat there, frozen and inert, and did nothing for a very long time—until the room phone rang, jarring me from my catatonic haze. I forced myself to pick up the handset.

"Hello?"

"It's Gil Carlisle."

I offered the only words I could think to say.

"I'm so sorry."

"You should be, you son of a bitch."

Gone was the deceptively honeyed twang in his voice. Gone, too, was any semblance of the weeping, disconsolate father. The Gil Carlisle on the other end of the line was a man, in the parlance of his native West Texas, fit to be tied. He told me he couldn't believe it when Savannah called him, to tell him we were getting remarried. He counseled her against it, he said, told her I was a loser, and that's what I'd always be. But she wouldn't listen to him.

"Why did you have to go and find that airplane?"

"I've asked myself that question a thousand times, Gil."

"Why didn't you call me back?"

"I was going to."

"When?"

I didn't know what to say.

"You didn't call me when she got taken, either," Carlisle said. "I could've done something. Brought in help, you son of a bitch."

"I should've called you. I'm sorry."

"Stop saying that! 'Sorry' don't bring my daughter back, goddamn it."

"I don't blame you for being mad at me, Gil."

"You don't *blame* me? Well, that's mighty white of you, Logan. I'm gonna tell you something, son, that I should've told you a helluva long time ago: the worst day of my life was the day my cherished, beautiful daughter crossed paths with your sorry ass."

I couldn't much blame him for saying that, either.

"She told me she was pregnant. Couple months along. That true?"

"Yes."

"You were gonna get married, make a decent woman out of her. That true, too?"

"She already was a decent woman."

"Well, whoopty-damn-do. You thought she was decent. That don't mean a damn thing to me, you know that? *You* don't mean a damn thing to me."

Carlisle told me he would dispatch his private jet to retrieve Savannah's remains as soon as the coroner released them. Her funeral would be in Las Vegas, where he lived. I wouldn't be invited. If I showed up, Carlisle vowed, he'd have Nevada authorities arrest me on the spot for trespassing.

"And one more thing," Carlisle said. "Don't even *think* about asking for any of her money. You weren't married. You don't get a dime. Not one penny."

"Do you really think I care about her money?"

"Well, you sure as hell didn't care much about her safety, did you?" He began to cry. "I don't ever want to talk to you again. Do you feel me, boy? Never!"

The line went dead.

I've lost comrades in combat, classmates, buddies I've flown with. At Alpha, I watched brother go-to guys die in action. But the sense of loss I suffered in their passing was little more than emotional potholes compared to the black hole of grief that threatened to consume me as a result of Savannah's death.

I called Mrs. Schmulowitz to tell her the news because I knew she'd want to know. She listened solemnly and told me she wasn't surprised. She'd had a dream the night before, she said, that Savannah was in heaven, sipping a martini and smiling.

"She's OK, bubby. She's in a better place."

"I hope so, Mrs. Schmulowitz."

I hung up the phone and wept. Somewhere in the night, as falling snow muffled the sound of passing cars and trucks, but not the rhythmic rooting and orgasmic moaning of the couple in the room above mine, I finally drifted off.

That's when they came to me—the ravens I'd seen that morning in the trees high above the ditch where Savannah's body was found. In subconscious revelation, I grasped what they'd been trying to tell me.

NINETEEN

In Greek and Egyptian legend, the presence of a raven portends bad weather. Some African and Asian cultures believe that the bird forecasts death. For Shakespeare, the raven was evil incarnate; for Poe, it was the embodiment of lost love and despair.

The only reason I knew all that was because of Lieutenant Commander Andy Ziegler.

Andy was a naval aviator with big teeth and a skull filled to overflowing with pointless trivia, which he was only happy to uncork with minimal provocation. He flew EA-18Gs off the USS *Nimitz*, with Electronic Attack Squadron 135—the "Black Ravens." With his hunger for useless information, he'd gone out of his way to learn everything he could about the deviously intelligent birds whose likeness he and his squadron mates carried into battle on the empennages of their warplanes.

We'd met stateside during a debrief after a particularly sensitive snatch-and-grab in which Andy and his squadron mates jammed hostile radars to cover Alpha's extraction by helicopter from a Middle Eastern nation that shall go nameless. We became friends after I mentioned to him that I'd flown A-10s during my air force days.

"Are you aware that the Gatling gun on the A-10 *Warthog* was developed by General Electric?" Andy asked me.

"I am aware."

"And you don't find that funny in an ironic way? I mean, c'mon, it's *GE*."

"I'm not getting it, Andy."

"The 'we bring good things to life' company? Developing a weapon to *end* life?"

I had to admit, it was pretty ironic.

Andy invited me to spend Christmas at his parents' 1,200-acre cattle ranch in eastern Montana after Savannah and I split. He was confident that big sky country and a break from greasing bad guys would do me good. We galloped Appaloosas across the frozen High Plains by day and chased local women by night in the saloons of Miles City. Two months later, on a routine night training hop, both of Andy's engines inexplicably quit on approach to the carrier. He ejected, but his parachute failed to deploy. The navy never found his body.

It was a grinning Andy Ziegler who'd come to me that night in my dream. He was flying his jet upside down between clouds as red as strawberries, mouthing the same advice he'd given me after Savannah and I divorced:

"Have no regrets," Andy said. "You can't move on, you can't think straight, can't see straight, if you're flying backward."

I awoke in a sweat in my silent and dark room at the Econo Lodge before the dawn. Andy's words reverberated on my tongue.

Have no regrets.

Regret and guilt consumed me after my divorce. Savannah had walked out, but not without cause. I'd grown brittle, short-tempered, and increasingly closed-off emotionally. I'd been unfaithful to her. I attributed my bad behavior to the stresses associated with the violent nature of what I did for a living, along with my inability to disassociate me, the covert operator, from me, the husband who could never tell his wife how he actually earned his living. At the same time, I blamed her, unfairly, for not understanding me better. I regretted my behavior and felt great guilt over the damage I'd wrought. All of that, along with anger, clouded my ability to function after we'd said our good-byes. I couldn't see straight, couldn't think straight. And, now, here I was, come full circle, seven years later, paralyzed by the same emotions.

For a full day and night, I had lain there in that cheap motel room, unable to sleep. I wept until I had no more tears left, my stomach aching from convulsive waves of grief that surged through me on a relentless, anguishing tide.

The next morning, I willed myself out of bed and into the bathroom. I tore the plastic wrapper off a plastic cup, filled it from the sink, and drank it down, then turned on the light. The eyes that stared back at me in the mirror seemed not my own, haggard and shot through with veins, older than when I'd seen them last.

Would Savannah still be alive, I asked myself, had I not caught that glint of sunlight from an all-but-forgotten airplane? Would she still be alive had I followed the instructions of her kidnapper? And there was Andy Ziegler, courtesy of those chattering ravens, still talking to me:

Have no regrets.

He was right. Was I really to blame for Savannah's death? Any pilot would've done exactly as I had done—reporting what appeared to be a crash site in hopes of saving lives. And even if I had done what Crocodile wanted me to do, there was no assurance that he would've let Savannah live. The only thing I knew for sure was nothing was ever going to bring her back. The only task left unfulfilled was to take my pound of flesh from the man who had taken her from me. But that wouldn't happen, I realized, so long as my mind remained a tormented mess.

I ran the shower as cold as it would go and stepped in. The stream of frigid water stung like needle pricks, robbing me of breath, but it forced me to focus.

At Alpha, we were taught that the most difficult question to answer is always the one to which the answer is obvious. Like peeling an onion, you start from the outside and work your way in. To me, standing there in that freezing shower, the obvious answer was either Gordon Priest or Preston Kavitch. Deputy Streeter had warned me about approaching Priest and interfering with his investigation. Fair enough. It was Kavitch I was more interested in, anyway.

My gut didn't buy Streeter's assertion that Kavitch was clean simply because the perverted little panty sniffer's ankle monitor showed he hadn't left his parents' B&B the morning Savannah disappeared. Anything electronic can be manipulated. There were other ample reasons to suspect Kavitch. He was no stranger to the criminal justice system. He was on a first-name basis with the psychopharmacology industry, and probably needed a lot of cash to maintain that relationship. And, if that weren't enough, he gave me the creeps every time we crossed paths.

From cold water to scalding hot, I soaped and scrubbed from my scalp to my toes, then rinsed off, my skin tingling, toweled dry, and lay back in bed, waiting for the sun to come up. I knew more ways to kill a man than I was willing to count. In Preston Kavitch's case, if my investigation proved fruitful, all I'd need was one.

✝

CONSTANCE, MY friendly divorced librarian, seemed genuinely pleased to see me again.

"I need some help," I said. "I'm doing some research on a local resident."

"Of course." She licked the tip of her index finger and slid a slip of scratch paper out from a small plastic bin sitting atop her desk. "What's his name?"

"Preston Kavitch."

"Any relation to the Kavitches who own that nice bed-and-breakfast across from the lake?"

"Their son."

Constance wrote down his name with the nub of a pencil, the kind you find in any library.

"Do you know how old he is, approximately?"

I told her.

"If you told me what kind of research you're doing, the purpose," Constance said, "I might be able to help you more."

"It involves a murder investigation."

She looked up at me slowly, with eyebrows raised and a slight downturn of her mouth that conveyed a sudden awareness of who I was.

"I read about you in the paper. Your wife was killed. She was pregnant."

"Ex-wife. We were going to get remarried."

"I'm so sorry."

I nodded.

"And this Preston Kavitch, he's a suspect?"

"Maybe."

Constance nodded, drawing her own conclusions. She typed on her computer. After about a minute, her desktop printer spit out a few pages.

"Can't find much on him, I'm afraid," she said, handing me the pages. "A couple of stories in the newspaper about him being arrested for this or that. Here's one about him being in a play at the high school. Ah, speaking of which, follow me."

She led me to a bookshelf crammed with South Lake Tahoe High School yearbooks, arranged chronologically. Constance picked out the one with 2006 printed on the spine, the silver cover featuring the image of a horned Viking hat. She flipped through the book until she found what she was looking for: two opposing pages of color photos highlighting the high school theater club's annual spring play—a production of "Monte Python and the Holy Grail."

Even disguised as a medieval knight, Preston Kavitch was hard to miss. Same stringy body. Same long, greasy hair. What caught my eye, however, wasn't so much his picture as it was the name that appeared directly above Kavitch's in the play's cast of characters—a schoolmate whose bullet-ventilated body would be found eight years later lying in the mountains high above South Lake Tahoe, beside a crashed, twin-engine Beechcraft:

Chad Lovejoy.

"Mind if I make a copy of this?"

"I'm sorry. Patrons aren't allowed to make copies of reference materials," Constance said, then smiled empathetically. "However, as head librarian, I can do whatever the hell I want."

✝

UNLIKE VICTIMS of random terrorist attacks, most murder victims die at the hands of someone they knew personally. I read that somewhere. Chad Lovejoy knew Preston Kavitch. Their shared history was one more nail in Kavitch's coffin, as far as I was concerned. And yet, the more I thought about it, the more I wondered whether meting out my own personal brand of payback for Savannah's death was the way to go. Perhaps it was the Buddha talking to me, or some newfound maturity in the wake of my grieving over Savannah that compelled me to realize I'd likely spend the rest of my days in prison were I to take the law into my own hands. Whatever the reason, it stopped me from stalking, beating a confession out of him, then killing Preston Kavitch.

I called Streeter instead.

"It's a small town," he said after agreeing to meet me at Steve's, the same coffee shop where we'd met the morning Savannah vanished. "So they went to high school together. It means nothing."

He slid the copy of the yearbook page Constance had copied for me at the library back across the table.

"So you've ruled Kavitch out as a suspect?"

"I told you. Kavitch wears an ankle monitor. And that monitor indicates he's never been within five miles of that downed airplane."

"He could've tinkered with the monitor."

"We would've known. The computer would've shown it. The bracelet he wears is state of the art."

"Such as that is in El Dorado County."

Streeter leaned back in his chair and folded his arms indignantly. "Despite appearances to the contrary, Mr. Logan," he said, "this isn't Mayberry."

Ruby the waitress shuffled over to take our order.

"I know what he's having," she said, tilting her head with affection at Streeter. "What about you, sugar?"

I ordered oatmeal—hold the raisins—and waited for Ruby to move on. I still wasn't convinced that the weirdo from the B&B was anything other than guilty, but I let it go for the time being.

"So, if it wasn't Preston Kavitch," I said, "who was it?"

"We're still operating on the assumption that it was someone Lovejoy did state time with," Streeter said.

I asked him if he'd contacted Jethro Murtha, the ex-con in Los Angeles who'd told me about Lovejoy's uncle, Gordon Priest, and Priest's supposed sketchy business dealings with members of Lake Tahoe's Iranian community.

"Not yet."

"What're you waiting for?"

Again, Streeter folded his arms and gave me that look.

"I don't mean any disrespect, Mr. Logan. I appreciate that you've lost someone very close to you. But I have to be honest and tell you, I resent your suggestion that we're not doing all we can to close this case as quickly as we can. We're moving as fast as we can, with the resources we have available."

My impulse was to tell him that his best wasn't good enough, though on some level, I suspected he knew that already.

"I want to know what you *do* know, where it stands," I said. "I think I have that right."

"I'm sorry. Department policy—"

"—Ever been in love, Deputy? So in love that all you could think about was her? Every waking minute of every day?

And when you weren't awake, you were dreaming about her, because you knew that was it, the one?"

Streeter stared down at his coffee, cupping the mug with both hands, and nodded solemnly.

"This was the woman I planned on spending the rest of my life with. If the shoe were on the other foot," I said, "I'd do the same for you."

He rubbed his chin and the side of his neck. He exhaled, then told me that the investigation showed Savannah had been strangled at some other location, and her body dumped in the grave where it had been found. He said that boot prints at the scene matched those taken at the site of the downed Beechcraft where Chad Lovejoy had been shot to death, strongly suggesting that the same suspect had been responsible for both killings. The prints were of a man with unusually large, wide feet—size 13EE.

"Tire tracks from both scenes also matched," Streeter said.

"What size were the tires?"

"I couldn't tell you offhand. The measurements are in my file. Big tires. Like on a pickup."

"Anything else?"

"Nothing that comes to mind."

"No arrests anytime soon."

Streeter hesitated. "Probably not," he said.

A good minute went by without either of us saying anything. Streeter sipped his coffee and methodically surveyed other diners, his eyes going instinctively to the bulges under their shirts and at their ankles where they might be concealing weapons. He was, I decided, a decent, if inexperienced, investigator merely out of his league.

I pulled a ten dollar bill from my wallet, laid it on the table, and angled for the door.

"I'm warning you, Mr. Logan, please don't interfere with an active ongoing police investigation."

"'Active.' Is that what you call it?"

I was out the door before he could respond.

— 221 —

The chill mountain air smelled of burning wood. A gray-brown smudge from hundreds of fireplaces clung to the tops of the pines. I sat in my truck. Maybe Streeter was right about Preston Kavitch. You learn while tracking terrorists that it's easy to become myopic. You convince yourself that that unconfirmed shred of a lead from some illiterate goat herder is true because you want to believe it's true. Soon enough, you're racing down camel tracks in Somalia, ignoring intelligence assessments that say the killers are in Spain. Then, a bomb goes off on a commuter train in Madrid, killing and maiming dozens, and you spend what years you have left haunted by your own intractability.

Lesson learned.

My phone rang. It was Marlene, the receptionist at Summit Aviation. She was crying.

"I read in the paper they found her body. I'm just so very sorry. I can't stop thinking about it." She cleared her throat. Then she said, "There's something I need to get off my chest."

"What's that, Marlene?"

"I wasn't exactly being truthful with you."

"About what?"

She hesitated. "You remember when you found Chad up near that plane?"

"Hard day to forget."

"Well, Gordon, he was . . ." She broke down, sobbing like she was in pain.

"Gordon was *what*, Marlene?"

"I'd prefer not to discuss it over the phone." She lowered her voice as though concerned she might be overheard—I assumed by Priest—and asked to meet in person.

"I'm here in Lake Tahoe. We can meet wherever you want."

She told me she was waiting for a callback from her husband—they'd quarreled that morning again over what she said were "money issues," and he'd stormed out of the house. She was hoping to hear back from him shortly and could meet me in thirty minutes.

"There's a grocery store on Lincoln Avenue, just south of Apache."

"I'll find it."

My old Tacoma didn't want to start. I cranked the ignition for a solid five seconds before the engine finally caught, then turned southbound on Emerald Bay Road, while a solid stream of cars and trucks bearing skis and snowboards inched along in the opposite direction toward the slopes at Heavenly.

I glanced up in my rearview mirror and realized I was being followed.

TWENTY

Most rolling surveillances are intended to be clandestine. The best ones involve multiple vehicles rotated in and out of the point position, such that the person being tailed never sees the same car very long.

This was not one of those surveillances.

This one was meant to intimidate.

A black Pontiac Trans Am circa 1977 with tinted windows quickly closed the gap. We drove that way for more than a mile, me doing the speed limit, him drafting my back bumper the way it's done at Daytona. A prudent driver might've put on his turn signal and pulled to the shoulder of the road to let the other driver pass and avoid a confrontation. Unfortunately, I've never been very adept at prudence.

I jammed on my brakes and he slammed into me. I cut the Tacoma's steering wheel right, then, hard left, locking my rear bumper to his front spoiler. With his muscle car stuck to my less-than-muscular truck, he had no choice but to follow me as I pulled over. My intent was to introduce myself to the Pontiac's driver by way of my fists to his face, before inquiring as to what he was doing, following me so closely. But it never got that far.

Deputy Woo threw open the Pontiac's driver-side door and took cover behind it with his pistol leveled at me through the open window.

I raised my palms to show him I was unarmed. "Burt Reynolds just called. The Bandit wants his ride back."

"Why'd you brake on me like that?" Woo demanded.

"Why were you following me like that?"

"To make sure you don't do something stupid." He holstered his weapon, closed his door, and walked forward to survey the damage. "Streeter texted me. He wants to make sure you stay out of trouble and stay out of the way as long as you're up here."

Cars speeded past in both directions without stopping.

"Sweet maneuver," Woo said, inspecting the damage. "Where'd you learn to drive like that?"

"My previous employer. We learned all sorts of fun stuff."

He asked me where I was going. I told him it was none of his business.

"I could make it my business," Woo said.

"If you want to arrest me, arrest me. My first call won't be to an attorney. It'll be to the local newspaper, to tell them in intricate detail how the local sheriff's department is incapable of making the slightest progress on a double homicide, and how the murderer is still out there, roaming free, capable of killing again at any time."

Woo studied me, his face expressionless, trying to gauge the sincerity of my threat. Then he stared down at our two bumper-locked vehicles.

"How do we get unstuck?"

"Easy. I'll show you."

Back behind the wheel, I fired up the engine and shifted into gear. When I gave it the gas, my truck pulled forward—ripping away the entire front spoiler assembly of Woo's Trans Am, while he stood there watching, wearing the same impenetrable expression.

I got out with the engine running and walked back to take a look.

"They don't make 'em like they used to," I said.

Woo didn't say anything.

Lira's Supermarket off Apache Avenue was no Safeway, but it was clean and well-organized. I ordered chicken tenders from the deli counter and ate them outside while waiting for Marlene to arrive from Summit Aviation. I wasn't really hungry, but I ate anyway. Chicken was protein. I needed protein to remain mission-focused. I wondered what part of the chicken a "tender" was and tried to block Savannah from my mind, the way her body looked in that ditch.

Marlene arrived within five minutes of the appointed time, driving a faded green Honda Civic with rusted sidewalls and a crumpled right front fender. She got out and looked around with noticeable trepidation, as if she, too, had been followed. From everything I could see, it appeared she hadn't.

"You doing OK?"

"Not really," Marlene said. "My husband's behaving a little crazy."

"Want a chicken tender?"

She shook her head no and glanced over her shoulder. Her face was flush. Her hand trembled when she ran it across her mouth.

"Can we go inside? I'd rather not be seen out here."

"Sure."

I followed her inside the supermarket. We stood in the bread aisle. There was bruising under her right eye. She'd tried to hide it with makeup, but you could've spotted it with a satellite.

"Does your husband hit you, Marlene?" I said gesturing toward her cheek.

"You mean this?" She blushed, embarrassed, and averted her eyes. "No. Of course not. I slipped on some ice, that's all."

"Somehow, I don't believe you."

"Look, I didn't come here to talk to you about my husband, or being a klutz, OK? I came to tell you about Gordon, my boss."

"What about him?"

"He wasn't telling the truth." Again, Marlene looked nervously over her shoulder. "You know how I told you he was at some big FAA meeting in Reno the day Chad died?"

"I remember."

"Well, he wasn't. Some guy from the FAA called, wanting operational stats from last month, takeoffs and landings, that sort of stuff. I told him Gordon took those stats with him when he went to the meeting in Reno. The FAA guy tells me, 'What meeting? That meeting got canceled.'"

"You're saying Gordon wasn't in Reno that day?"

"That's just it. I don't know." She bit a fingernail. "I lied to you about something else, too."

I waited.

"You know how I told you Gordon and Chad were like two peas in a pod?"

I nodded.

"Well, they weren't. Gordon hated Chad. Hated the way his sister made him hire him, hated him for who he was, the ex-con. He was always riding Chad, calling him lazy, a good-for-nothing criminal, how it was such a big waste, having to pay him even minimum wage."

"Why would you lie to me about something like that?"

"Gordon's my boss. I was just trying to be loyal, I guess."

"How did Chad react to all of that, when Gordon rode him?"

"Chad? All he tried to do was make Gordon happy. If what they said in the paper was true, that Chad went up to that plane to steal stuff, I could definitely see him asking Gordon to go with him, to try and please Gordon, because Gordon, he'd be all over something like that, knowing Gordon. He's definitely into making a fast buck if he can. And he's not beyond breaking the law to do it, either."

I asked her if she was aware of any business dealings Gordon Priest might've had with any newcomers living in the Lake Tahoe area. She started to say that she didn't know, then abruptly reversed herself.

"He gets a lot of calls from this one guy, now that I think of it." Again, Marlene glanced over her shoulder. "Talk about a crazy accent. I can barely understand the guy. Gordon always shuts his office door whenever he calls. He won't ever tell me his name. He just tells me to tell Gordon that it's his 'friend' calling."

"What kind of accent?"

"I couldn't tell you. Arab, maybe. I don't really know. Foreign. That's all I know."

"Iranian?"

"I don't know."

"Have you told the sheriff's department all this?"

"I was kind of hoping you might be able to tell them for me."

Marlene said she was afraid that if Priest found out she'd informed on him, she'd lose her job. Better that investigators find out about him from someone else, she said. Then, if they wanted, they could come to her for confirmation.

"I'll see what I can do," I said.

She checked her wristwatch. "I better be getting back. Got a flight landing in about ten minutes." Then she looked up at me, her eyes pooling. "Her father's flying in to take your lady back to Las Vegas."

☩

PRIVATE JETS don't interest me. They never have. I'll never be able to afford one, not in this life, which is why they all essentially look the same to me. But I easily recognized Gil Carlisle's airplane as it touched down. The gleaming white Dassault Falcon flaunted the Carlisle family coat of arms on its vertical stabilizer—a black knight's helmet above a yellow medieval shield embossed with a red cross. You've gotta have some major cojones to flaunt that much unvarnished ego.

I got out of my truck and leaned against a low chain-link fence as the jet swung smartly off the runway, taxiing to a stop in front of Summit Aviation Services. The door folded open and my former father-in-law, Gil Carlisle, bounded down the stairs, followed by his legal advisor, Miles Zambelli, both striding toward me.

"What are you doing here, Logan?" Carlisle said. He was wearing python-skin cowboy boots, a tan felt Stetson, carefully creased old-guy jeans, a white turtle neck and shearling coat. He looked like a bloated Marlboro Man.

"I came to say good-bye to your daughter."

"Haven't you done enough damage already?"

"I didn't kill Savannah, Gil."

"I have something for you," the smug, Harvard-educated Zambelli said. He dug into his stylishly distressed, $700 leather shoulder bag and removed an official-looking sheet of paper. "It's a restraining order, signed by the honorable Ronald Jablonsky of Clark County, Nevada. You can read it later."

He thrust the paper at me across the fence.

"Restraining me from what?"

"From participating in any funereal arrangements, or attending any graveside, chapel, or any other memorial service held in conjunction with the demise of Ms. Savannah Carlisle."

I wadded the paper and tossed it in his face.

"That's battery," Zambelli said, pointing an accusatory finger at me.

"Bullshit is more like it."

He picked up the crumpled restraining order, slipped it back in his man purse, and said, "You've been duly warned."

My issues with Zambelli were long-standing. He'd taken advantage of Savannah, enjoying a one-night stand with her after we'd divorced, for which her father apparently had forgiven him. I wasn't nearly so benevolent, but I knew that my impulse to forcibly remove the carotid artery from Zambelli's neck was nothing more than misdirected wrath. My fight was not with him or my former father-in-law. It was with Crocodile Dundee, the man who'd murdered Savannah.

"You have to leave," Carlisle said. "Now."

"Why is that?"

"Because I said so."

"We're not in Texas, Gil, and I'm not your son-in-law anymore. So I think I'll stay right here for the time being if it's all the same to you."

His face was turning red. "I can have you arrested."

"I don't think you can, actually."

A rolling, chain-driven security gate clanked open about thirty meters to my left, and a black hearse drove slowly onto the tarmac toward Carlisle's jet. He and Zambelli turned to watch it. The breath caught in my throat.

Marlene emerged from the offices of Summit Aviation and began walking toward the airplane, followed moments later by her boss, Gordon Priest.

It was time, I decided, to have a little chat with him.

I hopped the fence.

"Hey, where do you think you're going?" Carlisle yelled after me. "Logan!"

The hearse backed up to the jet. Two mortuary employees got out dressed in black. I ignored them, as I did Carlisle and Zambelli, hustling to catch up with me. Priest must've sensed me sprinting toward him from behind because he turned when he saw me and stopped in midstride.

"Mr. Logan," Marlene said with feigned surprise, like we hadn't spoken minutes earlier at the grocery store down the road.

I ignored her as well and focused on Gordon Priest.

"Did you have anything to do with this?"

His mouth was parted slightly, his eyes shifty, unwilling to meet my own. A muscle above his left cheekbone twitched. The fear in his lumpy face was unmistakable.

"I don't know what you're talking about," he said.

"You know exactly what I'm talking about."

I glanced briefly at the mortuary workers as they removed Savannah's casket from the hearse, an inexpensive metal box

— 230 —

that I knew Carlisle would exchange as soon as he got home for a far gaudier one befitting his obscene wealth and taste for the ostentatious. Had Savannah wanted to be buried in grand style or cremated? To my recollection, we'd never even talked about it. The lump in my throat felt as big as a baseball.

With Zambelli in trail, Carlisle came trotting up, out of breath.

"Who are you?" he demanded to know of Priest.

Priest told him.

"This is my personal attorney," Carlisle said, pointing at Zambelli, "and I guarantee you, he *will* sue your ass off and you *will* lose a shitload of money unless you have this 'gentleman,' and I use the term loosely,"—referring to me—"removed from the grounds of this airport forthwith."

Priest ignored him and told me, adamantly, that he'd had absolutely nothing to do with Savannah's death or that of his nephew. He said he was only too happy to cooperate with sheriff's investigators. I looked over at Marlene. She was staring nervously at the ground.

"I'm a law-abiding citizen," Priest said. "I've never even had so much as a parking ticket."

He was, I decided, one of those guys who *looked* guilty. He definitely bore further scrutiny.

Zambelli was yelling at him to call the authorities, demanding that I be arrested for violating his restraining order. I wanted to deck him but I knew that I couldn't. I wanted to watch the men in black load Savannah aboard that jet, in her metal box, but I knew I couldn't do that, either, not without giving my former father-in-law the satisfaction of seeing me cry.

I turned and walked away.

Carlisle's jet wasn't on the ground long. Twenty minutes, if that. It taxied to the south end of the field, passing me as I sat in my truck, then thundered into the crystalline blue, banking over the lake, departing the pattern to the east. I watched until it was no longer in sight.

So long, love. Blue skies.

A bitter burning taste filled my mouth. I couldn't decide if it was rage or my heart breaking.

✝

Buzz, my old Alpha buddy back East, had somehow already heard about what had happened to Savannah when I called him that night from my room at the Econo Lodge. How he knew, I have no idea, but he did. I told him I needed Gordon Priest's home address. He didn't give me any grief about it.

"We've been through a lot together, Logan, you and me. You need me to help you put the goddamn son of a bitch who did this out of his misery, I can be on the first plane out of Dulles and out there first thing tomorrow morning."

"I'll keep you in mind."

"Even if you just need somebody to talk to. I'm serious, Logan. Talking helps. According to Oprah, anyway."

"I didn't know you were an Oprah fan, Buzz."

"Who isn't?"

He told me all about what Oprah said regarding open and honest communications, how cathartic they can be. I listened, but not very well, thanked him for his support, and signed off. I pulled the covers up around me, not bothering to dress, and slept fitfully until just before dawn. My day, I decided, would be spent hunting. Hunting, like flying, requires complete focus. I liked that. It would take my mind away from my grief.

The complimentary continental breakfast at the Econo Lodge was the usual assortment of cold cereal, bad Danish, apples so mushy as to be inedible, and coffee so strong, you could refinish furniture with it. I ate quickly, zipped up my jacket, went out to my truck, scraped the frost off the windshield with my only credit card, and drove to Gordon Priest's residence in the dark.

Priest lived two minutes away in the Skylark Mobile Home and RV Park off Lake Tahoe Boulevard. His weathered, single-wide aluminum trailer, among about a dozen in the "park," exuded all the charm of a discarded beer can. Across the street was a large thrift shop. I parked in the lot, the rear of my truck facing his trailer, and established an eyes-on surveillance using my mirrors only. At 0750, Priest emerged carrying a small paper sack that I assumed was his lunch and exchanged angry words with a big-boned, bottle blonde in a red kimono robe who followed him out of the trailer, and whom I assumed was his wife. He got into a blue Ford Escort station wagon. I waited while he hooked a U-turn on Lodi Avenue, almost directly in front of me. That was followed by an immediate left onto Lake Tahoe Boulevard.

I followed him at a prudent distance, motoring north toward the lake.

He passed a lumberyard, crossed a creek, and made a right turn without signaling into the parking lot of a US Bank branch, while I deviated into the parking lot of the Denny's across the street so as to avoid suspicion. He withdrew some cash from the ATM and then proceeded to drive to the Iranian-owned Dutch Mart Gas and Grub, where he went inside.

I parked a block away and waited.

After ten minutes or so, Priest reemerged, accompanied by Reza Jalali. The two men spoke for a long minute, both occasionally glancing over their shoulders. They shook hands. Then Priest got in his station wagon and drove away. Jalali watched him go.

Neither man observed me.

We were headed south. At the intersection of Lake Tahoe Boulevard and Emerald Bay Road, a sign pointed in the direction of the airport, but he continued straight, picking up speed.

Odd.

I followed him for another three minutes or so, passing a fire station, the road out of town narrowing to two lanes, before Priest turned right onto a residential street called Stony Mountain Court that ended in a cul-de-sac. As I pulled over and watched, Priest proceeded to the end of the circle, and parked in front of a large, not unattractive custom home, the kind middle-class folks build to convey the sense to their neighbors that they've arrived.

Priest got out of his station wagon and walked up the driveway with his sack lunch. He must've been satisfied nobody was following him, because he never looked back.

As he walked up the driveway toward the front door, it opened. A woman stood inside the doorway, impatiently awaiting his arrival.

Gordon Priest, it seemed, had a big dark secret.

TWENTY-ONE

A sturdy brunette—mid-forties, big shoulders, big breasts, big hips—she stood with her arms sternly crossed just inside her doorway in knee-high leather boots, a leather miniskirt, and matching leather bra. A tattooed astrological sun took up the whole of her belly. In her right hand was a riding crop. In her left was what looked like a spiked dog collar. Gordon Priest tried to kiss her, but she backed away as he entered her house and whipped him once across the butt. He was getting down on all fours when she closed the door.

The manager of Summit Aviation appeared to be on a close personal basis with Lake Tahoe's resident dominatrix. Or at least one of them. Given the tongue lashing his wife had delivered to him that morning as he left home, I could more or less understand the appeal.

I telephoned Summit Aviation and asked Marlene when she expected him in.

"Probably not 'til late this afternoon," she said. "He called this morning and said he'd be away at meetings pretty much all day."

"The man is obviously dedicated to his work."

Marlene seemed anxious to know if I'd had a chance to pass along to the sheriff's department what she'd confided to me the day before about how Priest had lied regarding his whereabouts the day Chad Lovejoy was murdered, and how his relationship with Lovejoy was strained.

"Not yet," I said.

"Well, when you do, like I said, just don't say you heard it from me directly. I don't want to lose my job."

"No worries, Marlene."

I got out of my truck, walked up to the house, and put my ear to one of the two frosted glass panels that flanked the ornately carved oak door. From inside, I heard the following exchange between Priest and a woman whom I assumed was the dominatrix I'd seen standing in the doorway:

"You will lick my boots if I tell you to."

"Yes, mistress."

"You will get down on your knees before me if I tell you to. If you don't do what I tell you quickly enough, you'll be disciplined. Understood?"

"Yes, mistress."

Crack went the riding crop.

"Louder."

"Yes, mistress!"

I rang the door bell.

The house went conspicuously silent.

I rang again.

No answer.

I rang. And kept ringing until the dominatrix came to the door. She was lathered in perspiration, a black leather trench coat hastily thrown over her sadomasochistic accoutrements. Her fingernails were pointy and the color of the devil himself.

"I'm looking for Gordon Priest."

"I don't know any Gordon Priest."

"Tell him it's Cordell Logan."

"I just told you—"

"Tell him that if he doesn't come to the door," I said, pulling out my phone, "I'm calling his wife."

Her face softened with resignation. She sighed and yelled over her shoulder.

"There's some guy out here. Says his name's Logan. He's calling your wife."

Priest came sprinting. Imagine a barefoot, disheveled Fred Flintstone wearing a dog collar and a pink terrycloth robe that was ridiculously undersized.

"Can I help you?" he said sheepishly.

"We can take this inside," I said, "or we can stand out here and talk. That way all the neighbors can listen in."

Priest gave the lady in leather a look that was both pleading and apologetic.

"Come on in," she said. "I'm Mistress Elvira, by the way."

"Of course you are."

The living room was a testimonial to the American West. Cowhide-covered furniture. A pair of steer horns hanging over the fireplace mantle. Framed lithographs of horse-mounted Native Americans with feathers in their hair.

"Think I'll hit the can and let you boys chat," Elvira said.

Priest watched her disappear down a hall, her ample hips swaying side to side.

"It's not what you think," he said, looking back at me.

I shrugged. "Nice collar."

He smiled, embarrassed, and took it off.

"How'd you find me?"

"Followed you."

He nodded, hands stuffed in the pockets of his hastily borrowed robe, staring at the floor.

"You want a drink or something?"

"No, thanks."

"Mind if I do?"

"It's a free country."

He crossed to a wet bar and poured himself a full tumbler of vodka.

"You're not gonna tell my wife about any of this, are you?"

"Only if you don't tell me the truth."

"You mean about my nephew, Chad?"

I said nothing, waiting.

Another swig of booze, then Priest said, "I was at a meeting in Reno the day he was killed."

"There was no meeting that day in Reno."

"Of course there was."

"You're lying to me, Gordon."

He rubbed his nose with his free hand and folded his arms across his chest defensively, refusing to meet my eyes.

"How do you know that?"

"Your body language just told me."

Gordon Priest downed the rest of his drink. "OK, look, here's the deal." He hesitated, then exhaled. "I was here that day, OK? Most of the day, anyway. But, for god's sake, if my wife knew . . . She'll take everything I own. Please. You can't."

"You've got proof you were here?"

"My credit card statement."

"Your dominatrix takes MasterCard?"

"And Visa, and American Express," Mistress Elvira said, returning from the bathroom and disappearing into the kitchen. "I run a legitimate business. No hanky-panky. I'm getting the yogurt."

"OK," Priest said.

He told me he didn't use his personal credit card to charge his sessions with Elvira—nobody, he said, would be that stupid. Rather, he said, the charges posted to his corporate American Express account, the statement of which was mailed each month to his airport office, where his wife wouldn't see it.

I asked him about his going to see Reza Jalali at the convenience store that morning.

"Reza's a 'Niners fan," Priest said. "I'm a Raiders fan. The Raiders lost last week and the 'Niners won. I owed him $100. I went to pay him."

I didn't buy it. Murtha, the ex-con, had told me that Chad Lovejoy feared his uncle Gordon was involved in something sketchy with Iranians living in the Tahoe area. Chad was so unnerved, he couldn't tell Murtha what it was.

"You're lying to me again, Gordon," I said.

"I swear I'm not."

I dug the phone out of my pocket and punched in numbers.

"What're you doing?" he said, half-panicked.

"Calling your wife."

"Okay, okay, okay." Priest ran a hand through his tangled, sweat-soaked hair. "The truth. Just hang up. Please."

I hung up. He started walking toward the front door.

"Where're you going?"

"My car," he said. "Something I need to show you."

I followed him down the driveway. Barefoot, Priest navigated the snow-covered concrete gingerly, making little painful noises, like he was walking across hot coals. The station wagon was unlocked. Instinctively, I watched his hands and stayed close behind his right side as he leaned in and reached under the passenger seat with his left hand. If he did pull a gun on me, he'd have to turn awkwardly, drawing the weapon across his body before getting a shot off. I'd take him out long before he got the chance.

Only it wasn't a gun Priest was reaching for, as it turned out. It was a sheaf of papers—bills of lading from several foreign shipping companies, each listing replacement parts for Cessna and Piper airplanes.

"We run a company," Priest said, "supplying aircraft parts to Iran."

"In violation of US trade sanctions against Tehran."

"It's not military parts, nothing like that. They've got civilian pilots over there who like to fly small planes, just like we've got here. We're not hurting anybody."

"You could go to prison. You know that, right?"

"All we're doing is helping keep general aviation alive in a corner of the world that could use a little help, that's all."

I handed him back the papers. "What about nuclear material?"

He looked at me blankly.

"What're you talking about?"

"That Twin Beech we found up in the mountains was hauling enriched uranium."

"You think I was trying to export uranium to *Iran?*" He blanched, pumping his knees to keep his feet from freezing. "I wouldn't know anything about that. And if I did, I'd be on the phone to the FBI in a New York minute. I'm a proud American. I bleed red, white, and blue, OK? And I didn't kill my nephew. Or anybody else."

Two houses down, across the cul-de-sac, a garage door rolled up and a middle-aged woman in a burgundy tracksuit started to get into her black Mercedes SUV. She spotted Priest and stopped dead in her tracks, mouth agape.

"I'd say she definitely digs the robe."

"You're not gonna tell my wife about this, are you?"

"No."

"What about the feds?"

"I've got nothing against civilian pilots, in Iran or anywhere else."

Priest tilted his head up to the sky and exhaled like a great weight had been lifted from him.

"Thank you, Jesus."

We shook hands. "I'm real sorry again about your lady," he said. "And I know he and I didn't always get along, but I'm sorry about what happened to my sister's kid. I just hope they catch whoever did it before somebody else dies."

"Makes two of us."

As I watched him hotfoot it back inside, wondering what yogurt had to do with spiked dog collars and riding crops, my phone rang.

"Hello, bubby. It's Mrs. Schmulowitz calling."

As if I wouldn't recognize that nasally Brooklyn accent anywhere.

"It's not like I'm trying to be a Jewish mother," she said, "but, let's face it, I *am* a Jewish mother. I was just checking in to see how you're doing. Are you OK? Where are you? When're you coming home?"

"I'm fine," Mrs. Schmulowitz. "I'm still in Tahoe. Not sure when I'm coming back. Soon, I hope."

She also said she had news about my cat: he'd tangled with a snake.

"I'm sitting there yesterday, watching *Judge Judy*. Next thing I know, that *fakakta* Kiddiot comes running inside with this big black snake hanging out of his mouth. He crawls under the divan and they're flopping around under there, the two of them, like it's the World Wrestling Federation. So I go to the kitchen to get the broom, to get him out of there. By the time I come back, he's *eating* the snake."

The fact that Kiddiot could catch anything, given his weight and lack of smarts, was surprising. But actually eating a snake? Now, *that* is truly stunning. The cat wouldn't eat anything.

Mrs. Schmulowitz reminded me that the Denver Broncos, my favorite team, were playing on Monday night. She'd be making her usual brisket, whether I was there or not.

"No pressure," she said. "Plus I'm thinking about baking a pie."

"I don't recall you ever baking anything, Mrs. Schmulowitz."

"Last time I even thought about baking was forty-five years ago. Funny story: my dishwasher breaks, so I call a plumber. What a hunk this guy is! Tightens this, loosens that. Tells me no charge. 'No charge?' I tell him. 'I gotta pay you something.' So he tells me I can either bake him a cake or have sex with him. My third husband, may he rest in peace, comes home after work that night. I tell him what the plumber said. He's horrified. 'So what kind of cake did you bake him?' he wants to know. I tell him, 'What do I look like? Betty Crocker?'"

I knew my landlady was only trying to cheer me up. I appreciated her effort. But the last thing I felt like doing was laughing.

"Was he upset?"

"Was who upset?"

"Your third husband."

"Was he upset? What're you, kidding me? The man didn't talk to me for six months. But what're you gonna do? You can't go back, right?"

Special operators are taught to backtrack when they're in pursuit of a target and they've lost contact. In the haste of the hunt, little things often get missed along the trail. A broken tree branch. An overturned stone. Small clues.

You can't go back.

I realized I had to. I needed to double back, up to the mountains, to the crash site where my life had taken a turn toward hell.

"Thank you, Mrs. Schmulowitz."

"For what, bubby?"

"Being my compass."

┼

THE RUTTED logging road upon which I'd driven in with Deputy Woo to rendezvous with the sheriff's rescue team was now snow-packed and all but impassable. I drove as far as I could, fishtailing and grinding gears, traversing drifts, before getting stuck seemed likely.

I got out and walked, passing the same small, moss-roofed cabin I'd noticed that morning. The beat-up pickup that I remembered being parked out front was gone.

Forty-five exhausting, sweat-drenched minutes later, my unwaterproofed hiking shoes and feet cold and wet, I reached the trailhead. Without snowshoes, I knew that the climb up and back would easily take all day. The leg I'd scraped up after falling on my first ascent to the crash site was throbbing. I didn't care. I was trained to adapt and overcome, "see the hill, take the hill," no matter the odds.

Up the trail I climbed.

No one ever said being mission-oriented was synonymous with being smart.

I made it about two miles, fighting my way through snow that was at times waist-high.

Then I fell into the stream.

Anyone could've made the same mistake—losing their footing on slippery rocks and tumbling into icy, chest-high currents. That I did was more annoying initially to me than it was alarming. I slapped the water, angry at myself, waded to shore, and pulled myself out, drenched head to toe. Almost immediately, I began to shiver.

Shivering is the human body's first automatic defense against the cold. Shivering causes muscle contractions, which create heat to maintain homeostasis, or a constant internal temperature. I remembered a lesson I'd learned in escape and evasion training my first year at the academy: in water approaching fifty degrees, death can occur within the first hour of immersion. The water I'd fallen into was substantially colder than that.

My teeth were chattering uncontrollably. In another few minutes, I would begin to lose muscle coordination and have difficulty thinking straight. Drowsy disorientation would set in. I would sit down along the trail and, as they say, that would be that.

My truck, I knew, was too far away, and I couldn't very well call for help; even if there'd been adequate reception, I'd forgotten to take my phone with me, leaving it on the passenger seat when I'd started out on foot, up the trail. I needed to find someplace where I could strip down and warm up—and I needed to do it fast. There was really only one hope: the cabin I'd passed earlier.

By the time I got there, I was stumbling, willing myself forward one numb foot at a time, fighting with every waning ounce of willpower the urge to stop and rest.

I staggered onto the cabin's small, rough-hewn front porch and pounded my fist on the wooden door.

"Hello? Anybody here? Hello?"

No answer. A window with four small panes flanked the door. I turned away from it, shattering the lowest pane with my elbow, reached my hand in, and turned the deadbolt.

The cabin was dim and warm, the air sweet with the musk of pinewood. Embers glowed in a rock fireplace big enough that I could've climbed into it. Split logs were stacked high on the right side.

I threw two logs on, stoking the glowing coals with a charred iron poker, and stripped naked as quickly as I could. Standing there, the flames restoring me, I glanced around at my surroundings:

The cabin was essentially one large room. There was a small Formica-topped dining table and two spindly, ladder-back chairs. A green swayback couch. A sagging La-Z-Boy recliner positioned close beside the fireplace. A galley kitchen with filthy dishes piled high in a metal, pump-handle sink. A rumpled twin bed with a brass headboard. Foreign policy magazines and engineering textbooks scattered and piled everywhere.

The logs hissed and popped, shooting embers onto the blackened slate hearth and occasionally, my legs. I didn't care. I could feel the blood returning to my limbs, the cognitive function to my brain. I closed my eyes and began to drift amid the fragrant, delicious warmth of the fireplace.

Until the front door flew open.

TWENTY-TWO

There's a reason why professionals use short-barrel assault weapons when breaching buildings. A short barrel allows for greater mobility in close quarters; the shooter is less likely to get his weapon hung up in a doorway or have some enterprising bad guy snatch it out of his hands as he comes around a corner.

The man who came in shooting at me obviously hadn't gotten the memo.

Armed with an old lever-action Winchester, the kind of rifle you see in every John Ford Western ever made, he came storming in, firing wildly from the hip.

Cock. *Blam.*

The first round ricocheted with a spark off the rock fireplace and took out an old brass floor lamp, missing me by mere inches.

Cock. *Blam.*

The second round was considerably farther off-target, knocking a barn owl, stuffed and mounted, off the wall.

Cock—

I reached from behind the door before he could get off a third shot, clamped my hand around the wooden forestock, and relieved him of the Winchester.

"Old" didn't begin to describe him. "Ancient" did. He was bald but for the thatch of gray hairs protruding wildly from each of his Dumbo-sized ears. Baggy eyes. Yellowed teeth, missing in places. An insulated, one-piece army surplus snowsuit hung on his narrow frame like a kid wearing daddy's pajamas.

"Give me back my gun."

"So you can shoot me? I don't think so."

"It's my gun and you're in my house." He was looking at me funny, up and down. "What are you, some kind of sexual deviant?"

Then I remembered: I was in the buff.

"Fell in a stream, up the trail," I said. "Had to warm up before I froze."

"So you break into my cabin?"

"My apologies. I'll pay for the window."

"You're darned right you will."

I ejected all of the Winchester's remaining cartridges, the shells clattering on the wood floor, leaned the rifle next to the fireplace, then proceeded to put my clothes back on.

"What're you doing?" the old man.

"What does it look like I'm doing?"

"It looks like you're putting wet clothes back on." He watched me ring out my socks. Water sizzled and hissed on the hearthstone. "Wait."

He walked over, reached into a box beside the bed, and tossed me a dry, red flannel shirt, followed by blue jeans, and a rolled pair of socks, olive drab.

"I'd loan you some of my skivvies until yours dry out some," he said, "but I'm not a weirdo."

I thanked him for his kindness and put on his clothes while he propped a book against the pane of glass I'd broken, to keep out the cold.

"My name is Melvin Essex, by the way," he said, "and I'm as old as the hills."

"Cordell Logan. And I'm getting there."

"That your truck down the road?"

"It is."

"What're you doing all the way up here in the middle of winter with no tire chains, no nothin'?"

I told him. Essex listened intently.

"You've had a rough go of it," he said when I was done.

"I'll live."

"You hungry?"

"Now that you mention it . . ."

He had possum stew written all over him. Or fried squirrel. Something befitting a mountain man living the hermit's life. But that wasn't on the menu.

"Got some fresh croissants and a nice Brie. Just picked 'em up in town."

"Works for me."

He went outside to his truck and returned with a grocery bag, laying the food on the table, along with a quart of fresh-squeezed orange juice and two mismatched drinking glasses. We sat down and ate.

He told me he'd taught mechanical engineering at the University of Michigan, and had been indicted at the height of the conflict in Vietnam for allegedly helping orchestrate an antiwar protest in which several police officers were injured. Investigators, he said, manufactured the case against him out of whole cloth. He was denied tenure. Within a year, he'd lost his job. He never found work again in academia and ended up on a General Motors assembly line in Flint, Michigan.

"I vowed after that I'd never talk to another liar with a badge as long as I lived, and I haven't," Essex said. "More juice?"

"No thanks."

"It's like when the sheriff's department came around a couple weeks ago," he said. "They wanted to know if I knew anything about that boy you said got killed up the trail. Sure, I could've told them what I saw. But I wasn't about to."

"What did you see, Professor?"

He slathered Brie on his second croissant and looked at me over his glasses.

"How do I know you're not some undercover cop?"

"If I were, I probably would've shot you the second you came in here, blazing away with that saddle rifle of yours."

"Could be you didn't shoot me because you dropped your gun when you fell in that stream."

"Could be I didn't have a gun to begin with."

"You've got cop eyes."

I got up, walked over to my wet jeans, pulled out my FAA-issued pilot's certificate from my wet wallet, and showed it to him.

"I'm a flight instructor."

He studied the plastic, credit card-size certificate, chewing slowly, then nodded like I'd convinced him and handed it back to me.

"About ten o'clock the night before that boy died, I heard a car go by. Nobody comes up here that late. The engine sounded kind of strange. A dull, rotational knock, like he had a loose main bearing. I didn't bother getting out of bed. Then in the middle of the night, I hear the same engine. Now he's coming back down the road, and he's coming fast. This time, I get up. There's a good moon, and I see him out the window: a van. Green."

I stared into the fire, my memory flashing on the high school kid who'd been shoveling snow outside his family's house the morning Savannah disappeared from the B&B. I remembered his name—Billy. He'd called later to say he'd seen a woman who looked like Savannah trying to escape from a man parked outside a Mexican restaurant in South Lake Tahoe.

The man, Billy said, was driving a green van.

We chatted for another few minutes, mostly about airplanes and aeronautical engineering, with which the professor seemed endlessly fascinated, until my clothes and shoes were no longer wet but merely damp. They'd have to do. I changed out of Essex's shirt, jeans, and socks, and into my own. My wallet held one twenty dollar bill. I tried to give it to him, to cover the cost of the window I'd broken, but he refused to take it.

"I'm happy my cabin was here for you. And, besides, I don't get many visitors these days. I enjoyed the company."

We shook hands.

"Peace, love, and rock and roll," he said, flashing me a V-shaped peace sign as I started down the road, toward my truck.

"Groovy."

Was the green van that Essex had observed after Chad Lovejoy was shot to death the same green van that Billy, the snow-shoveling, snowboarding teenager, said he'd seen outside the Mexican restaurant? The same green van from which a woman who Billy said resembled Savannah tried to escape?

I didn't know, but I most definitely intended to find out.

✝

Streeter seemed mildly interested when I called him about the possible van connection.

"Did anybody get a license number?"

"No."

"We'll check it out," he said.

"When?"

"When time allows. We're working a couple of new angles right now that look extremely promising."

The FBI's lab in Quantico, Virginia, he said, now was actively involved in the investigation. I assumed that the feds were assessing such evidence as tire tracks and boot prints, but I didn't ask. Streeter would've been reluctant to provide any details, given the ongoing nature of his investigation, and for once, I didn't feel like pressing the issue. I was tired. Beyond tired.

I found a low rise overlooking the south end of Lake Tahoe and sat in my truck, the heater on low. The sky was clear. Whitecaps rippled the water, while the pines swayed fluidly on a stiff south wind. The trees reminded me of Savannah, the way she used to dance to samba music on the radio, her hips keeping perfect, seductive time to the beat, her arms snaking gracefully, always coaxing me with her hands and her smile to join her. I tried to block the memory from my head. I tried not to think of her. Only masochists seek that kind of pain.

I needed to focus and find that green van.

The kid who'd first told me about it, Billy, had said he'd get back to me if anything else about what he'd seen that night outside the Mexican restaurant bubbled up from the recesses of his adolescent brain. I never heard from him after that. Maybe it was time he heard from me.

✝

Billy wasn't home. His mother was. She stood inside the front doorway with her arms crossed, staring at me like I was trying to sell her a subscription to Pedophile magazine.

"Why do you want to talk to him?"

"It concerns a criminal matter."

"*What?* What kind of criminal matter?" She was in her early fifties, short and busty, with glittery nail polish, and frosted, severely jagged blonde and black hair that appeared to have been cut by a stylist in a foul mood.

"He may have witnessed an abduction," I said.

"An abduction. Yeah, right. Look, whatever you think my son knows, or 'witnessed,' he didn't, OK? He has a very active imagination. Besides, if he saw something, he would've told me, or his father."

"Billy may have information that could help identify the person who did it. Look, I'm not a cop."

"Then who are you?"

"The victim was someone very close to me."

"My son knows nothing."

"If I could just talk to him for a—"

"—I told you, he's not here, OK? We don't want any trouble. Please don't make me call the police."

She shut the door in my face.

In most foreign places, you can't simply hang out in a vehicle and wait for your target to show up. I tried that once with two other go-to guys in a Citroen along the Rue Charles de Gaulle in downtown Tunis. We were tracking a bagman working for a radical Salafist group, waiting for him to make a money drop outside the Monoprix supermarket. Several local men mistook us in our berkas for female Tunisians and began making what could best be diplomatically described as "amorous advances." We broke off the surveillance and drove on, but not before one of my colleagues reached through the window and crushed the windpipe of one would-be suitor who'd gotten a little too fresh.

Waiting for a high school kid in South Lake Tahoe would be cake by comparison.

I parked a block up the street, affording a view of both avenues of approach, and settled in. Dozens of cars and trucks passed by, along with two dog walkers and several joggers. Nobody even so much as looked in my direction.

After about ten minutes, a primer-gray VW bug came putputting down the street and passed by.

Billy was driving.

I fired up the ignition, made a hard right turn, and followed the VW into his parents' driveway. Billy parked behind a fire engine red Dodge Ram pickup with chrome wheels and got out of the Volkswagen, lugging his trumpet case.

He didn't see me initially as I pulled in, jumped out, and approached him.

"Yo, Billy, you got a sec?"

He turned toward me, brushing the hair out of his eyes. The expression on his face was a blend of surprise and fear.

"You remember me?"

"Yeah."

"When we talked on the phone, you said you'd let me know if you thought of anything else you saw that night. Remember that?"

"Yeah. Pretty much." He licked his lips. "All I saw is pretty much everything I told you."

"'Pretty much' suggests to me there might be more."

— 251 —

His eyes darted side to side. "Uh, no. Not really. That was pretty much about it. Can't remember anything else. Anyway, I better get inside."

I blocked his path.

"There's something you're not telling me, Billy."

"I don't know what you're talking about."

Clearly, he did.

I stood aside anyway and let him pass. As I did, the front door opened and a short, bald man with gray sweat pants, a black "Harley of Reno" T-shirt, and a Fu Manchu moustache came charging out, spitting angry, with a claw hammer in his hand.

"Get off my property."

"It's OK, Dad," Billy said, grabbing him and holding on, trying to stop him from coming any closer to me. "He's not the guy."

In the wake of Savannah's disappearance, I'd been attacked by a man with a gun, another with a knife, and now one with a hammer. What in the hell, I wondered, was going on?

"There's no need for violence," I said, which would've sounded mildly humorous had Billy's father known my personal work history.

"I said get off my property!"

Billy looped his arms around his waist and dug his heels in like a rodeo cowboy wrestling a steer, struggling to hold on.

"Dad, stop! It's not the guy!"

"It's not?"

"No. I told you. This is the guy who showed me the picture."

"Oh." Billy's father drew a deep breath. "Sorry," he said to me. "I thought you were somebody else."

"Which guy?" I said to Billy.

"Billy, no," his father pleaded. "Don't. Please."

The kid looked over at him like he was trying to make up his mind, then, finally, at me.

"The guy who took your girlfriend," Billy said. "I saw him again."

TWENTY-THREE

Billy's father, Gary, was an unlicensed contractor who'd recently been indicted for allegedly defrauding several residents of the Lake Tahoe area by billing them for home repairs that never were performed. Which explained, Gary said, why he'd sought to prevent Billy from contacting authorities about what he knew of the man in the green van.

"I didn't want it jumbling things up and messing up my trial," Gary said. "You know how juries are."

I said I understood, even if I didn't, and asked Billy to tell me what he knew. It went something like this:

Several days after Billy called to tell me he'd seen a man forcing a woman back into a green van outside the Los Mexicanos restaurant, he'd spotted what he was convinced was the same van outside an auto parts store in the town of Truckee, where he'd gone to price out a new muffler for his VW. He was standing behind the van, tapping the license plate number into his phone, when the van's owner appeared and demanded to know what the hell he was doing. Intimidated, Billy couldn't think of anything to say other than, "Nothing." The guy snatched Billy's phone away, demanded that the kid divulge his own name and address, which Billy did, then threatened to come pay him a visit if anyone, particularly the cops, contacted him for "any reason."

Frightened, Billy promptly raced home and told his parents what had happened in Truckee. He also told them about me, how I'd first approached him the day Savannah went missing, and about what he'd seen that day after school outside Los Mexicanos.

"I swear I was gonna call you back," he told me, "but . . ."

"His mother and me, we told him not to," Gary said. "We don't want any trouble from that man."

"That man," I said, "may be responsible for two murders."

"Well, we don't want to be number three."

"I still remember the dude's license number," Billy said.

"No, Billy," his father said.

"But, Dad—"

"I said no, son! Now, go inside."

"I need that number," I said. "And I'm not going anywhere until he gives it to me."

"Do you have any children of your own?" Gary asked me.

His question stung like a punch. I could've told him about how Savannah was pregnant when she died, but I didn't.

"No."

"Well, maybe if you did, you'd understand better. It's not that I don't want to help you. It's just that we can't. My son should've never talked to you to begin with. Now, please, go away. Leave us alone."

"But why can't I give it to him, Dad?"

"Get in the damn house, Billy."

The kid rolled his eyes and reluctantly headed for the house.

"Before you go, Billy," I said, more to his father than anyone else, "you might want to consider your options. You can give me that plate number, and I'll give you my word that I won't tell another soul where I got it. Or you can call the sheriff's department and tell them yourself. If you don't tell them, I'll tell them we had this talk, and they'll arrest you for withholding evidence. And, if you *do* tell them, they'll put it in their official file, where they got the number. When they arrest that dude with the van, it'll all come out in open court, how the cops came to find him. And when the dude gets out of prison early—and everybody in California gets out of prison early—I guarantee, he'll come looking for you."

His father stood there in silence, blinking at me, unsure what to do, then at his son.

"Please, Dad."

His father hung his head and nodded, then went back inside. Billy seemed almost relieved to give me the plate number, proud of himself for remembering it. I asked him if he remembered seeing any signs or stickers on the van when he was in Truckee, anything that might provide me a better notion of who drove it.

He said he didn't.

Could he offer any more specific details about the owner himself?

"He was pretty big," Billy said after thinking about it for a few seconds.

"You mean heavy?"

"More like, you know, tall."

"How tall?"

"About your height. Maybe an inch more. Or two. Something like that."

"Anything else you can remember?"

Billy looked down at his red Chuck Taylors and thought hard.

"Not really," he said after awhile.

"You did good, Billy."

He smiled shyly. We shook hands.

The sun was setting. The air was chilled. I zipped up my jacket and watched Billy head inside, then called Buzz. It was pushing 2100 hours on the East Coast. The phone rang four times before his machine picked up, with a personal greeting from the man himself:

"I'm trying to avoid somebody I dislike," Buzz's voice said. "Leave a message. If I don't call you back, you'll know it's you."

Beep.

I left the license plate number Billy had given me and asked Buzz to run it.

✝

My WALLET held less than twenty dollars in cash. I was $105.43 short of maxing out the credit limit on my Visa card, according to the pleasant-sounding young Indian woman on the other end of the 1-800 customer service number printed on the back. She said her name was "Kimberly."

"How may I assist you today, Mr. Logan?"

I kicked off my soggy hiking shoes and lay back on my bed at the Econo Lodge. I had enough credit for one more night's lodging, and barely enough for gas to get home. Unless Mumbai saw fit to up my limit, I'd have no choice but to leave Lake Tahoe in the morning, surrendering any hope of finding Savannah's killer on my own anytime soon, if ever.

"You can start off by telling me your real name," I said. "Not the anglicized version you give out so that geocentric Americans won't be quite so intimidated talking to a non-American. I like to know who I'm really talking to."

A long pause.

"I am called Nirupama."

"Pretty name."

"Thank you. How can I be of service, Mr. Logan?"

"I need you to raise my credit limit, Nirupama."

"I understand you would like your credit limit raised on this account. Is this correct?"

"Yes."

Another long pause. She was no doubt on the computer, studying my sketchy payment record—or, perhaps more accurately, *non*payment record.

"I'm sure we can accommodate your request in some fashion. May I kindly place you on brief hold while I consult my supervisor?"

"Sure."

— 256 —

Elevator music ensued. It soothed my brain. How long I was on hold or when Nirupama hung up on me, I couldn't say, because I fell asleep. When I awoke, I was on my stomach and my phone was ringing on the carpeted floor. Daylight was sneaking in through the curtains. Morning already.

"This is Logan."

"This plate number you left on my machine, is this the booger eater who did your lady?" Buzz asked, his voice faint and static-charged from 3,000 miles away.

"Possibly."

"Well, if it is, save a piece of him for me, will ya?"

"Roger that."

"You ready to copy?"

"Go."

Willing my eyes to focus, I grabbed an Econo Lodge pen off the nightstand and a slip of paper from a wafer-thin, motel-provided notepad.

Buzz had tapped into California Department of Motor Vehicle files. Had he violated privacy laws in doing so? Most certainly. But it wasn't like I was Al-Qaeda. A covert operator had shown his former covert operator friend a little love. Happens all the time.

The plate linked to a green 2003 Chevy Astro Cargo Van and was registered to a Nevada corporation—Patriot Flow Professionals, LLC. The company showed a corporate address in Reno, about an hour and a half away, depending on how snowy the roads were.

"And I already know what your next question is," Buzz said.

"What is Patriot Flow Professionals?"

"Like I said, I'm one step ahead of you."

Buzz had pulled up Nevada Secretary of State corporate records. Under "type of business," Patriot Flow was described simply as a "wholesaler." The company's registered agent was identified as D. B. Anderson. He or she also was listed as the company's president, secretary, and treasurer.

"You're wondering who D. B. Anderson is," Buzz said, "and that's where I can't help you."

The name, Buzz said, was too common to research without extraneous effort. I never would have asked him to put in that kind of labor in my behalf, given the pressures of his seventy-hour workweek, saving the free world as a counterterrorism analyst.

"That's one Pavarotti CD I owe you anyway," I said.

"We'll call this one even. Good hunting, Logan. You lemme know if you need any backup, you hear?"

"You're a man among man, Buzz."

"That's what I keep telling my wife."

I showered quickly, packed, slurped down a bowl of Cheerios in the dining area adjacent to the motel's lobby, left my plastic room key on the front counter, and headed north to Reno.

✝

THE CORPORATE headquarters of Patriot Flow Professionals was situated on the edge of a complex of prefabricated concrete warehouses hunkered north of Interstate 80 on the west side of the "Biggest Little City in the World," as Reno likes to call itself. There wasn't a green Chevy van in sight. I got out of my truck and walked to the office door of the warehouse that corresponded to the address Buzz had given me. On the door's glass insert, I could see the faint outline of stenciled letters, scraped clean: *atr ot low Pr f   n ls.*

I peered through the window. The office was empty. Random pipe fittings, brass and PVC, alongside an unrolled string of plumber's Teflon tape, littered the floor.

In the glass, I saw the reflection of a uniformed security guard striding toward me.

"Can I help you, sir?"

He was clean cut and buttoned-down, mid-twenties, five foot ten, 160 give or take a few pounds, with a pimpled complexion, mirrored aviator shades, and an all-business attitude. Riding his waist was a black leather duty belt that held handcuffs, a walkie-talkie, and Mace spray, but no pistol.

"I'm looking for Patriot Flow Professionals."

"May I ask why?"

"It involves a criminal investigation."

"Are you a detective?"

"Do I look like a detective to you?"

"Yeah, you do, actually."

"So, what can you tell me about Patriot Flow Professionals?"

"They took off, about two weeks ago."

The guard told me that the company owed several months' back rent. They'd stripped the office bare and skipped out in the middle of the night.

"Do you remember any of the employees, what they looked like?"

"Only one I can think of was this one guy. Sort of waved when he'd see me."

"What did he look like?"

"Tall, white. I didn't see him up close. I just started a month ago."

"Any idea where they might've moved to?"

"Personally, I don't. But somebody else might." He unholstered his walkie-talkie, held it to his lips, and pressed the transmit button. "Unit One, base."

"Base, go ahead," a female voice said over the radio. She sounded young and bored.

"Yeah, Lisa, I've got a gentleman here, he wants to know if we've got a current ten-twenty on Patriot Flow Professionals."

"He probably owes him money too," Lisa said, chuckling.

"He may be wanted for questioning in a double murder in Lake Tahoe," I said.

The guard peeled off his sunglasses. "Are you kidding?"

I shook my head no.

He held the walkie-talkie to his lips and pressed the transmit button again. "He says the dude is wanted for murder."

"Really?" the dispatcher said.

"That's what he says."

"OK, stand by one."

Cars and semitrucks rolled past on the interstate, a quarter mile away. Overhead, a hawk circled, trying to ignore the crows that were harassing him. We waited.

His walkie-talkie crackled to life.

"Dispatch, unit one."

"This is unit one," he said.

"Yeah, Ryan, the only thing anybody around here knows," the dispatcher said over the radio, "is that Patriot Flow might've moved to the Tahoe area. Clarice in billing thinks the CEO was from somewhere around down there."

"Copy that."

He volunteered that he was waiting to get into the Reno police academy and asked me what department I was with.

"None."

Ryan looked dismayed. "You told me you were a cop."

"On the contrary, Ryan. *You* said I was a cop. Do me a favor. Ask if she's got an address in Tahoe."

"I would if you were a cop."

"Look, I'm pretty certain this guy murdered my wife."

Ryan searched my eyes and saw my pain. Slowly, he brought the walkie-talkie to his lips and keyed the transmit button.

"Lisa, any chance we got an address in Tahoe?"

"Stand by."

"How'd he kill her, you don't mind me asking?"

"Strangled her."

"That bites."

"You have no idea."

"Dispatch, unit one."

"Go ahead, Lisa."

"Yeah, Ryan, Clarice doesn't have a specific address or anything. But she says the skip tracer thinks it's on Airport Road."

Airport Road. Where Summit Aviation Services was located. Where ex-con Chad Lovejoy labored for his shady uncle, Gordon Priest, before being shot dead beside the ghost of an airplane in the snowy mountains of the Sierra Nevada.

TWENTY-FOUR

Some say the drive between Reno and Lake Tahoe is among the prettiest in the country. Bald eagles. Gurgling, unspoiled streams. Verdant mountains majesty. All of that nature stuff at every turn of the gently winding, perfectly maintained road. I was too focused and too much in a hurry to play tourist. I needed to get back to Lake Tahoe, find Gordon Priest, and extract the truth from him by whatever means necessary.

Buddhists consider impatience and anger to be poisons that cloud sound judgment. I won't deny that I was well beyond both. The baser parts of my brain were running the show, the "fight or flee" parts, and I wasn't about to flee. Should I have contacted Deputy Streeter to tell him what I'd learned in Reno, then backed off and let law enforcement do its job? A prudent man would've done exactly that. But prudence was the last thing on my mind. I craved revenge, cold and sweet, and I needed it right then, more than anything I'd ever needed in my life.

What is normally a ninety-minute drive took me less than half that.

I stormed into Summit Aviation Services. Priest's office was dark, the door closed. Marlene was sitting at her receptionist's desk, eating a cookie.

"Where is he?"

She turned toward me, a little flustered, breaking off the friendly conversation she was having with two clear-eyed, clean-shaven young men garbed in charter pilot uniforms—black pants, white, short sleeve shirts, with captain and first-officer bars on their epaulettes. I could see their gleaming executive jet parked on the ramp outside.

"I'm sorry?" Marlene said.

"Your boss. Where is he?"

"He's at a meeting."

I came around the counter and planted my palms on her desk, invading her personal space.

"Where?"

"I don't know. He didn't say."

"Does he own a green van?"

"A green van? Not that I know of. Why are you so upset?"

"What is Patriot Flow Professionals?"

Marlene sat back in her chair, breaking eye contact, looking away, pretending to shuffle papers. "I have no idea."

"I think you do. I think it's that business he runs on the side, smuggling airplane parts to Iran. Isn't it?"

"I don't like the way you're behaving, Mr. Logan."

"Why are you covering for him?"

"I'm not."

"I want the truth, Marlene, and I want it now."

One of the pilots, thin-shouldered with long sideburns, walked around the counter and put his hand on my shoulder, trying to look tough.

"You heard the lady," he said. "You're scaring her. Why don't you take a deep breath and try to chill out a little bit?"

I looked over at his hand, then into his eyes. What he saw in my own eyes caused his Adam's apple to bob up and down as he swallowed fearfully. He backed off without me having to say a word.

I turned and walked out.

✝

GORDON PRIEST'S dominatrix was wearing a white lab coat with her name stitched in cursive, followed by the initials, "M.D.," and, below that, "Internal Medicine."

"Not you again," she said, pursing her lips, standing inside her front door.

"Is he here?"

"If he was, do you really think I'd be dressed like this?"

"Are you really a doctor?"

She tilted her head and fired a condescending smirk.

"Board certified."

"If you see him, tell him I'm looking for him. It's important."

"Will do. Listen, if you're ever inclined to expand your horizons . . ." She reached into the pocket of her lab coat and handed me a business card. "We could have a ton of fun."

The card featured a bullwhip coiled around an abstract rendition of what I assumed was the male reproductive organ.

"Doubtful," I said, "but thanks."

I drove to the Skylark Mobile Home and RV Park, pulled into the thrift shop lot across the street, and walked to Priest's trailer. His station wagon was gone. Nobody answered the door.

As I returned to my truck, a young Latino couple emerged from the thrift shop. The father holding their daughter in his arms. She was perhaps two years old, bundled against the cold in a one-piece pink snowsuit and matching woolen ski cap with a fringed pom-pom on top, and strings that tied around her chin. I paused to watch as the mother opened the back door of a rust bucket Volvo. The father lovingly strapped the wriggling toddler into her car seat, smothering her with kisses that made her squeal with laughter. I tried not to fantasize about what it must feel like, the intensity of that kind of bond. My chances of ever experiencing it had been denied me, stolen with Savannah's last breath.

I turned away from the happy little family, got back in my truck, tilted my seat back, and waited for Priest to come home. Was he Crocodile Dundee? My gut told me no. But my gut also told me Priest knew who Dundee was. And I had ways of extracting that kind of information in short order.

Pacifists question the worth of so-called "enhanced" interrogation techniques. They argue that such methods don't work because people subjected to waterboarding, for example, or made to sit for hours on their knees, will eventually 'say or do anything to avoid more pain. As such, the critics say, any intelligence derived by using these methods can't be trusted. They're right. Because if the person being interrogated knows that his questioners are playing by humanitarian "rules," then it's usually nothing more than a big time suck for all parties concerned. The only way it can work is if the guilty detainee fully understands that he may be maimed or even killed if he's not fully forthcoming.

Now, I'm not saying I ever personally relied on those kinds of tactics, techniques, or procedures. Nor am I saying I saw others use them. I'm not saying that at all. I wouldn't want to spend the next several years in federal custody. But I've heard that much good actionable intelligence can be quickly derived by shooting off a toe, or a finger. You'd be amazed how swiftly that can get somebody's attention.

Or so I've heard.

My phone rang. It was Marlene from the airport.

"Gordon's here." Her voice quavered with nerves. "He says he'd like to meet with you."

"When?"

"As soon as possible."

"Does he own a gun?"

She lowered her voice. "Not that I know of. Gordon can be a little gruff sometimes, but I don't think he's capable of real violence. He's a real teddy bear inside."

"I'll be there in five minutes."

I called Streeter as I drove to brief him about what I'd learned, but he wasn't in. His machine picked up. I left a message.

+

Marlene was standing outside without a coat, eating cookies, one after another. The temperature hovered in the low forties, but the wind chill factor was closer to freezing. Still, I could see sweat rings under the arms of her tan Summit Aviation T-shirt.

"It's been one heckuva day," she said. "You want a cookie? I just made some fresh."

Eating sweets was the last thing on my mind. I strode past her, toward the office door.

"He's not in there," Marlene said.

"Where is he?"

"Down the way." She pointed. "In one of our hangars. We've got a big charter coming in. There'll be a lot of people in the office. He just thought it might be better if the two of you could talk in private."

I followed her down the flight line. The walk seemed to tire her. She was breathing hard, perspiring even harder.

"Gordon says he's got nothing to hide," she said without looking at me.

"We'll see."

We passed two rows of prefab metal hangars painted aquamarine. At the third row, Marlene took a right turn. I followed her midway down the line, to the door of a hangar that was partially open. She paused before stepping inside and glanced back at me.

"I just feel so bad," she said, "what's happened, all of this."

Something didn't feel right. Maybe it was her words, or the way she said them, how the left corner of her mouth turned down, her downcast eyes. In combat, you learn to heed that inner voice that tells you when there's unseen trouble ahead. But I hadn't been in combat in a long time. I ignored the voice. The only one I wanted to hear was telling me that Gordon Priest was on the other side of that door, waiting for me to prime him like a pump handle.

I followed Marlene into the hangar.

The first thing I saw in the dim light as I looked past her was a green van, then various office desks and chairs that looked as if they'd been randomly dumped inside the hangar. Leaning perpendicularly against one of the desks was an aluminum sign painted red, white and blue, about three feet long, the kind you hang outside a place of business. It said, "Patriot Flow."

I sensed movement and turned to glimpse a blur that came up on me fast from behind, partially blocked from my sightline by Marlene's wide body. I brought my right arm up in a defensive position, but too late. Something hard and heavy came crashing down on the left side of my head.

I could feel myself falling.

✝

In Hollywood, people get knocked unconscious all the time. A karate chop to the neck, a jab to the jaw, and you're incapacitated for hours. In truth, it usually takes considerable effort to turn off most people's lights for more than a few seconds, mine included.

The blow that felled me didn't knock me out completely, but it did leave me stunned and incapacitated long enough that I could feel my arms being yanked behind my back and handcuffs being slapped painfully around my wrists.

There was nothing I could do.

My vision had blurred temporarily from the blow. As my eyes cleared, I fully expected to see Gordon Priest, especially given the handcuffs and what I knew to be his sexual predilections.

Only it wasn't Priest.

The man with the weather-beaten face standing over me, stuffing a .40-caliber Glock into his belt, which he'd apparently just used to club me silly, wore hiking boots, jeans, and a battered straw cowboy hat.

"You don't recognize me, do you?"

It took me a second to read the name stitched on his denim work shirt:

Dwayne.

"The Roto-Rooter guy," I said.

"G'day mate," he said in a mocking Australian accent. "Glad you could make it to our little party. Might have to throw another shrimp on the barbie, eh?"

He ordered Marlene to go close the door. She was biting her left index finger and fighting back tears.

"I don't like this."

"I don't care what you like or don't like," Dwayne said. "I told you to shut the fucking door."

Cowed, Marlene did as ordered.

Dwayne squatted down beside me.

"You had your chance, dickhead," he said, the accent gone. "You could've left it alone, done what I told you to do, and your lady would be alive today. But you blew it. You blew it bad."

He stood up and booted me hard in the ribs.

"Dwayne, don't, please," Marlene pleaded.

"You shut your mouth." He glared at her. "You're the reason we're in this goddamn mess, Marlene. I can't believe I'm married to a cow like you."

"I never wanted this to happen. I just thought we could make some money, that's all."

She began to sob.

"You stop that, Marlene, right now. Stop it or so help me God . . ." He cocked his fist like he was about to hit her.

Marlene recoiled, shielding her face, clearly used to it.

"I'm going to thoroughly enjoy killing you," I said.

Dwayne paused and redirected his focus on me.

"You're gonna enjoy killing *me*?" He laughed, then bent down beside me, his hands on his knees. "Seems to me, friend, that you don't fully comprehend what's happening here."

"Maybe you can enlighten me."

"Well, number one, you're gonna disappear. Forever, OK? And this whole shit storm, which I only got involved in with that punk, Chad, because my sweet 'little' wifey here told me how we could turn a quick buck salvaging some airplane? It's all gonna blow over like a bad dream."

Dwayne was one of those guys who didn't know when to shut up, the kind who couldn't help but remind everyone how brilliant he was, and how he could've been wildly successful in life, if only the Vatican and the Jews and the Trilateral Commission hadn't conspired to screw him over.

He said that after his wife, Marlene, told him about the crashed plane, they decided there might be some money to be made by salvaging a few choice aircraft parts and selling them on eBay. Marlene knew that Chad Lovejoy was familiar with the area, so they got him involved. Dwayne had served in the navy, aboard a nuclear-powered, ballistic missile submarine, which often made port of call in Australia. It was his naval training, he boasted, that allowed him to instantly realize the fortune to be made after he and Chad found the Twin Beech and made the unexpected discovery of the crated, weapons-grade uranium that had sat untouched inside the wreckage for decades.

"My mistake," he said, "was that I told the little punk what we had."

Chad promptly demanded a higher percentage of the jackpot by virtue of his having led Dwayne to the crash site. Their argument turned violent.

"He picked up a rock."

"So you capped him three times in the chest."

"Self-defense."

Hauling forty pounds of uranium down a snowy mountain single-handedly proved no easy task. Fortunately for Dwayne, he'd been a Boy Scout. He found a couple of stiff pine branches lying on the ground and made a travois like the Plains Indians once used, throwing his coat over the poles to serve as a makeshift cargo platform, then dragging the canister down to his van.

"Piece of cake when you got half a brain," he said.

"And finding a buyer?"

"Easy as turning on my computer."

He'd posted anonymous "uranium for sale" notices on a handful of anti-Semitic websites. Within a day, he said, he was in active negotiations with three prospective suitors. One group openly boasted in their e-mails of wanting to build a bomb big enough to wipe out Tel Aviv. They offered $100,000, to be wired directly to the bank account of Patriot Flow Professionals, Dwayne's fledgling plumbing supply company.

Arrangements were made for the buyers to drive from Los Angeles and to pick up the uranium in Santa Maria. Everything was going smoothly, right on track, Dwayne said, until I balked at completing the delivery.

"Is that when you killed Savannah?"

I couldn't believe how dispassionately I asked him the question.

"She killed herself," Dwayne said. "She wouldn't shut up. She kept trying to get away. I warned her. 'One more time, and you're gonna regret it.' But she wouldn't listen. That woman, she had a mouth on her, and if there's one thing I can't stomach . . ." He turned and looked over at Marlene who was standing near the van, muffling her sobs.

"You were never going to let her go, were you?"

He grinned.

"Remember that morning in Tahoe? When you first came walking up to me in the snow, all freaked out cuz she was gone, and you showed me her picture? Remember that?"

"I remember."

"She was right there, man, right in the back of my van! I was inside, taping her up just before you showed up. So close and yet so far, right? Is that a fuckin' hoot?"

Lying there, facedown, handcuffed, listening to him laugh, the killer of Savannah Carlisle and Chad Lovejoy, something cold and primitive came over me, an instinctive, reptilian-like response that prods one to move without thinking. I rolled, shifting my weight, and forcefully kicked the back of his right knee with my left foot.

He buckled and collapsed to the concrete floor.

Again I rolled, this time trying to scissors kick him in the face, but he rolled, too, and I failed to connect.

He got to his knees and drew his pistol.

Then he pulled the trigger.

TWENTY-FIVE

The round skipped off the hangar floor, kicking up shards of concrete between my feet, and punctured the van's left front tire. The hiss of air escaping reminded me of the sound Kiddiot made when he was dissatisfied, which was often.

How Dwayne missed putting a bullet in me from can't-miss range wasn't a function of poor marksmanship. It was a function of his beleaguered wife picking up a T-handled airplane tow bar and swinging it at the side of his head like a baseball bat just as he fired.

The pistol skittered under the van as he pitched forward onto the concrete. Blood trickled out of his right ear.

He lay still.

Marlene unclipped a fat key ring dangling from one of her husband's belt loops and singled out a short, thin handcuff key.

"I'm just so sorry," she said, struggling to free my wrists. "Dear lord in heaven, please forgive me, I'm so sorry. I never wanted this to happen. I just wanted to make a little money and make him happy so he'd stop beating me for once and blaming me for everything. That's all, just a little money. I never wanted anybody to get hurt. Please, you have to believe me."

"It's all right, Marlene. We'll sort everything out later."

She was weeping, having trouble unlocking the handcuffs. While Dwayne was starting to come to.

"C'mon, c'mon, c'mon," Marlene said, fumbling with the key. Try as she might, she couldn't persuade the key to fit.

Dwayne was groaning, beginning to move his legs.

"Get the gun, Marlene."

"What?"

"The gun. It's under the van. Forget about me. Get the gun."

She scuttled over, got down on all fours and peered under the van.

Dwayne was starting to move his arms.

Marlene got down on her stomach and strained to snag the pistol. It lay inches beyond her fingertips. She tried to wriggle under the van to extend her reach, but she was simply too rotund to fit.

"I . . . just . . . can't . . . get it."

"What the hell's going on?" Dwayne was rubbing his head as he came to, still trying to sit up, growing more agitated by the second. "Marlene, what the hell're you doing?"

As he gazed groggily at his wife, distracted, I rolled to my knees and stood in one fluid motion, my wrists still handcuffed behind me, while Dwayne scraped himself off the concrete.

"You son of a bitch," he said, now looking over at me, "I should've shot you dead the second you walked in here."

Ignoring his wife as she stood, Dwayne staggered to his van and pulled out a bolt-action hunting rifle equipped with a web sling and recoil pad.

I rammed into him with my shoulder. He slammed face-first into the van's running board.

Only this time, he didn't relinquish the grip on his weapon.

Marlene was already running, halfway out the door.

I was right behind her.

The bullet tore through the leather of my jacket sleeve, missing flesh by an inch at most. As the booming echo of the gunshot receded, I heard the *click-clack, click-clack* of a spent shell being ejected and a fresh round being chambered. Before Dwayne could get off another shot, though, I'd exited the hangar.

Any sense of safety lasted about two seconds. Dwayne emerged almost immediately and began chasing us.

I could hear an airplane, a twin-engine by the sound of it. Though I couldn't yet see it, I knew by the sound of it that the plane was likely taxiing out for takeoff from behind the long metal hangars ahead of me and to my left.

"Where're you going, Logan?" Dwayne yelled, bringing his rifle to bear. "It's over!"

Try running for your life alongside an out-of-shape, middle-aged woman, with your hands bound behind your back and a homicidal maniac on your heels. It's not easy.

At Alpha, my buddy Buzz enjoyed reciting prose to younger operators when instructing them on ways to more effectively kill bad guys. Mother Goose rhymes were among his favorites:

> For every evil under the sun,
> There is a remedy, or there is none.
> If there be one, seek till you find it;
> If there be none, never mind it.

With sudden clarity, I realized that the one viable remedy to the evil on my tail lay in that airplane taxiing behind the hangar ahead of me.

I heard a gunshot. Then Marlene went down.

"He shot me," she said almost matter-of-factly. "I can't believe it. The son of a bitch shot me."

A blood blossom spread across the back of her left calf where the bullet had entered, and the front of her shin where it exited. Maybe Dwayne was a bad shot, or maybe the sun was in his eyes. I didn't know. What I did know, though, was that his next bullet would be mine.

"Clamp your hands on either side of your leg," I yelled over the engines of the approaching airplane that was still obscured by the hangar. "You're gonna be OK, Marlene."

Her face blanched, shock beginning to set in.

Dwayne was fewer than twenty meters away, jogging quickly toward us, clutching his rifle with two hands in front of his chest at the port arms position, from which he could readily fire from the shoulder or hip. Running would've been pointless. There was no place to hide.

I turned and faced him.

He slowed to a walk and approached me warily, clearly wondering what the hell I was up to. His rifle was pointed at my chest. Then he flipped the rifle around and butt-stroked me hard in the stomach. I fell to my knees, unable to do anything at that moment, really, beyond groan in pain, while Dwayne turned his attention to his wife.

"Don't you *ever* raise a hand to me again, Marlene, or so help me I'll put you in your grave. Do you understand?"

"You shot me."

"You had it coming."

"Fuck you, Dwayne."

"You don't ever talk to me that way, Marlene. I'm your husband, goddammit."

He raised his rifle to club her with the butt.

"There's a way this can all go your way, Dwayne," I yelled over the airplane engines that were growing louder by the second.

"The only way this'll end is you dead," he said.

I got off my knees. "You still want that uranium?"

"Yeah, right," Dwayne sneered. "Like *that's* gonna happen. You must think I'm pretty goddamn stupid."

I stepped left. He quickly raised the rifle to his shoulder, shifting his footing, keeping the barrel trained on me.

"And you must think *I'm* stupid," I said, taking another step left. "I knew what was in that canister from the start. Do you really think I would've given it all back, knowing how much that stuff's worth on the black market?"

"You're telling me you've still got the uranium," Dwayne said like he didn't believe me, his field of view never leaving his gun sights.

"That's exactly what I'm saying." Another step left.

"Fine. Then where's it at?"

— 275 —

"Here's the deal," I said. "You agree to let me go, and I'll take you right to it. It's all yours. Just let me go."

He pivoted as I slowly circled him. The muzzle of his rifle was less than a foot from my face.

"I got a better idea, mate," Dwayne said, reverting to his Crocodile Dundee alter-ego. "You tell me where the shit's at, right now, then I'll let you go."

"How do I know you'll keep your end of the deal?"

"That's just it. You don't."

He was now turned away from the airplane that I knew would emerge at any second from behind the hangar.

"OK," I said over the roar of the engines. "You got a deal. But before I tell you, I have a question."

"What's that?"

"How's it feel to get what's coming to you?"

From around the corner of the hangar, directly behind him, the nose of a twin-engine Cessna 421, white with red accent stripes, came rolling into view, loud as a freight train. Dwayne started to turn his head instinctively to the source of the deafening noise.

That's when I rushed him.

My primary assignment when I played football at the academy was wide receiver, but I'd filled in enough at defensive back on the scout team to know how to properly tackle. You use your arms. You wrap them up low. With my wrists still handcuffed behind me, textbook technique wasn't an option.

In truth, that was never the plan.

I slammed my shoulder into his waist, lifting him up and driving him forward—straight into the Cessna's whirling starboard propeller. Envision a Cuisinart and a raw pot roast, pureed, with the lid off. That's what Dwayne looked like.

Enough said.

I rolled as the wing passed over me, narrowly avoiding having my legs crushed by the right main landing gear. That I wasn't shredded with him was, in itself, something of a miracle.

The pilot, a stocky blonde in her late twenties with those oversized aviator shades that are all the rage these days, hurriedly brought the Cessna to a stop. She shut down both engines, jumped out, her windscreen splattered with gore, and came rushing around the nose of the plane as I got to my feet. She gaped at what was left of Dwayne, bent at the waist, and vomited.

"Oh, my God."

"It wasn't your fault."

"Oh, my God."

"Everything's gonna be OK."

Frozen with horror, she couldn't stop staring at the killer's shredded remains.

"What's your name, cap'n?"

". . . Hailey. It's Hailey."

"Hailey, I need you to call 911. Tell them we need paramedics. Think you can do that?"

"My phone's in the plane."

"Might be a good idea if you went and got it."

Transfixed, she forced herself to turn away from the body and returned to the cockpit while I went to check on Marlene.

The receptionist was holding her lower leg with two bloody hands and staring blankly into space, like she'd just been through a war.

"I'm sorry you had to see that, Marlene."

Slowly, she raised her eyes to mine and thanked me. Then, softly, she began to cry.

I wished I could've comforted her, but my hands were still bound behind my back.

Some might wonder what it feels like, deep down, to kill another human being, especially in so gruesome a fashion. The easiest answer is that you typically rationalize your actions. You took out the garbage. Did the world a favor. Payback's a bitch. In truth, I felt no satisfaction killing Dwayne Anderson, no sense of relief. Only exhaustion.

I sat down on the tarmac beside Marlene.

"Keep applying that pressure, Marlene. Help's coming. Be here any minute."

I tried not to think about Savannah and the child I would never know. The sun was out. It felt warm and good on my face. I turned my gaze to the snowcapped mountains to the south and a place called Voodoo Ridge, where my life's journey had been changed forever. Try as I might, I couldn't remember what I'd had for breakfast that morning.

✝

THREE UNIFORMED sheriff's deputies were tasked with placing plastic tarps from their patrol vehicles over Dwayne Anderson's mangled body parts, while a paramedic unit drove Marlene to South Lake Tahoe's Barton Memorial Hospital. As the cops went about their grisly work, I rubbed circulation back into my newly unhooked wrists, courtesy of Detective Streeter and the universal handcuff key he carried in his pocket.

"We would've identified him eventually," Streeter said. "You just beat us to the punch."

I'd wanted to believe that he wasn't merely spouting cop bluster, but there was no denying the fact he would've been investigating my homicide as well, had I not gotten lucky.

Woo came walking up from the hangar where the green van was parked, toting dead Dwayne's .40-caliber Glock, bagged in a plastic Ziploc.

"Found it right where you said it would be," Woo said.

I said nothing.

Streeter wanted me to drive with him to sheriff's headquarters, to record chapter and verse everything that had led up to my confrontation with the man who'd killed Savannah, our baby, and Chad Lovejoy. I told him I would.

"You've been through hell," he said. "We can do it later if you want."

"Now's as good a time as any. I need to be getting back to Rancho Bonita. My landlady misses me. Wish I could say the same for my cat."

In the end, the Buddha believed, only three things matter: how much you loved; how gently you lived; and how gracefully you let go of those things not meant for you. Had I loved? Certainly. How much and how well, though, those were questions I wasn't prepared emotionally to address at that moment. Had I led my life in a gentle manner? Not hardly, but I'd saved lives in the process, and that was a fair trade, in my opinion. The more pressing question was how, if ever, I'd get over losing Savannah. How does one accept that the seminal romantic relationship of your life, with a woman so beautiful, so complete, that you could think of nothing but her day and night, was never meant to be?

I didn't know.

I doubted I ever would.

TWENTY-SIX

Whether Kiddiot was oblivious to how I was getting along emotionally, or was trying to comfort me, I couldn't say. He lay on my chest giving himself, not me, a bath that went on for easily a half hour. He may have been dumb, but at least he was well groomed.

I leafed through *Flying* magazine, pulled a copy of Whitman's "Leaves of Grass" from my bookshelf but found it too depressing, tried to sleep, did 100 push-ups, scrambled three eggs and ate them watching an infomercial about how to dance your belly away, tried to sleep, took a hot shower, and stared out at the moon. Anything to stop from thinking about how close I'd come to saving Savannah's life.

If only I'd been more observant when I had initially approached Dwayne Anderson's van.

In the movies, there's always that scene. You know the one: where the good guy stands over the bathroom sink, usually stripped to his chiseled waist, leans down to splash cold water on his face, then slowly looks up at himself in the mirror, staring into his own anguish-filled eyes, searching deep down for whatever the hell it is he's supposed to find in there.

I gave it a shot. I splashed water on my face. I stood looking at myself in the mirror. All I got back was an overpowering realization that I'd succumbed to weakness, to whining, that I'd forgotten how to be a man.

I also noticed I needed a haircut.

It was after 0500 when I finally dozed off. I was awake for good at 0535.

THE LITTLE bell over the door tinkled. My barber, former light heavyweight contender Primo Zacapa, glanced over, cutting another customer's hair as I walked into his tiny shop downtown on Cortez Avenue.

"*Que pasa*, Logan?"

"What's up, Champ?"

"It's all good. Have a seat. Be with you *momentito*."

At sixty-two, Primo remained every inch the fluid, graceful puncher he'd been back in the day, when he'd gone the distance with WBA legend Pipino Cuevas at the Forum in Los Angeles and lost on a split decision that every bookie on the street said was rigged. I sat down on the worn leather couch opposite his shop's one barber chair and watched him work: snipping and moving, snipping and moving. The customer, an older man with sad blue eyes, sat under his smock, head tilted forward. He possessed little hair on top, but that which he did have, Primo used to full effect, trimming and layering with such skill that, at least from where I was sitting, you'd have never known the guy was hurting for follicles. When Primo was finished, and the customer had left, he quickly swept up the trimmings with an old broom and a metal dustpan, unfolded a fresh smock from a wicker basket, and ushered me into the old swayback leather chair.

"An oldie but a goodie," he said, offering me a tattered, twelve-year-old *Playboy*.

"Not today, Champ."

"Not today? How 'bout another one? I got Miss June."

"I'm good."

His narrowed eyes told me he knew something was wrong, but he said nothing. He pinned a disposable sanitary strip around my neck and flapped the smock high into the air, letting it settle gently around my shoulders.

"So, how would you like your hair cut today?"

"Whatever you feel like, Champ."

He paused from pumping up the chair's pneumatic lift with his foot, wearing his usual spotless sky-blue Mexican wedding shirt, his own luxuriant black hair combed straight back, and looked at me hard.

"Every time you come in here, I give you a *Playboy*. Every time, I say, 'How do you want your hair cut?' You say, 'In silence,' cuz you want to catch up on your 'reading.' Every time. Today, no *Playboy*, no silence. What's going on with you, brother?"

"It's been a bad couple of weeks."

Primo was an excellent barber. Not so much because of the way he cut hair, but because he knew when to talk and when not to. He shrugged, then turned me in the chair, facing the big wall mirror, and went to work. I closed my eyes, my head filled with the comfortingly distracting perfume of talc and bay rum, and slept.

"All set, boss," Primo said after what seemed like no more than a couple of minutes.

He pivoted the chair and handed me a mirror so I could check the back.

"You do good work, Champ."

Off came the smock and the sanitary strip. I stood, got out my wallet. A Primo haircut ran fifteen dollars. I realized I only had nine dollars. I offered him what cash I had.

"Looks like I still owe you six, plus a tip."

"Keep it. You need it more than I do."

"I'm good for it. You know that."

He waved dismissively as if to say, "Don't give it a second thought," and walked me to the door.

"It's about your lady, isn't it?" Primo said.

I swallowed down the golf ball in my throat and nodded.

"You're not gonna see her again, are you?"

"No."

Primo rested a hand on my shoulder. "My wife passed three years ago. Cancer. We was married thirty-one years. Trying to forget that one woman is like trying to remember somebody you never met. You don't never forget her, OK? But you move on, you know what I'm saying? You got no choice, brother. None of us ever do. You feel me?"

"I feel you, Primo."

He smiled and struck a classic boxer's pose—slight crouch, face guarded by raised fists, the left slightly ahead of the right. His two front teeth were whiter than the others. I wondered how many times they'd been punched out of his mouth when he was a younger man.

"Remember," Primo said, "fists high, elbows low, and always, *always*, keep your head moving."

"Thanks, Champ."

We shook hands and I left, but his words of advice lingered long after. Savannah was gone. I could never forget her. I had to move on.

A BIG red digital "0" was flashing on my answering machine at the airport. No new messages. No new students. My flight school was dying. Truth be told, it had been for a long time. The pragmatic side of my brain screamed that it was long past time to fold the tent. Hell, I was no businessman. What was I thinking, trying to start a small business amid the nation's worst economic downturn since the Great Depression, and in a town that already had three other flight schools up and running? The quasi-optimistic side, the side that rarely weighs risk to reward, the side which made me a good fighter pilot and an even better special operator, told me to give it another week. Keep hope alive.

Larry had solved the *Ruptured Duck's* electrical issues, refusing to charge me. An alternator wire had frayed. The repair, he said, had taken him twenty minutes.

"Not even worth my time, filling out a bill," he said. "You owe me nothing."

I knew that the real reason Larry didn't bill me was because he felt sorry for me. He nodded, "Yeah, whatever," when I promised to pay him back someday. He'd heard it before. Many times.

Mrs. Schmulowitz felt sorry for me, too, and insisted on giving me a few bucks. "Just to tide you over," she said, "until you get on your feet."

She'd made similar overtures in the past, which I'd always politely but firmly turned down. You have to be pretty desperate to start taking handouts from little old ladies. But with my bank balance approaching negative integers and a monthly retirement check from the government that barely covered my rent, I didn't have much choice but to say, "Thank you."

I went flying, if only to distract myself.

The air offshore at 3,000 feet was cool and smooth. The *Duck* may have been nearly as old as I was, but he took to the sky that morning as if he'd just come off of the assembly line in Wichita where he'd been born more than forty-five years earlier. No creaking. No groans. Every flight instrument functioning solidly in the green as we burned lazy eights in the sky.

We orbited surfers and wakeboarders and, farther out, sailboats running with the wind, their spinnakers puffed out over their bows, in full bloom. We spotted no whales, unless you count dolphins, and we saw hundreds of them, a huge pod all surfacing and diving as if one, churning the ocean into creamy foam.

Shimmering blue sea. Green mountains, seemingly soft as lambs' ears. And, along the water's edge, extending inland among sun-kissed hills and arroyos, the Spanish-tiled roofs of Rancho Bonita. For an hour, I allowed myself to forget everything but how to fly an airplane and what a privilege it was to see the planet from so rarefied a perch. Sometimes you forget how beautiful the world really is, if you allow it to be.

Whatever euphoria I felt lasted about as long as it took me to land.

By THE end of the second quarter, Tampa Bay was trailing Carolina 24-3. The Buccaneers lined up for a twenty-nine-yard field goal attempt with no timeouts left and the clock about to expire. Good snap. Good hold. The kicker stepped into it, planted his right foot, swung his left leg . . . and missed.

"That ball was so far right," Mrs. Schmulowitz remarked, "it nearly took Rush Limbaugh's head off. More brisket?"

"No, thanks, Mrs. Schmulowitz. I'm beyond full."

"How 'bout more green beans? I got enough in there to feed Patton's army."

"I couldn't handle another bite. Everything was delicious, as always."

We were sitting in her living room, on her blue mohair couch, in front of her old Magnavox that hummed like a transmission tower, watching Monday Night Football with the volume turned down and eating dinner off of TV trays, like we always did.

"I *know* you saved room for dessert," Mrs. Schmulowitz said. "I made German chocolate cake. If you don't eat some, we're gonna be in big trouble."

"Why is that, Mrs. Schmulowitz?"

"Because it's a giant cake, that's why. You remember that little guy from 'Fantasy Island?' Always running around, yelling, 'Da plane, boss. Da plane'? This cake is so big, that little guy, he could hide in it, no problem."

"How could I resist? I'll take a small slice."

"Now, you're talking, bubby."

Off the sofa she sprang like no octogenarian I'd ever seen, a wonder of nature and superior genetics.

"Oh, I almost forgot," Mrs. Schmulowitz said, "I got you something." From behind a sofa cushion, she extracted a small box wrapped in blue foil paper with little stars of David. "Call it an early Hanukah present."

It was a gold Cross pen with my name engraved on it.

"So you can write the next chapter of your life," she said.

"You're the greatest, Mrs. Schmulowitz."

I tucked the pen in my shirt pocket as she padded into the kitchen and started telling me about her first husband, the one with the sweet tooth, and how she bought him a dozen Hershey bars for Hanukah one year, and how he ate them in a single sitting, which prompted innumerable cavities, along with an onset of adult acne that ravaged his face like a Biblical plague. Truthfully, though, I wasn't listening. I was thinking about where I'd been, and wondering where I was going.

The second half started. The cake arrived. I gorged myself on sugar while 300-pound men in pads and helmets pounded each other senseless as Mrs. Schmulowitz provided her usual expert, play-by-play commentary on the game. By the fourth quarter, consumed by memories, I'd turned inward and silent.

Mrs. Schmulowitz looked over, her dark eyes filled with compassion. She rested her hand on mine and said, "Tomorrow's another day, bubeleh."

"Think I'll take a little walk."

"Late-night stroll. A fine idea. Fresh air, burn off some of that brisket, get the old ticker pumping. I could use a little exercise myself. How 'bout a little company?"

"I'd really rather be by myself tonight. You understand."

"Do I understand? Of course, I understand! Don't give it another thought. Go. Just promise me one thing."

"Name it."

"Look both ways before crossing the street. This town is filled with *meshugener* old people. I haven't seen one yet who knows how to drive, especially in the dark."

I assured her that I'd look both ways.

╪

The moon that night was a silver sliver hanging low in the western sky, bracketed by Venus and some faint star, the name of which I didn't know. A dark and still night save for the throaty rumble of a motorcycle on a nearby street, its exhaust chopped to make the bike sound deafening—a not-so-subtle flipping of the bird to the rest of staid, refined Rancho Bonita.

I'd left Mrs. Schmulowitz's house and was halfway down the block when a large man came charging out from between two parked cars and tackled me to the sidewalk.

His right arm was around my throat, his biceps and inner forearm pressing against the carotid arteries on either side of my neck, while his right hand hooked into the inside elbow of his left arm, which was clamped around the back of my neck. A classic sleeper hold. We practiced the same move frequently on each other at Alpha. I knew that I had no more than about three seconds before I lost consciousness.

I brought my right hand back over my head to rake his face, but he seemed to anticipate my intentions and shifted his weight to the left, keeping his head just out of my reach. I attempted to tuck my chin into his bicep so that he could only squeeze my jaw and not my neck, but he forecast that move, too, adjusting his hold and maintaining pressure.

Then I remembered the gold pen Mrs. Schmulowitz had given me.

I grabbed it from my pocket and gouged the tip deep into the soft tissue above his right elbow. He yelped in pain and immediately relinquished his hold, rolled onto his left side, and shouted, "Son of a bitch!"

I'd have recognized that voice anywhere.

"Buzz?"

"Jesus, Logan, you *stabbed* me?"

"What was I supposed to do? You attacked me."

"You call that an attack? That wasn't an attack," he said, sitting up and clutching his arm. "If I had *attacked* you, god-dammit, you'd be dead."

He was built stout as a whiskey barrel, with a crew cut and a leather patch over his right eye.

"What're you doing out here, Buzz?"

"They sent me out, to see if you still had it."

"Had what?"

"You know what, Logan. The good stuff. Your mojo."

I looked at him, not fully understanding.

"Who's *they*?" I said.

He winced. "I can't believe you stabbed me. Jesus Christ, this thing hurts like a mother. Help me up, will ya?"

I helped him to his feet by his good arm.

"We're putting the band back together," Buzz said.

"Alpha?"

"Something new. A variation on the theme. It's got your name written all over it."

"I appreciate the offer, Buzz, but I'm really not in that line of work anymore."

"You're not in *any* line of work, from everything I've been able to gather."

I had to admit, he had a point.

"You got nothing else going on, Logan. We both know that. Nothing holding you down. Nothing to come home to at night except what, that cat of yours? I'm offering you a chance to do good work again, to get back in the game. Maybe even save the world."

A porch light came on. From behind the front door of the house came an older woman's voice:

"I'm calling the police if you don't get off my property right now."

Buzz looked back at me. "How about I read you in and give you the full brief while you drive me to the emergency room?"

"Sounds like a plan."

The Buddha said that uncertainty along the path of life is the only certainty there is. I had no way of knowing at that moment where my path would lead me. But Buzz was right about one thing: wherever it led, I had little to keep me from following it.

We started back toward Mrs. Schmulowitz's house and my truck.

"Sorry I stabbed you, buddy."

"Hey," Buzz said, "once a badass, always a badass."

And then he grinned.

For the first time in a long while, so did I.